HEAT

Also by Matthys Levy

Building Eden, a novel

Why the Wind Blows

Why Buildings Fall Down (with Mario Salvadori)

Why the Earth Quakes (with Mario Salvadori)

Structural Design in Architecture (with Mario Salvadori)

Books for Young People

Engineering the City (with Richard Panchyk)

Earthquakes, Volcanoes and Tsunamis (with Mario Salvadori)

HEAT

**A Tale of Love and Fear
in a Climate-Changed World**

Matthys Levy

Distinction Press
Waitsfield, Vermont
www.distinctionpress.com

Heat

A Tale of Love and Fear

in a Climate-Changed World

Matthys Levy

Published by Distinction Press
354 Hastings Road, Waitsfield, Vermont 05673
https://distinctionpress.com/

Photos: water by Dmitry Makeev, CC BY-SA 4.0 <https://creativecommons.org/licenses/by-sa/4.0>, via Wikimedia Commons; Miami skyline by joiseyshowaa from Freehold, NJ, USA, CC BY-SA 2.0 <https://creativecommons.org/licenses/by-sa/2.0>, via Wikimedia Commons

Cover design and interior by RSBPress

Library of Congress Catalog Number 2022907650

paperback ISBN 978-1-937667-27-6
ebook ISBN 978-1-937667-28-3

Acknowledgments

This story developed from my strong-held belief that we have mistreated the planet on which we live. Scientists tried to warn us that we could not continue to allow the atmosphere to be polluted by carbon products that would eventually enclose the planet in a warm blanket resulting in a hotter climate, the melting of glacier and polar ice and rising ocean levels.

I want to thank all the readers who have given me encouragement and useful comments to help me bring this story to life. I also want to thank Kitty Werner who provided the artistic and editorial guidance to bring the book to publication. Of course, my wife, Julie Simpson deserves credit for her forbearance along the way.

Dedication

To Nic, Okna, Shae, Edison and Austin

Contents

One fall day
The world will change forever
The forests will burn
The seas will return
To a land that now lies fallow

1
THE MANOR
Monday

IN THE SILENCE OF SPACE, a lone satellite focuses its electronic eye toward the surface of Earth, surveying its current state after a century of catastrophic transformations caused by climate change. After one circumnavigation, the satellite moves to view the next strip of the earth's surface, until one strip after another, the condition of the whole planet has been mapped and recorded. It is just another fall morning in the mid-twenty-first century.

Valeria Lopez looked out the window of the helicab as it approached a rise, west of Miami and saw lights leaking from open windows of a widely scattered handful of houses and a lone three-story building that was her destination. Situated on a quiet street far from the former bustle of the Miami beachfront and separated from abandoned buildings on both sides, the Duck Cove Manor, wrapped in faded ochre stucco walls stands waiting for her. She gripped the armrest in an unconscious reflex as the helicab descended to land precisely near the entrance, setting down on a pad marked, *for staff only.*

Exiting the vehicle Valeria carefully avoids stepping into a water puddle that seemed lately to be everywhere on the rolling surface of the pavement. She blinks in the bright sunshine but welcomes the light wind that blows in from the ocean that nevertheless fails to relieve the crippling heat. While holding her suitcase tightly in her right hand, she uses her left hand to brush away strands of her loose, rust streaked hair that was blowing wildly against her face in the downdraft from the vehicle's whirling blades. By the time she reaches the front door of the Manor, the autonomous vehicle has already departed. As usual, there were no cars parked in the front of the building this morning, since for months the road to the Manor had become impassable. Whenever Dr. Weiner, the consulting physician, would get a call from Valeria concerning the health of one of the remaining residents, he would fly in, and his helicab could be seen parked, waiting for him to complete the health evaluation of his patient. Apart from Valeria, there were no other staff members still working at the Manor, except, of course, Albert Drake. He is the building's owner, whose principal occupation these days has been to find new homes for the few remaining residents of the Manor. He would habitually fly out at the crack of dawn and return late each morning to restock the refrigerator with boxes of food that Valeria would later have to prepare and serve.

As Valeria pushed open the front door pulling her small rolling suitcase behind her, she crossed the empty entrance hall; the reception desk with no one to monitor the passage of visitors, the paradise palm tree potted plant that had begun sagging and turning brown from lack of care, the prints on the wall, a blue Picasso, and the blur of a Pollock. The chairs that usually accommodated visitors had weeks earlier been removed because the ceramic floor was constantly wet, and the legs of the wooden chairs had begun to rot. On the far side, she looked out onto the sad, drooping garden and remembered the warm days of the past when afternoon teas had been served in the shade of umbrellas as the many residents mixed contentedly and chatted in small groups. But the garden, formerly rich with dogwood and multicolored flowers was no longer visited since the heat was too oppressive and saltwater incursion had wilted most of the decorative plants. Valeria also sorely missed the elevator that no longer operated, as power had been cut off except for minimal service on the second floor, the only floor still occupied. The third floor had already been emptied of residents as had the penthouse that Drake had occupied before moving down to a vacant apartment on the second floor. *I don't know why I agreed to come back*, she thought, as she reached the stair that would lead her to the remaining residents of the Manor.

The Manor had been the prime destination for retirees looking for a stimulating atmosphere, attracting residents from all professions vying to stay there. Drake, the owner/manager selected people who were at the top of their professions to whom he offered attractive financial terms, enticing them to move in. Of course, his calculations still made certain that the Manor remained profitable. What he had not anticipated was that two years ago, it became clear that rising ocean levels would eventually make the facility unlivable forcing him to stop accepting new residents. As a consequence, Drake had systematically moved most of the residents to similar facilities far from the sea and north of the heat zone. Over this time, the Manor remained one of the few buildings left in the neighborhood that was even partly occupied. Now, only eight residents remained!

Valeria labored to climb the stairs located to one side of the reception desk, jumping her rolling bag one riser at a time. *Five more days and I'm out of here.* Even though her husband had not yet retired, she had planned to stop working but director Drake convinced her to stay a little longer while the home was emptied of all remaining occupants. After twenty years caring for the residents of the home, Valeria could not suddenly walk away when those who remained needed her. She had invested too much of her life to their care and many had even become her friends. Nevertheless, she resented having to leave her family by being called back. She stepped onto the second-floor landing, breathing heavily. *Maybe after next week I can lose some weight and get back into shape. One flight of stairs shouldn't be that hard. I'm not even sixty!* Valeria was of modest height and perhaps a little heavy, but no one would call her fat! Her husband often said he was seduced by her curves as well as her sparkling eyes and full lips that animated an oval face. Her dark hair accented with russet highlights dropped down to the top of her shoulders and was in constant motion except when she was working and pulled it back into a bun.

Reluctantly, Valeria had made up her mind to move back to the home for this last week before it was to be completely vacated, rather than shuttling back and forth daily from her own apartment that in any case had also soon to be vacated. The only sound she heard in the empty hallway was the whirr of her rolling suitcase on the tile floor. She shook her head in disapproval when again seeing the faded green walls, a color she despised. Reaching room 210 that had been vacant since Ms. Holmes died eighteen months earlier, she dropped her bag and looked around. The room was small, with only a single bed, a chair, a dresser and a small closet next to the bathroom. It was clean but not up to her standards. So, she immediately started wiping down the surfaces and remaking the bed. It depressed her to be there, and she was struck by a gloom of inevitability that permeated the atmosphere in the home. Death had always been a natural event throughout the home's existence. After all, Valeria remembered, it was simply expected that the residents of the home would walk in but never walk out … it was part of the cycle of life. But this! … the encroaching sea that had taken over in the past few years was different. It marked the death of a way of life, of the environment that had been considered as perpetual. It was an invasion of the sea onto the land, ever so slow but unstoppable. *Come on now*, Valeria snapped, *pull yourself together, you've got a job to do.*

Leaving her temporary quarters, she heard voices coming from the commons room where the remaining residents gathered for meals and to socialize. The main kitchen on the ground floor had closed when the cook left months earlier but attached to the commons room there was a small pantry/kitchenette that Valeria used to prepare meals for the few remaining residents.

As she walked down the hall, Julia Smith's sonorous contralto was heard, dominating the voices coming from the commons room.

"I warned you. It's coming soon, the end of time. It's written right here." Pointing to the open page with her index finger

"And there shall be signs in the sun, and in the moon, and in the stars; and upon the earth distress of nations, with perplexity; the sea and the waves roaring[1]"

"Look out the window, can't you see it. The water's getting closer every day." Julia was a spinster in her mid-eighties and spent most of her days poring over the Bible looking for answers to what was happening. She had stopped fussing over her grooming so that with her wild, unkempt white hair and razor-sharp nose, she appeared witchlike. When she saw Valeria approach, she grabbed her arm, "Val, you're a believer, you understand. These others, they don't know the truth."

"Good morning, Julia," said Val as she untangled herself from Julia's enveloping arms, "We'll have to talk a little later. I've got to check on the others and then I'll come back and see you."

1 Luke 21:25

Julia turned away looking confused. "But…"

"Later," said Val moving briskly into the pantry where she prepared a simple breakfast of coffee, tea and muffins and set them on a side table in the commons room so that the residents could help themselves.

The commons room was not large but accommodated the reduced needs of the few remaining residents. Windows on the west wall faced the skeletal remains of the distant towers of Miami Beach and nearby there was an increasingly bleak landscape of sad palm trees and magnolias with yellowing stalks and leaves guarding abandoned houses along flooded streets. Facing these windows were three tables surrounded by four chairs each and against one of the sidewalls was a couch while the middle of the room was occupied by three lounging chairs. A large telescreen dominated the wall adjacent to the double door leading to the corridor. Two large ceiling fans circulated the oppressive warm air bringing little relief from the heat. The residents in the room missed the air conditioning that had been turned off a month earlier to conserve the limited available power.

Holding a mug of coffee, Jim Robinson sat at one of the tables writing on an open pad. He was a retired engineer in his mid-seventies and had lived in the home for almost ten years. His pale brown face was lined from years of spending time in the sun on construction sites around the world, but he kept his body strong with daily exercise. As he scratched his stubbly salt and pepper beard, he was explaining to Henrietta Barker the inevitability of the current situation. "Look here please, follow me on this. I've started a new graph showing the progression of the high temperatures moving north, it should be clear even to you that we're doomed."

"What do you mean by 'even to you'? "said Henrietta. "Don't you think that's a bit insulting. After all, I've studied the environmental sciences all my life, so I know something about climate. Also, you forget that the UN has been making great progress lately to bring all the world's governments into agreement… ever since they sent a set of scrubber satellites into the upper atmosphere to try to remove some of the carbon that's causing this terrible hot weather." As she spoke, she absentmindedly pulled down at the edge of the tan turban that she always wore. Although she was only on the cusp of seventy, and had a classical Mona Lisa face, her hair had been thinning for the past decade causing her to adopt the turban headdress.

"Don't be naïve," replied Jim, "That's too little and too late and isn't going to make a difference. I know you scientists don't have much respect for us engineers but don't forget that without us, you wouldn't have your built environment. Remember what von Karman said, 'A scientist studies what is, whereas an engineer creates what never was'. Anyway, if you come to my room, I can show you exactly what's happened these past ten years." Jim had covered three walls of his room with a graph. A horizontal line represented ground level and an ascending line, sea level from the time he moved into the home. It was not a straight line but wiggled up and down with periods indicating minimal rise followed by sudden spurts of an increase. Pointing to one, he would explain, 'this was when a chunk of the Antarctic glacier collapsed', and pointing to another, 'that's the Greenland slide.'

Henrietta had been invited a number of times to see his wall-graph. "You've tried to show it to me before, and it's too hot in here to argue with you today. Maybe, another day." She rose to leave the room and wanted to remind him of the story surrounding the ozone layer that shields earth from harmful ultraviolet radiation. Back in 1996 all the world's governments cooperated to ban CFC's (chlorofluorocarbons) that were used in aerosols and had been escaping and destroying the ozone layer for fifty years. At that time scientists predicted that, by banning CFC's, the damage to the ozone layer would heal within less than fifty years and they were proved right. She also wanted to tell Jim that the scrubber satellites that were recently launched might, in a similar way, reverse global warming. But there was no point in arguing with this stubborn man whom, in any case, she would not see after this week. For a smart, good-looking man, he certainly was thick headed. As she left the room, she winked at Valeria who returned a knowing smile.

Sitting on the couch to watch a news program on the telescreen Frank and Diane Weill tried to ignore both Julia's biblical pronouncements and Jim's doom and gloom outlook. Diane was often confused and forgetful and held on tightly to Frank's hand and now closed her eyes in fear as images appeared on the screen of caravans of climate migrants carrying people fleeing from the Mississippi coast. The announcer described it as part of a migration that was taking place along every coastal region of the world, involving millions of people moving to higher and dryer ground away from the coasts and moving north away from the hellish heat. Frank switched channels to a cooking demonstration hoping that Diane would quickly forget the disturbing images in the news. "Open your eyes," he said gently, pointing to the screen, "you used to make meatballs just like that."

For a moment she looked puzzled but then smiled and nodded her head up and down. "I…yes…my mother taught me."

"If you've finished your tea, maybe you want to take a nap since you slept so badly last night," said Frank."

Julia, standing in the open doorway suddenly raised her voice and screamed out,

"This know also, that in the last days perilous times shall come[2]"

Startled, Diane buried her face in her hands as Frank pulled her close to comfort her by holding her tightly in his arms.

"Julia, dear, maybe it's time to put away the good book for a while and let your friends enjoy their morning coffee," said Valeria as she nudged Julia out the door and led her down the hallway to her room.

"But I want to warn them," Julia said pleadingly as she tried to resist.

It was no use! Valeria held her arm tightly and with her free hand, held the Bible out in front of her so that Julia was forced to reach out to follow and try to catch the moving book.

"Good morning Don," Valeria said as she passed Donald Garland holding his dog, Girl, in his arms. "How's your little Girl this morning?"

"She was quite fussy last night, and didn't like going out this morning as she had trouble finding a dry spot to do her business." Donald had moved to the home four years ago, long after his partner had died of AIDS. The two had been together for almost twenty years when Paolo was diagnosed with AIDS, a disease everyone assumed had been eradicated. Unfortunately, the virus that had previously been treated with anti-viral drugs had suddenly mutated in the mid 40's into a more virulent strain for which there was yet no cure. Shortly before he died, Paolo had given Donald the Bichon Frisé in remembrance of

2 Timothy 3:1-17

their love. When Paolo finally succumbed to his illness Donald depended on the dog for comfort.

As he entered the community room, Don waved to Jim Robinson who seemed annoyed as he looked up from the pad he was writing on to say, "Do you have to bring that dog in here. This is not a Paris bistro where dogs are welcomed."

"Girl has as much of a right to be here as you do. In any case, she likes to watch the morning news with me as you well know." With that Don sat down in one of the chairs facing the telescreen and in his usual smooth as molasses voice, turned to speak to Frank. "Do you mind if I change to the news channel?"

"Not at all! We were actually just leaving for Diane's morning nap."

When the Weills left the room, Donald flipped through the channels until he found the one he favored. Before retiring, he had been a news anchor for one of the major networks. With his trim body, chiseled profile and handsome, all-American appearance, he had been a popular feature on the evening news for more than thirty-five years. "Look at that man, Girl. I remember when he was first hired as a reporter. That was almost twenty years ago," and in a conspiratorial tone, he added, "I'll bet he gets the ax soon." Donald hated having to leave his profession, but the management told him that the audience was looking for a younger viewpoint and that his time had passed. Passed! How is that possible? But there was no denying the fact that he looked back nostalgically more than he looked forward and that the world seemed to be moving so fast that he didn't have time to catch up. Also, since Paolo had died, Don no longer had the drive to keep working. Looking up at the screen, he saw the weatherperson in front of a map of Miami-Dade County, announcing clear blue skies for the next few days. She also pointed to the coast of West Africa where a tropical disturbance was forming that until the next weekend should not affect the east coast of the United States. You hear that, Girl. No problem until we leave.

WHEN HE RETURNED TO HIS room, Frank Weill sat in his rocker looking out the window while his wife took her morning nap. *I worry... I worry all the time!* He reached into his dresser drawer and pulled out a worn, leather-bound notebook with a title written in beautiful cursive script: Mon Journal; Bertrand Weill Moreau. It was the diary of his great-grandfather's last days in France in 1940, that other time over a century ago when the world appeared doomed. As he began reading, he occasionally stumbled over French words that he could not immediately translate into English. He leaned back in his rocker and looked out the window as his great-grandfather had looked out a window from his house in the Paris suburbs...

May 10, 1940

Ever since the Germans attacked this morning, rolling over Belgium and Holland, bypassing the sacred Maginot line that was thought to be impenetrable but proved to be only a minor obstacle, it was clear to me that the enemy would eventually reach Paris and I would be forced to leave. The war had at first seemed so unreal that everyone called it the 'drôle de guerre'. Thank God that when the war started eight months ago, I sent Madeleine and the children to Switzerland to stay with my mother. But I could not immediately abandon my music students, so I remained in Croissy, but now most of my students have left with their families and there is no more reason for me to stay.

May 20, 1940

It's so quiet here that I still keep trying to work, I have time before I must leave! Just this morning, I stared at the blank sheet of music paper while my right hand hesitated, suspended over the keys of the piano, fingers bent, ready...but for what? The sounds in my head were still too jumbled to define a clear path. I forced myself to shut out the extraneous sounds of the birds outside the window behind my piano stool. Impossible! Too many sounds... To muffle the offending sounds I pulled the heavy wool drape that blocked off the view to the small garden outside the house. It was so dark that I had to switch on a lamp above my music stand. I then walked around the room as tones from the bird-sounds I had heard rolled around in my head. Three tones, two climbing quarter notes and a descending half note became a theme, the beginning of a musical line. That was a start and I sat at the Bechstein Grand, played the tune and started to write....But!... It was impossible in this threatening atmosphere, and I put the pen aside. I will try again on another day.

June 5, 1940

Today, I'm deathly afraid for the future. The unprepared and under-equipped French army seems to have collapsed before the superior mechanized enemy resulting in a rout toward Paris. It's clear that I will be forced to leave my lovely little home and join one of the caravans of migrants fleeing Paris. I must prepare!

As Frank read this, he thought, *I don't suppose we'll ever learn!* In those days over a century ago, man was fighting an evil enemy, whereas this time, nature is waging war against us. In both cases we should have seen the signs and acted to prevent a catastrophe. The history of the mid-twentieth century would have been completely different if the governments of France and England had taken the threat posed by Hitler's bluster seriously and had acted to stop him. In the same way, in the early twenty-first century, governments of the world had the opportunity to contain the advancing threat of climate change but chose instead to delay action until it became too late. These thoughts rolled around in Frank's head as he stared out at the bleak landscape that now seemed so menacing. In the distance, he saw the abandoned skyscrapers behind Miami Beach whose ground floors were now mostly submerged. Of course, the Manor was located on somewhat higher ground, but he had watched the Spoonbills abandoning Florida for the past five years. *If the birds won't stay, why should we. And... why has it taken so long for Drake to find us a new home away from this bleak place?*

Frank and Diane were both in their late seventies, had been married for almost fifty years and had raised two sons in their home in Scarsdale. Every weekday Frank commuted to New York to his desk as the editor of a weekly news magazine while Diane worked at home writing book reviews for a literary journal while simultaneously fulfilling the role of housewife, taking care of their two sons. Of course, their housekeeper Doris performed most of the actual work, cleaning and cooking for the family while Diane read and prepared her reviews. It was Doris who first noticed that Diane began to show signs of forgetfulness; missed appointments with colleagues, weekly paychecks not prepared, misplaced possessions and a decrease in her meticulous appearance. Frank at first ignored these early signs of dementia until Diane began to show poor judgment driving and had a small accident in her late fifties. A visit to their physician confirmed the diagnosis of early dementia that also caused Diane to lose her driver's license. Within a dozen years Frank found that caring for Diane made it impossible to keep up with his work responsibilities and decided to take early retirement and move to Florida. After an extensive search of facilities that appeared caring and friendly, he decided on the Manor. He never regretted that decision since Diane seemed happy and a little calmer after moving there.

Suddenly startled, Diane called out, "Frank!" as she awoke from her nap. "Where are you?"

"Shush, it's OK, I'm here," Frank turned away from the window and walked to the bed where Diane was resting, while cursing the arthritis that pained his knees with every step. She's having a good day. At least she remembered who I am. As a consequence of her dementia, Diane occasionally did not know where she was and sometimes treated Frank as a stranger to be feared. As he took her hand to reassure her, he said, "You must have had a bad dream. Would you like to get up now?"

"Yes! Can we go down to the beach? We haven't been there in such a long time."

"I'm sorry, but the beach is closed. In fact, I can't even see it anymore."

"What do you mean?"

"Sorry sweetheart, I shouldn't have said that... Look, Albert told me that we were going to move very soon to a beautiful lake with a little beach where you can walk around and put your toes in the water. And, it will be close to our sons. Doesn't that sound wonderful? He'll be here later, and I'll ask him to tell you all about it."

Diane looked at Frank and seemed puzzled. "Is Albert our friend?" she asked.

"You remember Albert. He runs the Manor and we've known him ever since we came here almost ten years ago."

Diane lay back on the bed. "I don't know?" She closed her eyes tightly trying to remember and slowly let herself dispel her fears and descend once more into a restful sleep.

Frank gently released her hand from his and laid it on her chest as the rhythm of her breathing steadied. *Thank God our exodus is only five days away.*

AFTER SETTLING JULIA IN HER room, Valeria walked over to the Simmons' room and knocked on the door. Dolores de la Vega and Alexander Simmons, both in their early nineties were used to sleeping late and did not respond immediately to the insistent knocking. Dolores's faint voice could barely be heard through the door. "Yes," she said.

"It's Val, can I come in?"

"Just a minute." A chair creaked against the tile floor and an airy rustle of bedsheets sounded through the door that opened slowly. Alex, his long grey hair tied carelessly with a rubber band into a ponytail, opened the door a wide crack. With his body bent forward as a result of a deteriorating spine, he looked up at Val. "What can I do for you this morning?"

"I thought you might want to join the others in the commons room," said Val.

"Dolores is not quite dressed but we'll join you in a while."

Once the door clicked shut, Dolores, sitting on the edge of the bed, looked up at her husband. "Why do we have to play this silly game every day. I'd rather read than have to talk to some of those people". Dolores had been a celebrated prima ballerina and although she now used a cane because of a fall some years ago, she was still blessed with a lithe, supple body without a superfluous ounce of fat. "This is no life," she said, "and now we will have to move again. I don't think I can take it. I'm just tired of it all."

"We'll work it out," Alex said. "We always have."

After being chosen as the new prima ballerina in the New York Ballet, Dolores felt she needed a business manager to deal with contractual matters. Her financial planner recommended Alex as someone who was totally honest and whom she could trust to represent her. When they first met in person, Dolores was not particularly impressed with this man, no taller than she, about her age but somewhat shy and seemingly put off by her celebrity. However, when she observed him in business dealings with the administrators of the ballet, she saw a different person, one who was forceful and direct and stubbornly supportive of her best interests. After hiring him as her manager, they became friends and after several months, best friends and later, lovers. Within two years they were married by a justice of the peace in his home overlooking the Pacific Ocean. It was shortly after a performance in which she had performed the role of Giselle in San Francisco.

Alex had long suffered from back problems and a constant pain in the abdomen that he attributed to all the exercise Dolores made him do. To find out what he could do to alleviate the pain he had months earlier been examined by Dr. Weiner. After reviewing the results of the tests. Dr. Weiner warned Alex that he needed to totally abstain from any more alcohol to give his liver a chance of healing from what the tests showed was advanced cirrhosis. If he didn't, he was at a high risk of dying. Ever since becoming Dolores's business manager, he was in the habit of drinking at lunch when negotiating contracts, drinking when they were on the road and having more than one scotch at dinner. Nevertheless, when he heard that he needed to give it up, Alex thought, a drink or two is one of the few pleasures I still have at my age. He decided not to tell Dolores.

"Do you realize how many times we've moved since we've been together," he asked.

"How many?"

"I have no idea, but it is surely many dozens, New York, Paris, San Francisco, Rome, …God, do you remember Rome. We had this great apartment there while you were performing. It was not too far from the Tiber, and we used to walk along the riverbank among all the other young lovers. Well, we weren't exactly that young anymore but we felt it."

"What do you mean, we weren't young!" Dolores said with a wicked smile, "I had barely passed forty and was still in my prime."

"We've been so lucky to have had such a great life. This is such a rotten way to end it."

"Don't talk like that and forget what I said about being tired. This is not the end, just another transition."

"But this is different. We've never been in a situation where nature conspired against us, forcing us to move because the damn ocean's moving in. I sometime think that Julia's right about this being God punishing us."

"Nonsense! …. here I was complaining about moving again and

now you're trying to frame our situation as a biblical prophecy. If you're going to blame anyone, blame all the lackadaisical governments who never had the guts to act to do something to deal with this climate problem"

"Of course, you're right…. Let's forget about this now and go out to see the others."

Somewhat irritated, Dolores sat down at her dressing table and said, "Give me a minute while I make myself presentable."

AFTER LEAVING THE SIMMONS', VALERIA continued around to each of the remaining residents' rooms and knocked on each door asking them to join her in the commons room. They slowly gathered; first Henrietta followed soon thereafter by the Weills' who immediately took possession of the couch. Val busied herself rearranging the chairs on either side or the couch so that a rough semicircle was created with a seat for herself at the apex. As a consequence, she asked both Robinson and Garland to stand temporarily while their chairs were moved. The two men were glad to end up far from each other at opposite ends of the seating arc. As the Simmons arrived, the whack-whack-roar of a helicab landing, rattled the windows. Reacting to the vibrations of the arriving helicab, Val said, "That must be Mr. Drake. Would you all excuse me while I go and meet him! Jim, could you help me carry in the food that he usually brought these days." Val, followed by Robinson, went down the stairs and out to meet Albert Drake, the manager of the Manor as he stepped out of the helicab.

The trimmed beard Drake had grown over the past year was speckled with patches of grey that matched his intense eyes. "Can you give me a hand with these boxes," he asked.

Robinson stepped forward, bent down to avoid the wind from the overhead blades and lifted a heavy box and carried it toward the door. "Hey," he said, "a case of wine. I guess you're planning a party?"

Drake ignored him and as Val was handed another box she asked, "You're early, Mr. Drake. Is anything wrong?"

Carrying the last box, he answered, "I'll tell you when we get inside out of this noise".

The three of them carried the boxes upstairs to the little pantry adjacent to the commons room. "Would you give us a minute," asked

Drake as he gently nudged Robinson out the door. When they were alone, he turned to Valeria. "This is the situation," he said. "I've been warned by the weather folks that we have to leave earlier. There's a storm brewing that may hit this area hard. And you know what that means."

"We've been through hurricanes before. What's so special about this one?"

"First of all, remember that the hurricane that hit us two years ago was much stronger than previous ones. And, the weather guys tell me that the one that's coming is possibly even more powerful. I for one don't want to be around when it hits. So, anyway, I've brought more than enough food to last us for the time we'll still be here, so we should be OK!"

"You're talking about less than a week? In that case, when should I get the residents ready to leave?"

"On Thursday morning, so you've got three days. I've made arrangements to house all the remaining residents. I couldn't keep them all together and unfortunately had to settle them into different homes." Handing her a sheaf of papers, he added, "The details are all here. There's a set of travel documents for each of them. They will all be together as far as Atlanta and then they will split up. Relocation guides will help them to sort it all out after they land. Also, I've got a couple of helivans ordered for Thursday." Drake added, "Why don't you tell the residents while I put this stuff away."

"I'd be happy to do that later," said Val.

"No, no! I'll take care of it. You go ahead." Drake turned starting to unpack the boxes while Val left the pantry. When he was alone, he stopped and, feeling unsteady, grabbed the edge of the counter. What am I going to do without this home? It's been my whole life. I don't have anything else. He wiped his creased brow and ran his hands across his cheeks and down through his new beard. If that storm comes, I'm finished. I have nothing else left. God damn it! Why didn't I sell out years ago? They said the waters were going to continue rising but I didn't believe them; …Hell! No one believed it then. Now it's too late. He started mechanically to put away the food, the perishables in the refrigerator and the rest in the overhead cabinets. Thank God my parents are gone and don't have to see the death of their dream.

WHEN VALERIA CAME BACK INTO the commons room, she saw that the Simmons had seated themselves in two chairs next to Don Garland as Dolores held out her hand to pet Girl who excitedly sought to lick it. Henrietta had squeezed herself on one end of the sofa not occupied by the Weills'. Julia had not reappeared, but Val thought that was for the best and she would deal with her separately later.

She waited until all had taken seats and the buzz of chatter quieted. "Folks," she started, "Mr. Drake brought us good news. We will be leaving here a little earlier than we had originally planned. Actually, we will be out of here on Thursday."

"Don, can you stop that yelping dog, I can hardly hear what Val is saying," Asked Robinson. Turning to face Valeria, he added, "Is there a problem?"

"Not really. It's just that Mr. Drake doesn't want to take a chance with the weather."

Some of the residents looked around nervously as Henrietta spoke up. "Be honest with us. We're not blind. I heard the news this morning that spoke of a storm off Africa. I know perfectly well that those type of storms often become hurricanes that hit our shores." As she was speaking, Drake strode into the room.

"You're right," he said. "I just wanted to be cautious and not take a risk so I've ordered helivans to come and pick us up before there is any chance that this storm will be a threat. Trust me, you know I've always taken good care of you. I've already made arrangements for all of you with other homes away from the sea. I'm certain you'll all find them welcoming. Valeria has all the details and will speak to you individually. Now, if there are no questions, why don't we let Val prepare our lunch".

"Now, hold on a minute Drake," said Robinson as he stood and walked toward him, shaking an accusing finger. "Are you trying to brush us off again? We knew over a year ago that we had to move out, and we've been really patient (stretching out those words) while waiting our turn. Now it's suddenly become an emergency! I don't buy it." Both Don Garland and Henrietta Barker got up at almost the same time, prepared to leave the room as they did not want to take part in an argument between Drake, whom they respected and Robinson, whom they considered too volatile. The Simmons and the Weills' were too bewildered to move.

"Get that goddam finger out of my face and shut up." Red in the face, Drake grabbed Robinson's hand and roughly pushed it aside. His eyes blazed with anger. He was an inch shorter but twenty years younger than the resident who now stared at him with open mouth. "And don't talk to me about patience. I've had to deal with your unpleasantness for the past ten years and your drawing on MY walls with your silly graph. You think that's been easy…" Valeria was stunned at this sudden outburst and stepped forward to try to defuse the situation. Ignoring her, Drake continued, "I would have been happy to get rid of you a year ago when I was told that the Manor had to be vacated but there were priorities established and you were too damn healthy. I had to start with those in the poorest health…and you were on the bottom of the list. You think finding new accommodations for the residents was easy? It was a hell of a job. All up and down the coast, there was flooding and every facility like ours was looking to relocate their residents. I had to scour the eastern half of the country to find suitable places. You're in the last group and I'm tired and as far as I'm concerned, good riddance!" Drake stormed out of the commons room and headed to the safety of his own room.

Valeria was never completely comfortable dealing with confrontations but felt that she had to try and turned to Robinson. "You must understand that Mr. Drake has been under a great deal of pressure this last year and I'm sure he didn't mean to attack you."

"He had no right to talk to me that way." Robinson muttered as he pushed past Val to leave the room.

Alex turned to Frank and said with a wicked smile, "Well, there are four of us left here. How about a quick game of bridge while Val prepares our lunch?"

"I'd love to but I'm afraid Diane is not quite up to it today."

"Let me see if I can persuade Don or Henrietta to join us and then Diane can watch."

"Thank you. I think that might work."

2

GENESIS OF THE STORM

Ten days earlier, of the coast of Africa, warm humid air began to rise from the ocean's surface. As it cooled, it began to condense, forming a cloud. More and more such packets of humid air followed suit and the resulting clouds began a counterclockwise rotation around a center where cooler winds were pulled down toward the ocean's surface. Known as a tropical depression, such a storm can grow into an 800-mile diameter monster. The National Hurricane Center located in Memphis (they had long ago moved from Miami as rising sea levels were threatening), contacted the pocket aircraft carrier, USS Obama, cruising in the Atlantic off the coast of North Africa, advising them to collect data on this storm. On the flight deck of the carrier, a Short Takeoff and Vertical Landing (STOVL) jet was being prepared for the mission. In a briefing room adjacent to the command bridge of the carrier, Vice Admiral Barstow who was on his last assignment before retirement was showing two pilots the latest satellite image retrieved only minutes earlier. "As you can see, the storm off the coast of Guinea seems to be intensifying although it's still classified as a tropical disturbance. I've been advised that it will likely develop into a tropical cyclone. As you know temperatures in that region have been increasing for decades and our weather folks are concerned that it could generate into a devastating storm when it hits the US coast. We currently have a narrow range of projected directions of the storm's path from meteorology. What we need are more accurate wind velocities and pressure data to evaluate possible scenarios as to the projected landfall along the Eastern Seaboard. That's your job. Gentl…uh, people!" Lt. Alice Maynard smiled when she heard this little gaffe but from the moment she joined this air-group she realized that Barstow had not been comfortable dealing with female pilots. But she was not inclined to make it an issue now, since she realized that this was Barstow's last command.

"I don't need to tell you how important this is but at the same time, how dangerous such a storm can be. I want you both safely back aboard by 1700. Any questions?"

Without further discussion, the pilots left for the flight deck and prepared to take off heading south toward the cyclonic line of thunderstorms. The satellite image had already shown the counterclockwise rotation of the developing storm and the plane headed directly toward its center to collect the needed data of temperature and pressure that were not obtainable from a satellite and that might determine its future intensity. As they approached the edge of the storm the plane was buffeted by strong winds, but they pushed on until reaching the eye where a momentary calm permitted them to record the needed data.

Once back on board the Calhoun, the data that had been collected was forwarded to the Hurricane Center where it was analyzed by the meteorology service. They determined that indeed, this storm had the potential of delivering a severe blow to the United States coastline although where it would make landfall was as yet undetermined. Since the seas had already risen over five feet in the last fifty years, this storm, with waves reaching thirty feet could well overwhelm a large section of the southeastern coast of the United States with devastating storm surges. This was significant since one fifth of the United States as well as the world's population lives near coastlines. This storm together with a second one just forming in the Atlantic have the potential of making most of Florida unlivable. The Hurricane Center considered this information critical and immediately forwarded it to the White House for further action.

When the data summary was received at the White House, it landed on the desk of Dr. Andrew Carlson, the senior science advisor to the President. Carlson had earlier received the latest world satellite map that revealed the devastation caused by decades of climate change. Now looking at the images on his screen, Carlson saw that from the north to the south pole, the planet is in turmoil! In the Arctic, floating ice is seen ripped apart creating wide channels of open ocean; In the Antarctic and Greenland, myriad rivers appear, carrying melting ice to the ocean; The former shorelines of all the continents are gone, having long ago retreated inland, swallowing beaches, towns, and cities; Oceanside treasures of history such as Venice and New Orleans are revealed only as shadows in the mirror of the sea like so many mythical cities of Atlantis; The tropical paradise of Polynesia is gone, vanished beneath the sea; Vast stretches of the west coast of the United States, portions of Australia and Southeast Asia, South India, Pakistan and Afghanistan after years of fires, scorching heat and lack of water are uninhabitable; The Amazon is a desert as is much of central Africa and South America; Southern China is a dust bowl.

Feeling a sense of hopelessness after finishing his review of the satellite data, Carlson opened the urgent message from the hurricane center. After quickly reviewing the attached data, Dr. Carlson phoned to request a meeting with the President. Speaking to the appointment secretary, he emphasized the pressing nature of the situation. Within thirty minutes, he received confirmation of a meeting and walked in quick time from the west wing to the oval office. Arriving somewhat out of breath, he was ushered into President Margaret Davenport's office.

"You seem a bit breathless, Andy. Come in and sit down. When you've recovered, can you tell me what is it that can't wait until tomorrow's cabinet meeting?"

"Madame President, it…"

"For heaven's sake, Andy, we've known each other since college, so in the privacy of this office can we skip the formality?" It was over twenty years earlier that the two had met in Cambridge. Davenport was in her last year at Harvard completing a history and political science degree and Carlson was in his first year of graduate school at MIT pursuing a degree in earth and atmospheric sciences. Although in different schools, they met when they both attended a rally supporting action to deal with the climate emergency. They were attracted to each other and dated for a while until Davenport graduated and left for Indiana to begin her political career. When Davenport started her run for the presidency, they reconnected. Carlson was impressed with her understanding and respect for the issues facing the country and Davenport respected his ability to make complex scientific information understandable to the laymen. There quickly developed a deep measure of trust and respect between them.

Still breathing heavily, Carlson answered, "all right, Maggie, here it is! I just received a message from the hurricane center that may require immediate action."

"In the two years I've been in this office, it seems that every change in the weather becomes a major crisis. Honestly, we've lived through hurricanes before. What's different about this one?"

"I'm afraid this one's a real doozy. Probably one of the most powerful storms I've seen in all my professional life but also one of the most dangerous for the Atlantic coastline States."

Sitting forward in her chair, and with deep lines suddenly appearing on her otherwise smooth brow President Davenport answered, "All right, Andy, you've got my attention."

"You understand that what happens in the atmosphere is intimately connected to what happens in the oceans."

"Is this going to be one of your science lectures?"

"I'm just trying to put this in context."

"All right, go on."

"In the Atlantic, there is a circulation pattern moving warm water from the south to the north, losing temperature as it moves north. When it arrives in the arctic, the now cooler surface water drops down and begins a trek south, picking up heat in the process until it rises in the south to begin the circulatory process again. It's actually a little more complicated than that but in essence that is what happens. Air temperatures obviously interact with this circulation pattern as the warm tropical air adds heat to the water and the cold arctic air cools it down. Now, this has gone merrily along for hundreds and thousands of years until something else happened. Here, I'll make it specific. As a result of the catastrophic increase in carbon we've been pumping into the upper atmosphere, we've triggered a change. The atmosphere has greatly warmed, causing the melting of glaciers resulting in an input of fresh water being added in the arctic. As you know, one consequence of this has been the increase in ocean levels, but...and here's where I get nervous. Our little hurricane in the Atlantic, well, actually, there happens to be another one in the Pacific right now where they call it a typhoon.... I'm concerned that these two guys are going to be joined by a bunch of others triggering what would be a superstorm on a global scale... goodbye civilization!"

"What the devil is a superstorm?"

"It's the virtually simultaneous appearance of storms throughout the world with a catastrophic impact on weather."

"Andy! Aren't you being a little overdramatic? What is the possibility of such an occurrence?"

"Right now, I give it about a thirty percent chance."

"Is this a consensus from your staff?"

"Well, some of them think I'm crazy but I'm working on them."

"So, what are you asking of me? Is there some way we can prevent this from happening?"

"I honestly don't know. All we can do now is watch and wait and hope that more storms will not suddenly develop elsewhere in the world."

"Have you shared your concerns with other science organizations?

"Yes! I've advised the World Meteorological Group and they will keep me informed of any developing storms."

"All right! In that case, keep me informed as well." Carlson left the meeting to go back to his office to monitor the situation recognizing the reality that the President was powerless to take any action that would remove this threat to the world.

3
PREPARATION
Tuesday

O N TUESDAY MORNING THE SKY appeared almost totally covered with a blanket of grey clouds. Where the full sun should have been rising above the eastern horizon all that appeared was an orange-grey fuzz. On the ground, there was no letup from the incessant heat and humidity. Ever since the air-conditioning had been turned off at the Manor, to save the limited power provided by the roof mounted solar panels and batteries, residents had to make-do with open windows and fans.

Following the blowup on Monday, Valeria and Drake avoided each other but Val decided this morning that she needed to defuse the tension and knocked on the door to his room. "What is it?" Drake answered sharply causing Val to momentarily reconsider, but she was determined to act for the good of the residents. "It's Val and I wonder if you had some time to talk?"

"I'm really not up to talking today. Go away!"

"Look, Mr. Drake, we only have two days left here and I think it's important that we clear up the situation that you caused with your blowup yesterday."

The door flew open and Drake stood framed in the doorway in an open shirt hanging outside blue jeans. His hair, usually neatly parted on top of his head, was splayed out in all directions and his mottled face, short craggily beard and bloodshot eyes gave him the appearance of a man who had just woken from sleeping on a coarse pillow. "Damn it to hell, I don't know what situation you're talking about?"

Not about to be put off by this outburst, Val replied calmly, "If you're going to start screaming again, let's do it behind closed doors. Will you let me in or not?"

Somewhat flustered, Drake stepped aside and let her enter. Once in his apartment, she closed the door behind her and waited, looking around at the state of the apartment. In the sitting room which Drake had arranged as an office, papers from open file cabinets were scattered on the floor; Through an open doorway, she could see into the bedroom with its unmade bed on which lay three separate piles of clothes. An open suitcase lay on the floor adjacent to the bed. "Since you're in, sit in that chair next to the desk," said Drake as he absent-mindedly tried to button his shirt and added, "just push those papers to the floor."

Before sitting down, Val picked up the papers on the chair and put them on the desk.

"Now, suppose you tell me what's so important? "said Drake as he sat down and tilted back in his desk chair.

"To be perfectly frank, Robinson was really upset with your outburst and I feel you need to get back to him and possibly even apologize. I realize this is a difficult time, but you did not have to take it out on one of your longest-term residents."

Turning toward the window Drake pointed and said, "look out there! What do you see? What used to be a paradise is now a dying landscape. Soon it will be underwater! And this Manor, that my parents opened long ago is now going to die with it. They left it to me, and I've nurtured it all these years and in two days it will be gone and with it everything I own." Raising his voice, he added, "Of course, I'm angry. Who wouldn't be, in my situation? I'll have nothing left when we leave on Thursday. This has been my home as well as the residents', but the difference is that they will still have a home that I worked hard to arrange for them. Where's my home going to be? I'm not a rich man and most of what I had was tied up in this fucking Manor." Drake put the back of his hand up to roughly wipe his eyes.

Valeria respected this moment of silence and then asked, "What about your family?"

When he retained his composure, Drake answered quietly, "The residents, they were my family. I never married and never had kids. I've got a sister in Phoenix, but we weren't really close. And besides,

Phoenix is drying up and I wouldn't want to live there."

"What about friends? Surely, you must have some!"

Drake turned to face her. "I've always been able to talk to you and thought you were a friend, not just my employee."

"You never said anything before but..." feeling somewhat embarrassed, Val added, "you always showed me respect and I've always appreciated that. I'm flattered that you think of me as a friend." She took a deep breath and added, "Sooo, …as a friend, won't you consider talking to Robinson."

Drake stood up and walked to the window. "I'll consider it,… that is,… as a friend. Now, if you don't mind, I'd better get back to organizing this mess."

Val stood by the door before leaving and whispered, "Thank you!"

AFTER LEAVING DRAKE'S ROOM, VALERIA walked down the hall as she had done thousands of times and, as if for the first time, took notice of all the art that was hung at intervals. They were mostly prints of paintings by expressionist artists such as Picasso, Cezanne, Matisse, even a brightly colored geometric composition by Mondrian that Drake referred to as that bunch of colored rectangles. *Get rid of it!* he had said. More to his liking were the pastoral scenes by Pissarro or a Monet or Renoir. He particularly liked coastal paintings with boats. Yes! Boats made him think of the time he sailed along the Florida coast and crossed over to the Bahamas alone. It had made him feel so free and powerful, but that was before he took over responsibility for the management of the Manor from his parents. He never again felt that sense of exhilaration and connection to the sea. At the far end of the hall were a few paintings donated by departed residents. Most were somewhat amateurish but one, portraying a sloop in heavy seas with colors of blue, grey and black was particularly striking and Drake would often stand and stare at the painting for a long time. If asked why, he would simply say that he felt a connection to the scene that was portrayed.

Val stopped in the pantry and then went to Julia's room and knocked on the door. "It's Val! May I come in?" She spoke in a loud whisper as she could hear Julia pacing back and forth. "You missed dinner last night, so I've brought you a little something to eat. Also, there's something important I need to talk to you about."

After what seemed to Val an eternity, Julia opened the door and shouted, "I don't know why I'm always excluded when there's a group meeting?"

"Calm down, you weren't excluded yesterday. I just didn't want to upset you with Mr. Drake's news."

"What news?" Julia responded sheepishly.

"You'll be happy to know that we are going to be picked up on Thursday to move to our new homes. Mr. Drake has found a lovely place for you just outside Atlanta that's run by the Baptists. I think you'll find the people there very welcoming. I know you've been unhappy with some of the residents here so I think this move should make you much more comfortable."

"I've tried to show them that the signs are all there; the immorality all around us, the disaster we're living through, all the talk about the end of humanity. It's all in the book but they just won't listen." She then added in a conspiratorial tone, "I think it's because most of them are atheists…"

"Come now, they're not necessarilly atheists. It's just that they don't like to think of this as the end of time. Some of them still see signs of hope. Henrietta for instance."

"No, no! they're sinners, all of them, and they have to atone."

"Julia, calm down. I really don't have the time now to have a theological discussion with you. Why don't you enjoy the snack I've brought and perhaps after dinner we can have a serious talk? Also, since there isn't that much time before we leave, you have to decide what you plan to take with you and begin to pack. I'll be happy to help you."

"No, no! I can do it myself."

Valeria walked toward the door to leave when Julia grabbed her arm. "I still think they're all sinners!"

"Before I leave, why don't we pray to clear away your wrathful thoughts," said Val who had spent many evenings praying together with Julia ever since she learned of her past. Over several meetings, Julia described when she first grew up on a small farm in Eastern Kentucky. Her father whom she adored died of a heart attack when she was eight. Her mother and older brother took over management of the farm. It was hard work and her mother was always tired leaving Julia alone much of the time. When Julia was twelve, her brother began molesting her, becoming more forcefully sexual within a year. Disgusted with the abuse, Julia eventually fled into the bosom of the local Baptist church. They became her protectors and she never returned home. As she grew older, she shunned all men as fornicators and evil and was never able to form a healthy relationship with a man. Nevertheless, as she matured, Julia became a successful independent woman while always remaining in the shadow of the church. When she arrived at the Manor, she immediately bonded with Valeria who was the only one she found sympathetic toward her beliefs.

After a short prayer session with Julia, Valeria left and walked toward the Commons Room, hearing rhythmic sounds in the air. Entering the room, she saw Robinson sitting at his usual table absentmindedly drumming with a pencil on the edge of the table.

"James, do you have to do that?"

"When you call me James, I know I'm in trouble. It's just that I can think better if I hear a repetitive drumming sound."

"You're not in trouble, Jim. In fact, I talked to Mr. Drake about yesterday's incident and he is sorry to have lost his temper."

Raising his voice, Jim said, "Sorry? Who the hell does he think he is? Maybe he doesn't remember that he has an obligation to us… to me. I paid good money to spend my last years here in supposed peace and the least I expect from the management is respect for my opinions. Hell, I know this current situation is not his fault … he didn't create the problems caused by the weather, but at the same time, I've been very patient while he worked this out. Frankly, we should have been out of here a year ago when it was obvious that this city was gone. For years water had bubbled up through the porous limestone on which Miami was built. More recently, the city suffered from successive attacks as rising sea levels intensified by surging water pushed by annual hurricanes reached higher and higher until the city was no longer livable. Yet here we are!"

"You're not being quite fair. There were over two hundred residents here when it became clear that this part of the coastline was eventually going to be flooded out. Drake had a great deal of trouble finding everyone suitable accommodations and as he said he had to establish priorities based mainly on health conditions."

"Sure! And we went along with it even though it's been a little rough at times. It still doesn't give him the right to take out his frustrations on us. We're just as frustrated by this as he is! Look, Val, I'm sorry for you. You've been very patient with us through this and you've stuck with us after everyone else left. I can't imagine it's been easy on you and your family. I don't even know where you plan to go when we all leave?"

"I'll be fine. My husband has already moved to Nashville to set up our new home, so we'll be closer to our kids."

"OK, but Drake's got to understand. I'm an engineer and I like to deal with facts, and I don't like to be put off with a wave of the hand."

"He does understand and as I said he was sorry for yesterday. Now, let's put it behind us. I'll go and let you prepare to leave this dying place."

Once he was alone, Robinson looked at the graph he had depicted on the walls, and as he walked around the room turning from one wall to the next, he retraced with his index finger the line he had drawn. *It's really happening.*

Jim Robinson was the son of an interracial couple who lived on the South Side of Chicago. His mother was a nurse who never spoke of her parents both of whom had died in an accident when she was six. She was raised by her father's family until leaving for college. Jim's father was a black contractor and was an early influence. Walking around construction sites in Chicago with his father, Jim began to observe all the downtown buildings, and wonder what made them stand up. This led him to decide in high school that he would become an engineer and spend his life designing such structures. Watching his creations rise out of the ground as construction progressed, always gave him an unimaginable thrill. But now, as he looked toward Miami Beach, he could see a building he had designed decades earlier, abandoned and ravaged by the elements. It saddened him, especially as he thought about other structures he had designed in coastal areas around the world and realized that many of those must have suffered a similar fate! Over the years, his work had taken him all over the world, designing projects in Europe, the Middle East and Asia. This meant long absences from his wife and son and their home in St. Louis. Eventually this led to an irreconcilable break with his wife. After the divorce, Jim tried to maintain a close relationship to his only son, Mike, but that was thirty years ago, and their visits together became increasingly infrequent. He blamed it on the work and the long separations that also prevented him from developing any long-term romantic relationships. Once he had retired and moved into the Manor, he had written Mike and called but to no avail. His son now had his own family and did not seem to want to resume contact with Jim. So, the graph became his passion even though it too, was pointing toward doom, not the death of a relationship but of a familiar environment! Jim's insistence at following the unfolding of the climate's impact also isolated him from most of the Manor's residents. "Whatever happens, will happen. Don't make such a big fuss about it," was the reaction he received from all but Henrietta. Of course, she understood, given her background but even she didn't respond to his obsessive nature. *Someday*, he thought, *someday I'll get through to her.* For some reason, he felt closer to her than to any of the others. When she looked at him, he felt a warmth, a feeling that had eluded him for most of his life but, *I can't even talk to her*, he realized. In seventy-two years, he had never learned to be really close to another human being, not his wife nor his son. *In two days, she will be gone as well. I can't let that happen without at least making an effort.* He vowed to approach her again, but not to discuss technical issues rather to talk more intimately.

THE MORNING SUN PENETRATED DEEPLY into her room causing Henrietta to pull down the shade allowing her in the reduced glare, to open her computer and check her mail. Henrietta had retired as a professor in environmental science at Lehigh University and kept in touch with some of her colleagues to keep up with the latest thinking on the impacts of climate change. Before the screen flashed open, she glanced next to her computer at a photograph of a young man with a broad smile and a wave of dark hair suspended above his right eye. Henrietta had married Crandall Barker when she graduated from the college where they had met. It was the year before she started graduate school. Crandall lived off his family's inheritance and had decided to manage it himself and create a philanthropic organization. Unfortunately, he was reckless in his investments and when the panic of '31 hit, he lost a major part of his inheritance. This caused him to fall into a severe depression and within a year he committed suicide. Since Crandall was the love of her life, Henrietta never recovered from the loss as she blamed herself for not having been sufficiently aware of his pain. Consequently, although she had occasional relationships, she was never again able to commit herself to another man and instead, she concentrated on her career. When she retired, she reluctantly moved to Miami to be closer to her older sister. That was in the early fifties and only four years later her sister passed away.

For company, she now relied on the electronic tablet, that allowed her to remain in contact with her former students and keep abreast of the latest developments in the environmental sciences. Every five years, scientists had made predictions about the consequences of climate change that inevitably proved to be too conservative. A prediction in the early twenties for a four-foot rise in sea level by 2100 was almost half-way there by 2035 raising alarms in the scientific community. As a consequence, an interdisciplinary team of scientists RACE (Rapid Assessment of Climate Effect) had been established in the mid-thirties to come up with more realistic predictions of temperature increase and sea level rise and to focus on the 'race' against the consequences of climate change. Henrietta was an integral member of that team. In annual meetings, the team would review all the latest statistics from monitors around the world to update their projections. When she retired, one of her former students replaced her on the panel but continued to share with her the latest data. Knowing that sea level was rising and threatening the livability of the coast, she often regretted moving to Miami. After the loss of her sister, she rationalized it as a desire to live her remaining years where the land and the ocean collide.

Today, she studied the charts that appeared on her screen looking for hopeful signs of a positive change when a knock on the door interrupted her. "Who is it?"

"It's Albert, Albert Drake, may I come in?"

"Of course, Mr. Drake, please come in," she said as she opened the door. "What can I do for you?"

"I know you're a scientist and I wonder if you can help me look into the future concerning this coming storm?"

"As you, yourself said, we have to evacuate because of the possibility of disastrous flooding. I'm not sure I can tell you more than you already have seen on the telescreen."

"I know, but you've studied this whole climate change business and I don't know what to expect?"

"There's no good news, I'm afraid. Climate change is not a new subject. It's been going on for the last century. There was a chance when it was first identified, that the world could have taken action to reverse it but I'm afraid that didn't happen...the political will wasn't there and the special interests in the coal and oil industries fought against change."

"Yes, I know all that but what will happen tomorrow and the next day and the next weeks and months after that!"

"Mr. Drake, I'm afraid you expect too much. I can only repeat what you already know. The coastal areas of the continents will continue to be flooded and there will be few parts of the world not subject to increased temperatures. In the long term, the good news is that the far north of this continent and of Europe and Asia as well as the tip of the southern continent, will become the new habitable belts with cities thriving, filled with new arrivals and expanding agricultural areas."

"Forget about Canada! You don't understand! This home is all I have in the world and I can't believe I have to abandon it to the fishes."

"Believe me I understand, but we're doing the right thing by moving north and inland where we can re-establish ourselves. You have to hope that you can find a new future there."

"That means starting over ...and at my age..." Drake turned away from Henrietta and brusquely left the room saying. "How can I find hope when there is no hope!" This was not the direction he was seeking.

Henrietta was somewhat shaken by Drake's sudden departure and wondered whether she should have given him a different answer and perhaps a measure of hope? But she had long ago decided that it was important to accept the world as it is and not deal in the myth of false hope. That was the only way to engage people to take action convincing governments to oppose the special interests that stood in the way of curbing the use of fossil fuels. Among all the residents at the Manor, she felt that Jim is the only one who seemed realistic and understood what was happening. *If only he weren't so difficult to be with...so sure of himself and so unapproachable. He seems to wear a protective armor,* she thought. *I wonder what he's hiding.*

WHAT TO TAKE, OH, WHAT to pack? These thoughts were on the minds of all the residents. Drake had told each of them that they could only carry one suitcase for the trip. On top of what they had originally brought, there were so many memories attached to the objects that had accumulated since arriving at the home: Photographs, knickknacks, letters, notebooks, to say nothing of clothes!

"There's no way I can pack everything in one suitcase," said Diane, shaking nervously as she looked into the closet. "It's like we're being sent to one of the camps we read about in the big war during the holocaust."

Frank put his arms around his wife to calm her. "It's nothing like that! And besides, Mr. Drake said we could pack what's left in big boxes he gave each of us, that he would have picked up later and shipped to our new home. So, let's just concentrate on what you would need immediately. Here," he said walking over to the dresser and opening the top drawer, "let's start with this drawer."

Diane walked up to the dresser and looked down at the open drawer. For a long minute, she did not move until slowly placing her left hand into the drawer and pulled out a cotton top, holding it up for a moment before replacing it in the drawer. "Perhaps we could do this a little later," she said as she moved toward the bed to lie down.

"Of course. There's no big hurry and we can put it off for a little while. Why don't you close your eyes and rest while I start on my things?" Frank stood on the side of the bed holding her hand. He was also tired as he was reminded once more of the ravages of the disease that had turned a vibrant, vivacious woman into this fearful soul.

He thought back to their time in New York and when they first met. Since kindergarten, Diane had attended an all-girls school from which she had graduated at eighteen. To celebrate the event, she enticed two of her classmates to go to a lounge where her favorite jazz trio was performing. The three young ladies also hoped there, to meet boys that were outside of their usual dull social group. When they arrived and since they appeared too young to consume alcohol, their IDs were checked by a suspicious host who then reluctantly seated them near the stage. Frank, who was in town after his first year at the University of Pennsylvania, was seated at the bar with a friend and took note of the three young ladies who walked past him on the way to their table. He was immediately struck by Diane because of her grace and classical good looks and her translucent skin set off by her blazing blue eyes. He blushed as he gazed at the top of her breasts that were revealed by her off-the-shoulder dress.

"What are you looking at?" she said as she caught him staring.

Diane was accustomed to being admired and did not immediately succumb to this rude boy who then asked if he and his friend could join them for a drink. Only at the insistence of her friends, she agreed to let Frank and his friend join them as the music started. Later, she further put him off when he suggested meeting the following weekend. Frank was upset by this rejection but at the urging of his best friend, he called Diane later in that week and again the following week since she had twice claimed to be too busy preparing for a family trip. Finally, after three tries, Frank called to say that he had two tickets to a Broadway show that Diane had long wanted to see. She could not refuse! And she was not disappointed as Frank turned out to be a wonderful conversationalist and, as she later told her mother, not at all bad looking.

From that day forward he thought of her as his Diana, the Roman Goddess of the Moon, no longer a mere mortal but a princess.

But after the summer, they drifted apart as Frank, who had been a weak student when he started at Penn, was totally overwhelmed by the demands of coursework in the second year. In any case, Diane was far north at Smith College. He simply did not have the energy to pursue her while maintaining his academic standing. On a warm summer day before her senior year, they met quite by accident on New York's Park Avenue. Frank had just started working as a reporter for a weekly newspaper as he saw Diane, who was walking the family springer spaniel, approaching. She looked stunning in a light blue paisley print dress that appeared to vibrate as she walked. No longer was she the girl he dated three summers earlier, but she had matured into a beautiful young woman. "Diane," he called out, as she was about to pass him. "Remember me? It's Frank." Startled, she turned her head but did not suddenly stop until the dog pulled back on the leash as he started to sniff at Frank's shoes. She did not immediately recognize him as his upper torso had filled out resulting from years of rowing on Penn's crew. "Frank," she said tentatively, "what's happened to you? You look different," like a real man, and she liked what she saw!

"I've had to work out a lot to stay on crew while I was at Penn. If I didn't, I would have lost my scholarship. But you, my god, you look smashing, so… I don't know, sophisticated." The dog kept sniffing around Frank's shoes. "I didn't know you had a dog?"

"It's my mother's. She got it when I went away to Smith. Listen, I must run but give me a call sometime and perhaps we can go out. Let me give you my email." She called out the address and as he watched her leave, he kept repeating it to himself to embed it in his mind. He practically ran to his parent's apartment on 81st street and locked himself in his room to compose a message that he was certain Diane would answer. A week later, they met at a French bistro on Third Avenue.

"What is this great mystery you hinted at in your text? I've been dying to figure it out all week," Diane said when they sat down at a corner table.

"Let's order first and I'll tell you," said Frank.

"I don't like to be kept in suspense. If you don't tell me right now," she said, raising her voice, "I'm leaving." Diane pushed her chair back from the table.

"All right, all right! Don't go," he said, somewhat agitated, as he took hold of both her hands. "There is no great mystery. I just wanted desperately to see you again and was afraid if I just asked you in the normal way, you would turn me down."

Pulling her hands away from his grip, she sat bold upright and said, "For heaven's sake, Frank Weill, I would think you'd have a little more confidence in yourself and…a little more respect for me. If you don't even trust my judgment…."

"No, no, no. It isn't that." He took a deep breath. "You see, I've messed it up. It's just that I've thought about you many times since we met three years ago and then when we bumped into each other last week…I just think we have a future, and I didn't want to take a chance of missing it."

Well, that's how it started. After she graduated from college, Diane became a freelance writer for a literary journal while Frank was moved to the editorial desk at his weekly paper. They spent all their free time together. She became the love of his life and they soon married. Over time they had two lovely children before this gnawing illness started robbing her of her spark.

As he remembered that meeting about fifty years ago, Frank lay on the bed staring at the pebbled ceiling and pushed back his glasses as he blinked, his eyes shedding salty tears. *It will be better when we move North. Hopefully it will be far away from this infernal heat, and Diane will forget this last year. She was so much better a year ago. If someone had told me that she could decline so quickly, I would then have insisted that we leave this place...It's Dr. Weiner's fault! I blame him! He must have known or at least suspected.... But... the edge of a lake, mountains, that's what we need. Diane will like that. She'll be able to take walks with me, and maybe even go swimming. Oh, God! I just don't know any more!*

DOLORES DE LA VEGA SIMMONS was rummaging through her dresser when she came across a pair of ballet shoes that set off a rush of memories of her many years on the stage. She turned and called out to Alex, "Look what I found!" but he was in the bathroom and could not hear her. She stroked the silky smoothness of the top of the black ballet shoes and quickly realized that these were too big to be hers. What were they doing in her drawer? As she turned them over in her hands, she felt the rough spit canvas soles. He was rough as well, she remembered! It was so long ago. Her mind drifted to her performance at the Palais Garnier in Paris, so much more classical than that modernist monstrosity, the Opera Bastille. *Why wasn't Alex with me? It's so hard to remember. He should have been there. Of course, then I wouldn't have met Jean Claude. He was so lithe and graceful, and so self-assured. I was so tempted, oh God, more than tempted. I was lonely. Alex should have been there.*

Alex was in New York negotiating a new contract for Dolores's next season and needed to complete the details that were being argued over. By the time he obtained a final signature, it was almost time for Dolores to return home.

It started quite innocently. Jean Claude was the principal dancer with whom she had been rehearsing all day and needed to unwind. He invited her to dine with him in a little bistro on a side street near the Place de L'Opera. It was early May and the sweet fragrance of spring was in the air. After two glasses of a rich Bordeaux, she was feeling a little lightheaded, so they ordered a meal but naturally, also had to finish the bottle. When she awoke in his bed the next morning, she felt so ashamed. *How could I explain this to Alex?* Of course, she couldn't.... and didn't...until almost a year later. He was so hurt and would not talk to her for the longest time. To this day she still doesn't know why he forgave her, but the reality was that they needed one another and never spoke of it again. *The shoes? Why did I keep them? They're going in the garbage bag right now and I don't want to see them again... and remember!*

When Alex came out of the bathroom, he asked, "Did I hear you say something?"

"It was nothing. I just decided to throw out some old ballet shoes that I never want to see again."

"You're not still sorry that you retired," said Alex. "That was thirty years ago, and it was time for you to get some well needed rest and rehabilitation. You couldn't go on punishing your body the way you did, night after night. Also, I thought you enjoyed teaching those youngsters after that?"

"I did love it, but it also made me sad that we didn't have children of our own."

Alex enveloped her in his arms and kissed her neck. "You know, all those years, we moved around so much that it wouldn't have been possible to drag children along, and now...well, I'm glad we didn't. This world is falling apart. All this heat and the rising oceans making the seashores uninhabitable... Remember when we heard what had happened in Venice when piazza San Marco was flooded forever. Those fancy sea gates were no longer enough, and the city was eventually abandoned. What a tragedy! That was a real shock since only a few years earlier you had danced on the stage of La Fenice. Our kids would have had to live in this new unwelcoming world. It's too late for us, but I certainly would not have wanted them to have to deal with it."

"I know, but still," crossing her arms over her chest, "I miss never having held my own child to my breast."

"We don't have much time left," said Alex not comfortable in continuing this discussion, "So let's just get back to our packing. By the way, I've asked for some heavy rope to tie the boxes you wanted to send to your sister."

"Don't forget, we agreed to throw out what my sister would not want." Also, have you thought about what we would say to the others before…?"

"Maybe there is nothing more to say. After all this is our life and our decision," added Alex. "We've always led a dignified life and at this point that is not going to change.

'Ihey both returned to the task of emptying cabinets and drawers and packing the suitcases and the boxes with what would be shipped out, trusting that Drake would respect their wishes. In the garbage bag, Dolores added some worn clothes and hats that no one would want and miscellaneous knickknacks, so that the black ballet shoes although properly buried at the bottom of the bag…were no longer in her memory, forgotten…

THE AFTERNOON DRAGGED ON FOR all the residents as they dealt with making choices of what to keep for their future lives. By late in the day, they all felt exhausted. There was an eerie silence in the commons room when the residents gathered for dinner that evening. The two couples, the Simmons and the Weill's' sat at one table barely exchanging pleasantries. Jim, Don and Henrietta sat at the table nearest the open window benefiting from the occasional whiff of a warm breeze. Julia sat alone at the third table preferring not to mix with those heathens. Drake was absent, having decided to eat alone in his room. After serving the residents, Val sat down at Julia's table, of course after asking her permission to do so. "Well, Julia, how's the packing going?" asked Val.

Looking suspiciously around the room, Julia whispered, "They're all devils the way they're looking at me. You see them don't you, with their red eyes."

"No one's looking at you," answered Val, trying to calm her by putting an arm over Julia's shoulder while suggesting she might feel better eating in her room.

"Yes, I'd much prefer that. I just don't feel comfortable with those, those…"

Interrupting her, Val said, "Come along. I'll help you get set up in your room."

When they had left, Dolores turned to speak to Diane. "The poor woman seems to be somewhat delusional."

Frank jumped in to answer, "Well,…" and was immediately interrupted by Diane who, turning to glare at Frank, said, "I can answer for myself, thank you very much." Turning to address Dolores, she continued, "I'm afraid the strain of our situation, dragging on for so long has unhinged her a bit. She needs to be comforted, not mocked. I can sympathize with her as I've had similar moments questioning the reality of what is happening. It's not easy to be displaced at our age, moving out of a home that we've become attached to. I'm sure you've had similar thoughts." Frank sat with his mouth open, surprised at the sudden lucidity expressed by his wife.

"You're absolutely right," said Dolores, "I was just telling Alex the other day how upset I was at having to move once more when we had counted on this to be our last home. It's the uncertainty that makes it difficult to live with"

Having heard this discussion, Henrietta stood up and turned to interject, "You're absolutely right."

Both Frank and Alex stood up simultaneously to offer Henrietta a seat at their table. When he saw this, Jim waved to the two men and said, "why don't you two join Don and I, and let the ladies continue their discussion." They immediately took him up on this offer while Henrietta took a seat next to Dolores and continued, "Mr. Drake came to see me earlier today and asked me to predict what is going to happen next because of climate change. What he wanted was certainty and all I could give him was the best projection. He wasn't satisfied and I understand that, because as you said, uncertainty is hard to accept. When we get a weather forecast, there's a degree of uncertainty, but we accept it. Whenever we try to predict what will happen tomorrow there's uncertainty and we live with it, but this… these major changes that are happening in the world because of what our great grandparents and later generations did not take seriously, well, that's hard to accept."

"I know I haven't been well lately," Diane said, "but that's because my illness has been aggravated by all these changes that are happening so fast. I think about my boys sometimes and wonder how they're going to manage in such a crazy world."

"My god," Frank said, almost a whisper to his table mates, "she hasn't talked about our sons in weeks. Of course, they're not children they're grown men with families of their own."

"Where are they?" asked Jim.

"They are in northern Vermont. I don't worry too much about them because luckily they're in a part of the country that still has a breathable climate, not so damnably hot.."

"You're right," said Jim with a smile, "except the skiing isn't as good as it was in the past."

At the other table, Dolores asked, "How many children do you have?"

Diane answered, "two boys. Well, they're grown men now. One's a doctor and the other is a high school science teacher. I"...said Diane as her voice began to hesitate, "I haven't seen them in a long time."

"Maybe now you'll be closer to them and you can see them often," said Dolores. "You must have grandchildren as well, I imagine."

"I guess so?" The veil began to descend, and Diane suddenly looked confused and sat back in her chair as her eyes glazed over.

The women sat quietly for a long minute watching Diane with concern before Henrietta spoke directly to Dolores. "Just to finish my thought, I do have a great deal of sympathy for Julia. It's not her religious beliefs that I have difficulty with, because especially in this time, we all need to hold on to some belief. But, in her case, she's carried it too far, so it's become a fanatical obsession. I'm afraid it's made her ill."

"You can say that again," Jim spoke out. "The old girl's a bit daft, don't you think."

"It's not for us to judge," said Henrietta. "Let the good doctor make that determination."

Just then, Val returned to the commons room and Henrietta asked her, "Is Julia going to be all right?

"I'm not sure. I have a call into Dr. Weiner to ask his advice."

"I can give you my diagnosis," said Jim

"We all know what you think," said Henrietta visibly annoyed, "and I still say I'd rather hear from the doctor."

Jim realized immediately he had made a bad mistake by being so flippant and as a result had irritated the one person with whom he wanted to be closer. Damn it let's see if I can turn this around and not screw it up again and said, "I'm sorry! I didn't mean to make light of another person's suffering. I know I can be an oaf sometimes, but I hope you can forgive me just this once."

Henrietta was taken aback by this apology. "If you mean it? I suppose I can forgive you," and added with a smile, "but just this once."

"Absolutely! I wasn't thinking and my mouth moved before my brain could catch up." He stood and walked over to her table. "There is something I wanted to talk to you about and wonder if you would mind stepping outside for a minute."

Surprised, Henrietta looked up at him and asked, "can't you ask your question here?"

Suddenly feeling a flush of embarrassment, he answered, "It's perhaps somewhat, uhh, technical and I thought we should discuss it privately first."

"Couldn't it wait till later?"

"We don't really have that much time and ... No! I'd rather not wait."

"I can't imagine what can be so important," but she said in an exasperated tone, "Very well, if you insist!"

Jim led her into the hallway and asked, "Can we take a walk outside?"

"For heaven's sake, Jim," she answered. "You know the ground's all wet and it's very unpleasant out there. Why can't you say what you want to say right here?"

Jim was flustered by this time and finally said, "It's somewhat personal. Can we sit somewhere alone? In your room... or mine, perhaps?"

"This is ridiculous."

"Please?"

"Very well, we'll talk in my room...but with the door open."

I'm not trying to seduce her, or am I? "All right, we'll talk in your room...with the door open if you insist." Jim answered.

When they reached her room Jim asked, "you wouldn't have anything to drink, would you? My mouth is really dry."

What a big baby, but somewhat endearing in a way, she thought. Jim's face was lined from too much exposure to the elements but was softened by his close-cropped grey hair behind a half-moon bald front and his broad shoulders were somewhat bent forward with age giving him appearance of diminished strength. "There's water in the pitcher on the table …and a glass."

Her apartment was like all the others, a sitting room and an adjacent bedroom, both facing the garden. Henrietta had customized her sitting room with a comfortable chair and a recliner with a coffee table between them. Facing them was a closed cabinet with a small bookcase on either side. All the furniture reflected her Scandinavian taste for light wood and clean lines. The water bottle and two glasses sat in a brass dish on top of the cabinet. The walls were bare except for a large copy of Monet's Water Lilies above the cabinet.

Jim poured himself a glass of water and once he sat in the chair, said, "I know you must think I'm a bit crazy wanting to have this chat with you when we've barely spoken ten words together over all these years."

"Well…" interrupted Henrietta

"But there isn't much time left before we may never see each other again and I felt I had to tell you how I feel."

Henrietta reached for the other glass. *Oh my God, I hope this is not a confession?* "Would you mind pouring me some water too."

Picking up the bottle and pouring, Jim said, "We've had our differences over technical questions especially concerning climate and I realize you have much more knowledge concerning the science involved but I've spent a great deal of time studying the effects of what's happened so I'm not an amateur and I hope you recognize that."

"I didn't mean to belittle your work, but I just hadn't wanted to talk about it every day and that graph of yours…"

"I know and…" Jim didn't know quite how to express what he wanted to say. "I really respect you and I find you…" *why not just say that I desire you…* "attractive as well as smart and I wish we could be friends, close friends."

It was a confession. What can I say now? "I thought we were all friends here. Especially now, since we're going through this difficult period."

"You don't understand. I want to be your special friend. I want us to get to know each other better. I know I'm not making any sense but…"

"I understand and…" Henrietta looked Jim in the face and thought that he is really quite sweet, a nice man and not bad looking except for that stubble on his chin. "There's no reason we can't be friends."

Relieved, Jim stood and said, "OK, we'll be friends. I'm glad that's settled. I guess we can go back to the others now."

"Or," said Henrietta, "you can tell me more about yourself. In the years we've been here, I really haven't learned much about you."

Jim couldn't believe it. He had penetrated the ice shield. "I'd love that, and I really want to know more about you as well." She moved to the open door and began to close it but finally left it only slightly ajar.

During the next hour, Jim revealed something of his vagabond life. It was the first time since arriving at the Manor that he had told anyone of his past, but he found it easy to talk to this woman. He told her of his early marriage and the son from whom he was estranged. "I'm so sorry," Henrietta interrupted, "Maybe when you get settled in your new home you could try again to reconnect with him. It would be so sad if you spend the rest of your life regretting not having done so."

"Maybe," he said, " I used to contact Mike for birthdays and holidays and when I came back from my overseas trips, I would bring him a present. He always seemed glad, and I received thank you notes. All that changed when he entered his teens. He stopped responding to my letters and calls. I think he didn't care enough or was so angry at me because of my absences from his life. Eventually, my letters were returned, and his email blocked me." He went on to explain that in any case it was a difficult situation, and he did not want to intrude."

"You wouldn't be intruding and perhaps Mike's children would like to meet their grandfather." Henrietta told him about the loss of her husband and how devastated she was but that his estrangement from his son was different because he still had the opportunity to reconnect.

She was right and moreover telling her about his life and hearing about hers flowed so smoothly between them. More than an hour passed quickly and when they parted, they were both left with the thought that they had wasted so much time since arriving at the Manor being insular and detached from one another. They promised to continue connecting. As he retired to his own room, Jim realized it was late as all the other residents had already retired. He smiled to himself contentedly, with the thought that his life had taken a new turn.

4

THE DEVELOPING STORM
Tuesday to Wednesday

THE USS OBAMA WAS STEAMING northwest from its previous position staying a respectful distance behind the moving storm that they had been tracking for the past two weeks. Flights were sent every day to update data that was then forwarded to the Hurricane Center for analysis. Based on the dropping atmospheric pressure measured in the eye of the storm, the meteorologists were now projecting that this was going to be a monster storm and that the projected path pointed at the southern Florida coast. As a result of climate change, the intensity of storms had been increasing for decades so it was not surprising that this one was a killer storm. As it moves west, this type of storm usually approaches a clockwise rotating region of high pressure that sits over the island of Bermuda and is appropriately known as the Bermuda high. This causes what is now a full-blown hurricane to be whipped further west like a slingshot. The full impact of this particular storm on the coastline was now expected on the weekend although the exact point of landfall was still not clear. In view of the expected rain and storm surge, all communities along the Atlantic Coast were nevertheless alerted to evacuate.

Notice was sent to the few pockets of remaining population along the east coast of Florida, including the management of the Duck Cove Manor that they must seek shelter further inland by Thursday evening at the latest.

Andy Carlson, in his West Wing office, watched on his screen as images of the intensifying storm were received. On a second screen he pulled up images of the storm in the Pacific and was surprised to see that there were now two storms in that region. He then saw that there was another tropical disturbance developing off the coast of South Africa as well. It was time to act but what could he really do except to watch as nature moved destructively in her own way? Of course, he had to keep the President apprised of these developments and placed a call to the White House. Clearly, his fears of a developing superstorm were coming closer to reality and yet, as a scientist, he realized that there was as yet insufficient evidence. He decided to share his concerns with a former colleague and sent her an email.

As she was preparing for bed, Henrietta heard the melodic sound of an email arriving on her phone.

> From: Andrew Carlson
> To: Henrietta Barker
> Henrietta,
> First, let me apologize for not contacting you these past years. My only excuse is that I have been very busy in my new position and have had no time to contact old friends and colleagues. I hope this email reaches you as I don't know where you're living since you left Lehigh.
> I'm following a storm that is developing in a manner consistent with a prediction that you made in a paper some years ago and would like to discuss it with you. There is some urgency and I would appreciate if you either respond to this email or call me at 292 913 4587.

Reading the message, she wondered what Andy could possibly want that is so urgent. She assumed the paper to which he was referring was the one in which she postulated the possibility of multiple storms merging. Since it was too late to call, she emailed him back.

> Andy,
> You old dog! I'm mad at you for waiting so long to contact me. You were one of my first students and I thought that as we met at conferences year after year, we became friends. Of course, I've followed your recent career move into the political arena. Don't you miss the supposed civility of academia?

Anyway, to bring you up to date, I've been retired from Lehigh for some time, and am living in Florida, though not for long. Although I still read the journals, I may not be totally up to date with all the developments in the field. In any case, your note intrigues me, and I'd be happy to talk to you. I will give you a call at sunrise tomorrow.

Henrietta

When she awoke on Wednesday morning, Henrietta placed a call to Andy Carlson. After the fourth ring, he answered in spongy voice. "Who is this?"

"It's Henrietta!'

"Do you know what time it is? When you wrote 'sunrise' I didn't imagine you meant it literally. Give me a second to get a glass of water." He dropped the phone on the bed and came back after a few minutes. "How are you? You're obviously an early riser."

"You wrote that you wanted to talk urgently."

"I didn't think I had this early in mind, but since here you are, I might as well tell you what it is that concerns me. There is a storm moving in toward the coast…"

"Sorry to interrupt you," said Henrietta," but are you talking about the storm that is forcing me to leave my home to move north tomorrow."

"The very same! But that's not what concerns me."

"But it does concerns me!"

Ignoring the interruption, Andy continued, "There are a number of other storms that have popped up around the globe that reminded me of the scenario you postulated about the development of a superstorm."

"You know, Andy, that it takes more than a small number of isolated storms to develop into a worldwide storm. You need to collect much more data; ocean temperature as well as atmospheric wind information. It just isn't that simple."

"I know and I've assigned folks to collect all the necessary data for review and wonder if you'd be available to look at it with me in Washington?"

"I'm sure you're aware that we're being evacuated in the morning and I don't know when I'll reach my new home in Pennsylvania. Let me give you my cell phone number if you can't read it on your screen so you can contact me in the next few days, of course, assuming no disruption of cell service. What I can do, in any case, is to try to call you when I get to Atlanta tomorrow so you can update me."

She sat on the edge of the bed for some time after completing the call to Andy, trying to remember all the details of the scenario she had projected in the paper she wrote almost two decades earlier. *I'd better download a copy from the electronic file storage*, she decided, as she could not trust her memory.

A HOT WIND BLEW IN from the east on this overcast morning and Drake looked up at the sky and watched transfixed as the varicolored grey/white clouds appeared to be racing toward no clear destination. He had just received a message from the Hurricane Center confirming the need to leave the Manor. When he entered the commons room, he saw Garland sitting on the couch with his dog resting on his lap and on the telescreen, he saw a large map of Florida with a swirling grey mass shown moving toward the coast.

"Good morning, Don. I see I'm already too late. I was going to tell everyone that I just received confirmation that we are ordered to leave tomorrow morning. But, of course, you've already seen the latest news, so you already know."

"I've been up for a long time," said Don, "because I couldn't sleep thinking about our departure. Ever since you told us a year ago that we would eventually have to leave, it's been hanging over our heads and now that the day has finally arrived, it somehow seems like an anticlimax or," smiling and beginning to laugh, "somewhat anti-climatic, if you know what I mean." When he saw Drake scowl, he added, "Sorry! I couldn't help this little play on words. After all, a little levity at this time wouldn't be so bad."

"That's a good one," said Henrietta as she walked into the room. "And you're right, we could use a bit of humor." She was still disturbed from the news she had received.

"Don't you mean black humor, and I don't really think it's appropriate considering what's happening here," said Drake, gruffly.

"Lighten up," said Don.

Drake yelled back, "You people just don't understand! Anyway, just remind the others we're leaving tomorrow morning," and he added as he stalked out of the room, "tell them to be ready promptly at 9 a.m.!"

"That man has no sense of humor," said Don.

"That's true but maybe you shouldn't needle him," said Henrietta. "He has real problems. This home has been his whole life and he doesn't know if he can start again somewhere else."

"I suppose you're right. He certainly was unhinged when Jim challenged him the other day."

"You know Don, he's about to lose the only home he ever had. Now, if that happened to one of us, I think we'd be pretty upset. That's why I believe we need to give him a little space and not press him with little jokes," she said as she smiled, "...even though I thought that one was pretty cute."

"Of course," said Don. "I'll keep my sense of humor in abeyance. If everything works as planned tomorrow, I realize we'll owe him a debt of gratitude. He'll have managed to relocate us to dry land and, hopefully to a home equally pleasant as this one used to be. With this approaching storm, we're all a bit on edge. But you're right, when it hits, this place could be kindling"

"What's that?" said Val as she crossed the room heading to the pantry. "What has the storm got to do with kindling?"

"I was just saying," said Don, "that this building is not strong enough to resist the force of a strong storm surge. I remember when I was a TV newsman, our weatherman told me about coming super-storms resulting from higher sea temperatures and how destructive they could be. He made it sound like something unimaginable...something out of Dante's Inferno. Even concrete walls could crack like an egg! You must know all about that, Henrietta."

"Your weatherman was right. We've seen the strength of storms increasing in magnitude over the decades. What was experienced at the beginning of this century seems like nothing compared to what's happened lately. Remember four years ago when the storm surge from Hurricane Roberto caused almost ten billion dollars' worth of damage along the coast of Georgia and the Carolinas. And since then, on top of the rising seas, we've seen storms approaching category 5 almost every year."

"Maybe Julia's right," interjected Val, "when she says we've reached the end of times."

"You don't really believe that?" said Don

"I was brought up on the Bible," said Val, "and was taught to believe the word of God."

"But surely, not literally?"

"With what's been happening, I don't know any more."

"I believe in God, just like you," said Henrietta, "but this, what's happened over the last century, is the responsibility of man. We're the ones who put all that carbon in the atmosphere and…" She turned to see Jim enter the room and smiled. "Although, we cannot undo what's already taken place, I really believe that science is well on the way to implementing a way of reversing course."

"Are you talking about those carbon capture satellites you mentioned the other day? Do you really believe that they can reverse the current situation?" said Jim.

"Yes! That and the fact that there has been an increase in clouds due to evaporation. They are both contributing to slow cooling the earth's surface… which is needed if we're going to reverse the current disastrous heat. I read in a recent paper that it's also possible that this could lead to abrupt climate change such as happened in the past. In fact, there was a time, as recorded in ice cores, when a 16^0 C temperature drop occurred within a decade. Up or down, rapid temperature changes can occur."

Jim was not about to argue with her, yet he remained skeptical. "Thank you for clarifying that for me." As he went up to her, he put a hand on her shoulder sending shivers radiating through her body. It was an automatic reaction that she didn't fight or try to move away from, but she relished the warmth of the feeling. She wanted to share with him the news she had received earlier but now was not the time.

Meanwhile, Val had gone into the pantry to prepare breakfast for the residents and came out carrying a tray of coffee cups and toasted English muffins. "I'll bring out the coffee in a minute. I'm afraid there are no more fresh eggs, only that powdered variety that I know you all don't care for. But we still have butter and jam."

"No eggs, no eggs," cried out Julia as she walked in half naked. "They're God's children and we're not meant to eat them." Henrietta was shocked when she saw her while Don and Jim stifled a laugh.

Val immediately put the tray on a table. "Now Julia," she said grabbing her arm, "You know you can't walk around here like that. Let's go back to your room and put some clothes on."

Julia started screaming "leave me alone," and flaying around while Val tried to restrain her. "I have to leave now! It's too late to stop me. He's calling me and I have to go to him."

"Who's calling you?"

"God!

"Please, Julia, let's talk about this in your room," said Val while leading her away with Jim's help.

As Julia kept screaming out, "I'm coming, Lord!" Drake came storming out of his room. "What's all this ruckus about?"

Val quickly explained that Julia needed to be restrained so the three men helped Julia into her room and used a sheet to tie her to a chair as Drake asked Val to call Dr. Weiner for help in dealing with this situation.

"Oh God, I've been tied to the cross," cried Julia.

"Nothing of the sort," said Drake. "We just don't want you to hurt yourself accidentally, Miss Smith."

Dr. Weiner's office was located in Atlanta and when Valeria finally reached him, he explained that it was not possible for him to fly out today both because of the weather and because he had a full schedule. It would have to wait until they arrived in Atlanta. In the meantime, he asked her to hook up Julia to the portable electronic monitor that he had left for an emergency. He also told her to give Julia a cup of chamomile tea followed by a dose of lorazepam that he had left in the medicine cabinet for such an eventuality. He promised to monitor the patient's condition remotely, keep in contact and arrange to meet them tomorrow when they arrive at Atlanta airport. He would then escort Julia to the hospital for further evaluation.

The Weills and the Simmons's were getting ready to go to the commons room for breakfast when they heard Julia scream out. Frank and Alex, when they heard the noise, stepped out into the hallway and detained Val who was on the way to the pantry to retrieve the monitor. "What in God's name is going on," said Frank.

"It's Julia! I'm afraid she's had a breakdown, but we have it under control."

"The poor woman," said Alex. "Is she going to be all right?"

"I've been in touch with Dr Weiner. But," moving away rapidly, "if you'll excuse me, I have to get something to make her more comfortable."

"What's happened," asked Dolores as she pushed open the door that had been left ajar.

"It's Julia," said Alex.

"Obviously! The whole world knows that from her screaming voice. But what are they doing for her?"

"Val is taking care of her," said Alex, "and I heard Drake's voice a few minutes ago so I assume he is involved."

Just then, when he heard her whimper, Frank went back into his room to comfort Diane.

Alex thought, what's wrong with these women; one's screaming, one's whimpering. Thank God I married a sane one. "Dolly, let's go have breakfast, I'm starved."

"All you think about is food! I'm concerned about that poor woman. We should see if we can comfort her." Just then, Jim and Don came out of Julia's room. "Is she all right?"

"She's quiet now," said Don. "Drake is with her waiting for Val to return with some medication."

"Is there anything we can do to ease her suffering."

"She's not really suffering. She's just upset," said Jim. "Why don't we all go and have our breakfast and let Val and Drake handle the situation."

They all agreed that this was the best approach and started toward the commons room as Jim knocked on the Weills' door to tell them that they were going for breakfast.

Frank came to the door to explain that Diane was not well, and he would come out soon to get the food for the two of them to eat in their room. Jim offered to bring them breakfast, but Frank said he preferred to do it himself as he knew what Diane would want. Jim then joined the others stopping to pick up the coffee pot in the pantry. "This is a hell of a situation," he said as he poured out the coffee into the mugs that Val had left on the tray. "We're all going to go nuts if we stay here another day. Just look outside! It's gray and muggy and the air is so heavy you could cut it with a knife. It's just so oppressive."

"Now, don't you start to fall apart on us," said Henrietta, taking the coffee pot out of his hands to finish pouring. "Listen to Don. He had the right idea when he tried to inject a little humor into the situation."

"What did he say that was funny?" asked Alex. "We could use a little comedy to relieve this… I don't know… disaster, I guess."

"Yes, Don, what did you say?" asked Dolores.

Somewhat embarrassed, Don answered, "Well, I said this time, when we're actually leaving was anti-climatic."

Dolores looked puzzled.

"Anyway," added Don, "it wasn't that funny for Drake because the Manor, his home, may be destroyed and he feels lost."

"Oh, climate! I see," said Dolores as she picked up her coffee and muffin to sit next to Alex. They were joined by Don while Jim and Henrietta sat at another table.

"Do you know where you are going when we leave tomorrow?" Jim asked her.

"Yes, of course. It's a community near Lehigh, actually not far from my old stomping ground. It will certainly be cooler than it is here but much warmer than it used to be in the past. It's in an area that is not yet swamped with climate migrants unlike some of the northern cities that I heard have been invaded with people trying to move in."

"It sounds ideal." I wonder if they'd have room for me. "I can't believe that we'll actually be going tomorrow. It seems unreal after waiting for so long." Jim did not want to tell her that he would miss her company. *Damn! I'd better check my travel documents to see where I'm going to end up. I didn't really pay attention and maybe it's even the same place. If not….,* "I'll be right back!" Jim suddenly felt fifty years younger and practically ran to his room to look at his travel documents. When he saw the top of the first page his shoulders sagged, and he let out a sigh. There it was on the end of the first line: Ohio! He left his room and walked down the hall to knock on the last door. "Who is it?"

"It's Jim and I'd like to talk to you."

"I don't think we have anything to say to each other." Drake had returned to his room leaving Val to monitor Julia until she quieted down from the effect of the tranquilizer.

"Please Al, it's important."

Drake opened the door. "Since when is it Al? I didn't know we were on intimate terms."

"Can I come in?"

"Very well, but I'm retaining the right to throw you out. I'm not in the mood for complaints."

Jim stood just inside the door as Drake took a seat behind his desk. "This is not a complaint but rather a request. I'm not sure quite how to put it?"

"Just spit it out."

"Well, you see I've been talking to Henrietta and she tells me that she is going to a home near Lehigh and frankly, I've always wanted to go there because of the University and some of the professors whose papers I've admired. So, I wondered if there was the possibility of changing my destination to that home. You understand…"

"Let me stop you right there. Maybe you didn't hear when I explained how much trouble I went through to find you people new homes that were comparable to the Manor. And now, you want to make a change! You've got some nerve."

"Listen Al, I know we haven't always seen eye to eye…"

"That's an understatement. Have you forgotten what happened the other night?"

"I think I apologized for that and frankly we both went a bit overboard, but look, Val explained why you were so upset, and I understand that I may have been insensitive. Can't we start with a clean slate. After all we most likely won't have to deal with each other after tomorrow."

Drake turned his chair to face the wall and paused before standing and walking around the desk to face Jim. "OK, I'm listening."

"Thank you! If you're willing to give me the contact information for the Lehigh home, I could get in touch with them myself and explain the situation to see if they would have room for me."

"Sure, but I don't give you much of a chance. All these places in the North were pretty well filled up. Anyway, what's with you and Henrietta? I thought you two didn't get along."

"Actually, we're both pretty much in the same field and we have a lot to talk about."

With a knowing wink, Drake handed Jim a sheet of paper with the relevant contact information.

Back in his own room, Jim placed a call to the Lehigh home and explained who he was and what he was seeking, also mentioning that he knew Henrietta. The director's assistant explained that they had no single rooms available but that there was one two-bedroom suite that had to be occupied by two residents and had not yet been taken. Jim thanked her and promised to call back later. He now knew what he wanted but was at a loss how to approach Henrietta. He returned to the Commons Room and sat with Henrietta who asked him if all was well as he seemed somewhat agitated earlier. He explained that he was distracted but referred back to their wonderful conversation last night and told her that she was right, and he would definitely try to connect with his son and perhaps she could even help him with plotting the approach.

"Naturally," she said, "I'll do what I can but since we may end up far apart, that might be difficult."

"I just don't want to lose contact with you."

"There's always skype. Anyway, there is something I want to say to you and perhaps we can get out of here for a few minutes and talk privately."

"Of course, I'd love to," he said putting his hand on hers. She did not try to pull away.

ON THE RADIO, THE FIRST movement of Rachmaninoff's second symphony was playing. Dolores commented on the wave like sounds at the beginning of the largo and how it built up in the allegro sounding like mounting waves crashing down on the shore.

"Actually, I look forward to experiencing this storm with you one last time. We've lived through so many storms in our life together and I hear this one is going to be spectacular," said Alex.

"We have gone through a lot together," said Dolores

"I know! How would you like to take one last stroll around the area this afternoon?"

"I'd love to, but I'm afraid we'd need our galoshes. Even the sidewalks are wet."

Alex took her hand as if he were leading her onto the ballroom floor, as he had done so many times before when they went dancing together. She smiled at him and stifled a tear as they went back to their room as the sound of the music slowly faded.

Don turned on the telescreen to his former station saying, to Henrietta and Jim, "do you mind?"

"Of course not," said Henrietta. "Where's Girl this morning?"

"She was fussy last night and was tired this morning, so I let her sleep."

"By the way," asked Jim. "Do you know where you'll be settling in after tomorrow?"

"I'm scheduled to go to a place in Minneapolis. I know the area well because I spent my early career there as a newscaster."

"That's wonderful," said Henrietta, "but please excuse us if we leave you alone, as we have to finish a discussion." She had decided to help Jim map out an approach to reunite him with his son.

"No problem," said Don as Jim and Henrietta got up to leave the commons.

The telescreen featured a report of current conditions around the country. Don watched transfixed as images were shown of caravans heading north, crossing parched deserts in the southwest. The commentator was describing how hundreds of thousands of migrants from south of the border were joining residents of the border states escaping the well over one-hundred-degree temperatures and lack of water, all moving north as far as Canada to find areas still suitable for habitation. What started as a trickle had now become a deluge. As expected, with such a large movement of people, there was disturbing news that small gangs had formed in some areas to harass and rob some of the most vulnerable migrants. There were even reported cases of killings leading the governors of Tennessee and Kentucky to call up the national guard to restore order.

In other news, along both coasts, seaside towns and cities were being abandoned in the wake of rising seas. Almost a million homes had already been flooded. Similar movements of people were taking place on every continent. It was the greatest migration ever experienced in the history of the world. The commentator exclaimed, "The world is not just going to hell, we may be witnessing the end of civilization as we have known it." Don was not in a mood to receive all this negative news and switched off the screen. *Paolo should have been here to comfort him but now there was only Girl. It's not that I don't love her,* he thought, *but I really loved that man, and he shouldn't have left me so long ago. But, it's too late to obsess over what I can't change. It's just that I may not survive what's happening out there in the world and I wish I could share my distress with another human being. Maybe in my new home, there will be someone…. Let tomorrow come soon!*

WHEN HE CLOSED THE DOOR, after the ruckus in the hallway with Julia, Frank sat on the bed next to Diane and put his arm around her pulling her close. "It's all right. Apparently, Julia had some kind of breakdown, but Val is taking care of it."

"I was just thinking about her after what happened yesterday, and I thought about…."

"What did you think about?"

"My boys, my dear boys. Where are they? Why aren't they here?"

"Don't you remember, Mr. Drake was able to arrange for us to move to a home that is close to where the boys live, and they'll be able to visit you often. Won't that be wonderful? It's been over a year since we've last seen them because of this damn situation."

"It was so lovely when we first came here. There were green and colorful gardens and we would walk in the sand along the ocean. You remember? The feeling of warm sand passing through my toes. I miss it!"

"It will be different in Vermont but at least we'll get away from this oppressive heat. And, there is a lake and we'll be able to put our feet in the water. Also, we'll see our boys and those cute grandkids that must be so much bigger now. I know you'll love that."

"I don't remember them. How big are they?"

"Well, Frank Jr. has a boy of eleven and a girl of nine. Arthur has only one daughter who I think is thirteen and super smart as well as cute. I've already contacted the boys to tell them that we were coming so I'm sure they will arrange a get together soon after we arrive."

"I wish I could touch them and hug them right now." Diane closed her eyes and crossed her arms over her chest in an embrace.

"Soon, it will be very soon. Why don't you sit back a minute while I fetch our breakfast?"

She sat back obediently against the headboard as Frank left the room.

WHEN HENRIETTA AND JIM LEFT Don, they walked down the hall and stopped in front of her room. "Why don't we talk in here," she said.

"With the door closed?"

"Fine! I think I can trust you to be a gentleman. Especially since I wanted to talk to you about your son."

"Oh! And I thought you were going to talk about us."

"You move pretty fast for an old guy. There is no 'us', at least not from my perspective. We've known each other for…what is it, almost four years and we have one civil conversation and suddenly you think we're an item. Really?" Henrietta turned away from him to stand by the window and look out. "It's so bleak out there and last night I was lonely for a little human interaction. Perhaps I gave you the wrong idea?"

"No, no! It's my fault. I'm just not able to say the right thing and I always mess up. That's why my marriage broke up and why my son won't talk to me. The truth is that I feel we have a lot in common and I like you and I don't want to lose you too."

"Then act like a mature man, which you are, and not a teenager."

"OK, Henny, let's start again."

"Oh, my God, where did you get that nickname from. I haven't heard it since I was in college."

"Well, you know that we engineers are resourceful. You can't hide anything from us…actually, I found it in a bio online. If it bothers you, I won't use it."

"It's all right. I was just taken aback when you said it because I hadn't heard it in such a long time."

"Very well, then! You were going to help me come up with a way I can get together with my son….and you can see that I need all the help I can get."

"Sit down," she said, "and let's strategize. That's something as an engineer you should be good at, apart from finding people's nicknames."

Outside Henrietta's room there was a print of a painting by Vincent van Gogh called Starry Night that captured the view of an evening sky with swirling brushstrokes of blue and pools of white and yellow clouds. It was painted when van Gogh looked out the iron barred window of an asylum in which he was confined while recovering from a breakdown. Today, the sky seemed similarly angry, with grey and white clouds swirling around, hiding the late-morning sun. An occasional break in this grey ceiling sent a glimmer of sunshine illuminating the dying landscape.

The residents all waited for this day to end so that a brighter tomorrow could arrive.

5
THE LAST SUPPER
Wednesday Evening

O**N THIS LAST EVENING, VALERIA** wore a brightly colored print dress instead of her usual slacks and blouse. She was determined to make it a festive evening and had asked the residents to dress up for the occasion. She asked Jim and Don to help her arrange the tables, putting three of them in a row to make the equivalent of one long table. For the occasion, the two men had brought jackets that they dropped on the couch. From the cupboard Val had found a long orange runner that had been previously used for thanksgiving suppers and stretched it the length of the long table. As Val had decided that Julia was not well enough to be in company with the others, the table was set for nine people. She arranged the seating with Drake in the middle of the long side of the table, one couple on either side of him, Val, Don, Henrietta, and Jim on the other long side facing Drake and the two couples. For the wine that Drake had saved for the occasion Val brought out the last of the wine glasses that were still in the cupboard.

Val had prepared two dishes, one with an onion dip another with celery and carrot sticks that she placed on the table. The residents slowly gathered. Don and Jim were the first, followed by the Simmons and the Weills. Frank gently guided Diane to her seat on the outside, away from Drake. In keeping with the festive but informal atmosphere, the men donned their jackets even though it was so hot and humid...of course, no ties.

Once the others were seated, Henrietta made a grand entrance wearing an off the shoulder white satin gown decorated with meadow-like scattered blue flowers. On her head, she wore her usual white turban. All the men turned to look at her and Jim stood to pull out her chair. "Wow," he said and as they both sat down, he put his hand on her shoulder feeling the warm, naked flesh as he realized what a desirable woman she is.

Dolores tapped her cane on the ground as she turned to Jim and asked, "why don't you play a happy tune for us on the piano. I've heard you playing on many late evenings when you thought we were all asleep."

"I didn't know you played the piano?" said Henrietta. "Why have you kept that from us all these years?"

Jim looked down, feeling embarrassed. "I just play for myself….to relax. I'm not really trained and don't play in front of people."

"Oh, come on, we're not here to judge you and would love to just hear a little music before this last supper. Please!" pleaded Henrietta.

"Yes, please," Diane added. "I'd love to hear you play."

Don got up behind Jim, who looked resigned to his fate, and pulled him up off his chair and led him to the upright. The room became totally quiet as Jim sat in front of the keyboard and rubbed his hands together before the fingers of his right hand moved slowly tapping their way to a simple tune. Joined by his left hand finding a rhythm that became more and more elaborate, a familiar melody emerged.

"It sounds like Chopin," whispered Dolores.

"I don't know." Said Jim, continuing to play. "I just play what I've heard."

"It's wonderful! Don't stop," said Diane.

Don added, "and without any professional training!"

"I did have some lessons when I was very young. But… I never had much opportunity to play once I started traveling for work," said Jim as the music continued and the tunes became more complex. "I just feel the music."

While listening to Jim play, the residents had begun nibbling on the crudités, when Drake suddenly entered the room saying, "Well, isn't this a happy gathering, and with an undiscovered talent to boot." At this, Jim stopped playing and went to sit next to Henrietta. Drake stayed standing as he addressed the residents and Val. "Folks, here we are, together for the last time. I may not see any of you again after tomorrow so first of all, I want you to know that it has been my pleasure having you all as residents in my home…yes, even you, Jim." Jim raised his head as if to speak but Drake, held out his hand to stop him. "No! you don't have to say anything. I know I was a bit harsh the other day, but I was upset and shouldn't have taken it out on you. As for the rest of you, you've been really patient with a very difficult situation and I appreciate that. Frankly, we all have the right to be upset… upset and angry at what has happened to our world. I keep thinking I must have done something wrong…or maybe you did. But, it's not us is it? It's the stinking system. It's the politicians but it's not them either because they simply reflect us. It's our collective selfishness over all the years since this climate problem was identified. It should not have been allowed to deteriorate this far. Early in this century we could have changed the path leading to this disaster…I don't mean you and I, but our grand-parents and even great-grand-parents. Damn it! I blame them. I said it was selfishness and that's exactly what it was. They had a good life with their gas guzzling cars, their coal fired power plants, their farting cows, their wasteful practices…throw away and replace, throw away and replace, on and on. "

"What is he talking about?" whispered Diane into Frank's ear.

"I'll tell you later."

Drake ignored the interruption. "They used up this earth and we've had to pay for it. Sure, I know that we've all been good boys and girls for the last few decades once we got the world to cooperate and stop spewing carbon into the atmosphere, but it was too goddamn late to change course. We had long ago reached a tipping point and we couldn't reverse the damage so fast. So, there we were, thinking we were saved and suddenly, on top of the melting ice, methane, that had been safely stored frozen in the arctic for millennia starts spewing out as our world became hotter, wiping away all the good that had been accomplished and causing a new round of temperature increases to put us in the position we are in today, having to abandon our home. This Manor was my home for most of my life so yes, I'm mad, and you should be too. I'm sorry to go on like this but Ms. Barker, you know what I'm talking about."

Henrietta looked dazed at being singled out but raised her head to look directly at Drake. "Albert, If I may call you that, you're not telling us anything we don't already know. But, I'm more than a little surprised that you're being so morose on this last night we'll be together. I thought this was to be a celebration of our departure."

All at once others spoke up. "Yes!... Absolutely!... let's enjoy our last supper together!"

"You hear that," said Jim, looking directly at Drake, "no one wants to be reminded that the world is going to hell. Instead, why don't you pick up your wine glass and suggest a toast to our survival and to an improved future."

"Wake up, people," Drake interrupted, "I'm trying to warn you that if you think conditions are any better where you're going tomorrow, you are deluding yourselves."

"It's not up to you," shouted Alex, "to tell us what to expect. We're all intelligent people and are perfectly aware of what's been happening climate-wise. We have been living with it for years. And we are also aware of the fact that conditions in the rest of the country and even in the world, are not getting any better. So, don't insult us with your warnings. If we want to know about tomorrow's scientific forecast, we can ask Henrietta or even Jim who have studied it."

"Have it your way," Drake bellowed out as he left the room.

While this discussion was going on, Diane covered her ears with her hands and once Drake left the room she looked around and slowly put her hands down and smiled. "I heard, wine!" she said meekly.

"That's right," said Frank, "why don't we all have a glass of wine. In fact, I propose a toast. To our friends around this table and to a new phase of our lives."

They all raised their glasses to drink.

Don turned to Val and asked, "Well, what other surprise do you have for us...I mean, in the way of food?"

Val no longer felt the need to defend or even explain her boss's actions. "You can munch on these veggies while I bring out the food," Ten minutes later she brought out a platter of beef stew with mashed potatoes and a bowl of a rich gravy. "Please help yourselves while I bring Julia a plate in her room."

Don offered to serve everyone while Jim turned to Henrietta to say, "You look stunning in that dress. Why have you been hiding it from us?"

She had spent the past two hours in the shower and in front of her dressing table, creaming, powdering and coloring, all to make herself feel like a woman again. For too long she had given in to a measure of hopelessness caused first by the loss of her husband and lately by the oppressive changes in the weather. So, on this evening, she accented her lips with ruby red lipstick, put on her pearl necklace and earrings and a fresh white turban that set off her pink cheeks. Responding to the attention she received from Jim, she felt alive again and needed to revive her spirits by looking and dressing seductively. "I hoped you'd notice," she said.

"How could I miss such a fantastic transformation. No longer the professor, but the seductress."

"Now don't get the wrong impression." Said Henrietta. "I just felt this was an important occasion and needed to be celebrated. And, I saw another side of you as well, tonight."

Jim looked away, not ready to respond to this directly but said instead, "Don, don't you agree that our Ms. Barker looks smashing tonight?"

Before Don could speak, Frank interjected, "All our ladies look wonderful tonight, don't you think, Alex?

"Dolly! Isn't that what I said to you a few minutes ago?" Alex answered.

"Yes, dear," said Dolores, "but I feel badly for Julia who should really be here with us. If you don't mind, when I finish eating, I would like to visit with her for a while."

"Perhaps you should wait and see what Val says when she comes back?" said Alex.

"Of course," said Dolores.

While waiting for Val to return, the seven residents around the table began to eat their dinner trying to put Drake's rant out of their minds. Accompanied by generous quantities of wine, all agreed it tasted delicious. Diane was particularly enamored of the wine and kept asking for just a drop more. "Maybe you've had enough," said Frank, concerned that it would affect her negatively.

"It's not your wine," said Diane "and you don't have to worry that I'm taking it away from anyone else."

"That's right!" Don interjected, "And, besides, we're supposed to be celebrating tonight. So, loosen up a bit."

Frank glared at him. "I think I know what's best for my wife so please don't interfere."

"Diane, dear," said Henrietta. "Perhaps one more drop and no more. After all, you don't want to make a spectacle of yourself."

"Maybe you're right. I am beginning to feel a little lightheaded." After a few more minutes, she added, "Frank, maybe you could take me back to the room. Thank you all. You've been so kind."

Frank helped her get out of her chair and held her tightly as they walked her back to their room. Just then, Val returned.

"How is she?" Dolores asked. "Do you think I could visit with her for a little while?"

"I don't think that would be a good idea. I gave her a sedative and she's dozing off."

"Maybe I'll have a moment to talk to her in the morning before we leave?"

"I'm not sure, "said Alex, "we'll all be so rushed, but why don't we keep it open."

"Of course," said Val.

"This has been an interesting evening," said Dolores. "Not quite what I expected from a farewell party. Nevertheless, I wanted to say that Alex and I have been delighted having all of you as our neighbors…and friends and we wish you all the best in your new situations. Come along, Alex. Let's get some sleep."

"Good idea," said Don. "I've got to take Girl out for one last walk tonight. I'll see you all in the morning."

"I'll finish up," said Val.

With everyone else gone, Jim and Henrietta stood up to leave and walked down the hall together. "I guess I'll see you in the morning," said Jim, as he reached her door. "I want to say again how lovely you looked tonight. Do you mind if I kiss you goodnight?"

"I'd be insulted if you didn't."

He pulled her close and embraced her for a long minute before she turned to go into her room. Once the door closed, she began her preparations for going to bed. Fifteen minutes later she was ready but hesitated and putting on her nightgown over her pajamas, went out into the hall and walked to Jim's room and knocked. "Come in."

She stood before Jim for a moment before speaking. "I know you'll think this is crazy. But I want to ask you a favor." Suddenly embarrassed she stopped and turned to leave. "I'm sorry, I shouldn't have come. You're ready for bed."

"No, no," he said reaching for her hand. "Sit down and let's talk."

For a long time, they talked …. About his life, about her life. He thanked her for the suggestion she had made to help him reconnect with his son. She revealed the contents of the conversation she had with Andy.

"I didn't know you had such important friends?"

"Actually, he was a former student. He wanted my advice relative to a paper I wrote a long time ago. It's still up in the air as I'm re-reading it to refresh my memory. I plan to talk to him again when we get to Atlanta."

They continued talking about every subject other than the one she had meant to broach until finally, he asked, "You said something about a favor?"

"I know you'll think I have no right to ask you."

"For Christ's sake, just ask me?"

"I've been here for almost five years with you and all the others, and I don't know why, but I've been lonely lately, actually very lonely. It's not that everyone has not been friendly. I don't know how to say this. "

"Just say it!"

"It's been such a long time since I've been with a man and…I just want to be held….for a long time. What I'm trying to say is: Can I lie down with you tonight, holding me. It's for comfort, you understand, that's all."

Jim turned and pulled her toward him to kiss her.

She pulled back. "No! I'm asking as a friend. Nothing more. I'll understand if you say no."

"You're making it very hard to refuse but you understand that it will be difficult for me to be in bed with you just as a friend. I know we're not young anymore but still…"

Henrietta rose to leave. "I understand. It's too much to ask."

"Hold on! I didn't say no. I still have to brush my teeth and you know where the bedroom is."

When he finished in the bathroom the bedroom was dark and he slipped under the light blanket, nestled behind her and put his arm around her. She fell asleep long before he did but finally his eyes closed, and a warm, comforting curtain enveloped him.

When they settled in their room, Alex asked Dolores, "You haven't changed your mind about tomorrow, have you? When you started talking about seeing Julia, I wondered?"

"No! I just wish I could help that poor woman."

"I understand, but Val seems to be very caring and has made all the arrangements with Dr. Weiner to take over once they get to Atlanta. So, I wouldn't worry that she won't be well taken care of."

"Still…"

"We need to finish our preparations for tomorrow. There's a great deal still to do with packing and letters."

"Very well. You finish packing while I write the letters." She looked at her husband with love and regret. In over sixty years together, she never stopped loving him and only had that one regret when she was still young and … no! there were no real regrets that had not been dealt with a long time ago. Now, as they prepared to enter the last phase of their lives, she remembered all the wonderful times and looked forward to this as a new adventure, together forever.

They finished all that needed to be done and went to bed before ten o'clock, setting the alarm for five a.m.

By the time Diane reached her room, she could hardly stand, and Frank suggested she go right to bed. He helped her get ready and once her head hit the pillow, she was almost fast asleep. *Poor darling*, he thought, *I'm afraid you did have a bit too much wine tonight. You're simply not used to it. But you seemed so much more alive. Maybe I've been treating you too much like a crystal, always about to break. I promise you that after today, it will be different. I won't let your illness control either of us and I'll let you guide me more and not hold you back. We will have a wonderful life closer to our children and I so look forward to discovering our grandchildren.*

"Good girl," said Don when the dog had finished doing her business. The dog suddenly pulled hard on the leash and started barking. Out of the corner of his eyes, Don saw a black streak. "Damn rats, they're everywhere these days since all their hiding places are underwater." *As for the poop, there's no point in picking it up*, he thought, *as the ocean will wash it all clean.* "Come inside and I'll dry off your paws." In his room, Don fastidiously cleaned the dog, using a clean towel followed by a thorough brushing. "There! Now you look beautiful for our trip. I think you'll enjoy our new house. There will be a grass lawn nearby where you can run around, and a dry sidewalk for our daily outings. No more mud and water to worry about. We've had enough of this awful place that we should have left long ago. But we were trapped…we had a contract and would not have gotten our money back if we left. My pension…Yes, I think we'll both enjoy it up north. It will be full of people and dogs I'm sure, and we'll make friends with new people…and live a better life."

EACH IN THEIR SEPARATE ROOMS, Valeria and Albert were preparing for tomorrow's departure. Val packed the last of her belongings and then went to Julia's room to make certain that she was comfortably asleep. She watched her for a few minutes as Julia breathed regularly interspersed with light snoring and, confident that the sedative would keep her quiet until morning she quietly left the room. There was nothing more she could do for her until they arrived in Atlanta, and she could turn her over to Dr. Weiner.

Drake was restless and paced back and forth from his study to his bedroom. He warned them…that's all he could do. If they didn't heed his warnings, then let them all go to hell! This storm, this fucking storm! After all, the Manor has been here for fifty years and has survived many storms. Why do I have to leave now? What's different? Of course, he knew the answer. Fifty years ago, the sea level was almost six feet lower than it is now. That's why water from the bay occasionally licked at the foot of the Manor. It was clear that the expected storm surge from this coming hurricane could easily overwhelm the building. But maybe the hurricane could turn and veer off the coast and the building would be saved. But then, why did he even start to empty the building a year ago? He momentarily forgot that the sea was rising relentlessly and would eventually engulf the Manor. Once more he considered his options; he could leave with the others or stay and protect his property. There was no answer in his mind to this conundrum. But he thought of the line from Macbeth, *I will not be afraid of death and bane, till Burnam Forest come to Dunsinane.* He still had time as the waters had not yet moved against him.

6
EXODUS
Thursday

V AL WAS AWAKENED OUT OF a fitful sleep by the incessant chirping of one of the few remaining birds that sat on a branch outside her window. When she glanced at her watch, it read five and although she thought she heard footsteps outside her door, she turned over and waited for the alarm clock to ring at six.

The sun did not appear this morning in all its glory and instead took shelter behind a veil of grey clouds. However, this did not deter the residents of the Manor who experienced a sense of urgency, excitement and energy as they awoke early in anticipation of their imminent departure.

Henrietta was an early riser and gently disentangled herself from the arms enveloping her. She had not had such a warm and restful sleep in years, perhaps not since the death of her husband. Before leaving to go to her room she looked down at the sleeping form of the man in the bed and kissed him gently on the cheek. Jim stirred and groaned as he turned onto his stomach.

Unknown as yet was the fact that before dawn, the Simmons had quietly walked out of their room, walked down the stairs avoiding the one creaky tread and stepped out of the Manor. Using a flashlight to guide their way, they headed beyond the end of the road to the water's edge and spread the tarpaulin that they had brought along on the moist ground. They then lay down to wait for the dawn and the arrival of their fate. Looking across the bay, the partly denuded towers of Miami Beach stood like sentinels standing guard against the approaching hurricane that was nurtured by the roiling sea. But, for the time being all was silent other than the squawk of the sea gulls. In each other's arms, they both fell into a calm and restful sleep.

Don and the Weills made final preparations to leave, packing up their toiletries and placing their bags outside their doors. Jim was the last to wake this morning and was more than a little surprised to find Henrietta gone. He remembered last night with a sense of longing. He dressed quickly as he had to talk to her and tell her... He ran to her room and knocked. "It's me," he said, and not waiting for an acknowledgement, opened the door.

"For heaven's sake, Jim," she said running into the bathroom. "I'm still dressing. Please wait while I finish."

"I have something important to ask you."

"Can't it wait a minute?"

"No! I know you're going to a home near Lehigh. Well, I contacted them to see if I can go there as well. They told me the only apartment available is one with two bedrooms. So, I wonder if you'd be willing to share that apartment so we could be closer. I mean it as friends. No obligations!...Please!"

There was a long moment of silence until Henrietta came out of the bathroom. "I do have feelings for you, but I don't know if I am ready for such a commitment."

"I'm not asking for a commitment. You can think of it simply as sharing a home...even like brother and sister, if you want?"

"I'm just not sure but...after last night, it might work. Can I have some time to think about it?"

"No! I promised to call them this morning because they can't hold it."

"As friends?"

"Absolutely!"

"Very well, then."

Jim kissed her on the cheek and ran out of the room to make the call. When he received acknowledgement from Hillcrest, he returned to tell Henrietta. She wondered if she had been too quick to accept Jim's request. After such a long, carefully measured period in her life, there were suddenly so many quick changes. Perhaps she should have put him off...But!

The residents gathered in the Commons Room where Val had prepared coffee and muffins, the last meal they would have at the Manor. Noting that the Simmons were not among the diners, Val went to the Simmons' room and knocked. When she received no response, she opened the door slightly and called out, "hello, it's getting late." Still receiving no answer, she pushed open the door all the way and saw two suitcases and a bundled box on the floor of the living room. All the while calling out their names, she went to the bedroom and saw that the bed had been made and the bathroom was empty with nothing left on the counter. She ran back to the Commons Room and asked, "has anyone seen the Simmons' this morning?"

Everyone shook their heads except Don who said, "I thought I heard them last night saying that they might take one last walk outside."

Val ran to Drake's room to tell him. In response to her banging on the door he yelled, "What the hell is going on," as he pulled open the door brusquely.

"We have a problem," said Val. "The Simmons are missing."

"For Christ's sake why did they have to do this now. Have you looked around?"

"Of course! They're not here and they may have gone out for a walk."

"A walk? Where the hell can they go? There's only water everywhere? Did you check their room thoroughly?"

"Yes, but I'll go back and look again." Val went back and looked around carefully. She had already noted earlier that the bedroom and bathroom were clear and in the living room the suitcases on the floor indicated that the occupants were ready for departure. Turning around, she saw it, two envelopes tucked under the edge of the pad on the desk. One envelope was addressed to her that she ripped open nervously and read,

> Val,
>
> We're sorry that we will not be able to join you on this next voyage, but we have other plans. We're had a marvelous and fulfilling life and do not want to have to end it in a messy way. Our last few years here with you and our friends have been lovely and we are sad that it has to end. Clearly, nature is taking its revenge for our lack of appreciation of the damage we, all of us, had caused to our environment. We have been as irresponsible as anyone else in the world, and

it has caught up with us. Now we need to atone by doing the only thing we know which is to become one with nature. Don't be sad for us, be glad that we still have the strength to decide our own fate. And, as for you and the other folks, please tell them how much we had enjoyed the past few years in their company and hope that they will all find happiness in their new surroundings. Finally, please see to it that what we packed will be sent to my sister. I've left you her address. Thank you and God bless!

Dolores

The second note was addressed to Albert Drake and she ran back to his room and handed it to him while reading him her note. "The fools," he whispered as he opened his note.

Albert,

We heard from Henrietta that you are depressed having to abandon the home that your parents created. We just want you to realize that our experience in the dance world has been a series of successes and depressing voids. That's generally true in the arts. In the same way, we hope you will start again in another part of the country... somewhere up north, that is still not too hot and that has adequate water, to drink and not to inundate you. We hope that you will build another home for yourself and for people like us.....

Alex

He turned to Val; "There's no way we can even look for them. We simply don't have the time or the resources. I'll have to call this in and see if the authorities can start an aerial search... After all I've done for them, they do this to me! It's just so selfish of them."

As he talked, Valeria's eyes narrowed and her mouth tightened before exploding, "If anyone's selfish, it's you. After all you've done for them...hell, you did what they paid you for and no more. You have a nerve tearing them down. They were the sweetest people, always kind and considerate, unlike you...you selfish bastard. Maybe after a long happy life, after all they were in their nineties, they had enough. Sure, my faith may not condone choosing your own end of life, but I've been around death long enough to know that sometimes folks know better when it's time." She stormed out of his room and into hers and stayed a long time before calming down sufficiently to go to the Commons Room to tell the other residents what had happened.

"Shouldn't we go out and look for them?" said Jim.

"Absolutely," said Don. "They couldn't have gone too far since last night."

"There really is no time since we're being picked up within the hour. And besides we don't know where to look," said Val.

"We just can't leave them out there," said Henrietta.

Frank kept his arm around Diane to keep her from getting agitated and did not say a word.

Val left to check on Julia whom she found curled up on her bed. "Are you awake? We have to get ready to leave. Would you like a little breakfast before we go?"

Julia stretched out but kept her arms crossed over her eyes. "The day of reckoning has arrived. I'm ready, Lord."

"I asked if you wanted some food?"

"There's nothing more I need before I meet you, Lord."

"Very well," said Val. "I'll come and fetch you when the transport is ready."

THE MORNING AIR HUNG HEAVILY over Miami. Alex awoke with a start as he felt something nibbling his toes through the thin blanket that covered them both. When he looked down toward his feet, he stifled a scream. There was a black rat chewing the corner of the blanket. He kicked it and watched the rat scampering away, joined by another rat. Shaken, he leaned over and gently kissed Dolores on her brow as she stirred and slowly opened her eyes. "It's so quiet here," she said.

"Did you sleep well?" asked Alex.

"Quite well, although I wouldn't have called the ground, a comfortable bed."

"You don't want to go back, do you? We could, you know. We're not that far."

"Absolutely not, unless you're having second thoughts?"

"No, but I just saw some rats…"

"How disgusting," Dolores screamed. "We can't stay here."

"I know, but actually, we should move to a more protected place in case the folks from the Manor decide to look for us. There's a small grove of trees not too far if you're up to it."

"What about the rats. Will they be there as well?"

"No, I don't think so. I can scrape the ground to make a little trench around the place. I can use a cup to put water in it...just like a moat that they can't cross." It was a fairy tale that he tried to convince himself was true. "Shall we go?"

"If you really think it will be OK, give me a minute to get the kinks out and let's go."

They picked up the tarp and walked toward their destination about a quarter mile away and further from the Manor. "I'm sorry I didn't bring any food," said Alex.

"I don't believe there's any reason to eat today." Dolores had some difficulty walking since her cane kept sinking in the wet soil. With her free arm she took her husband's arm and held it tightly. As they walked slowly, they tried to avoid the myriad puddles that Alex thought were as big as mini lakes. Their shoes became wet, then their socks and then they were in water up to their ankles. There was no way of avoiding getting wet although they tried to stay close to the shores of these shallow puddles. Around the base of the stand of trees that Alex had chosen as their final destination, it was relatively dry for a short distance in all directions. So, when they arrived at the grove, Alex spread out the tarpaulin on the ground. He then proceeded to dig his little moat, which was not difficult since as he scraped the ground, it filled with water. It took him over an hour to complete, by which time he was exhausted and happy to stretch out. Dolores nestled in her husband's arm, looked up at the slow-moving grey clouds and listened to the sounds of the few birds that had not fled the approaching storm. Alex felt secure that with the cover of the trees, there was no chance they could be spotted. With his free hand, he held on tightly to the rope he had brought along...for later!

PUNCTUALLY AT NINE, THE WHACK-WHACK sound of the transport could be heard approaching. Drake came out of his room. "All right folks, let's get everything downstairs and ready to load onto the helivan."

"Aren't we going to wait and see if the Simmons will return?" asked Jim.

"For God's sake, Robinson, don't make any more problems for me. We don't have time for that and besides, I'll be staying behind to wait for the next van to take all the remaining boxes you folks packed."

"Sorry, it was a simple question. No need to make an issue out of it," said Jim as Henrietta tugged at his sleeve to pull him back from another possible confrontation.

Val turned to Don to ask, "after you have brought your bag downstairs, would you mind giving me a hand with Julia's belongings while I get her settled in the van."

"Of course, and why don't you seat her next to me? I'll keep her occupied during the flight to Atlanta."

"Thank you. I'd appreciate that."

Both Val and Drake, helped the residents to take their suitcases down the stairs and out to the helivan. The Weills had not yet left their room when Val came and told them that it was time. Diane was sitting on the bed as Frank tried to coax her to get up as she kept pulling back. "Please, sweetheart, we have to go," he pleaded as Diane whimpered.

Val decided to intervene and firmly took Diane's left arm to pull her up. "Come on, sweetie, you have to get up and walk down to the van. You don't want us to carry you, do you?"

Unable to resist the pull from two people, she said, "all right, I'm going. Please don't pull me so hard. Frank, tell her not to do that!"

Everyone was finally standing next to the helivan after all the baggage had been loaded.

The helivan was designed to accommodate sixteen people in four rows of two on each side with a central aisle. A large baggage compartment was situated in the back.

The pilot-monitor sat in front of a display screen that featured the view in all directions as well as a series of gages and a continuingly updated weather monitor. The vehicle was fully automatic; once the destination was punched into the computer, an automatic sequence was initiated. The pilot-monitor was there to provide backup should a problem occur.

The Weills boarded first and took the two seats in the back row on the right. Jim and Henrietta boarded next and took the two seats in front on the left. They were followed by Julia accompanied by Don and Val. Don took the window seat in the second row on the right and put the carrier with Girl on his lap. Julia was next to him on the aisle. Val then disembarked to talk to Drake.

"Are you sure you shouldn't come with us now? There's plenty of room since we're missing the Simmons and even the baggage compartment is half empty."

Drake was still undecided whether or not to go. "I said I would wait for the next van to take all the remaining boxes and anyway, I think I should give the Simmons a chance to return or be found. A search team has been scouring the area with drones and they might be lucky." "Come on, Mr. Drake, I know you're not being honest with me. Please promise me you will go when the next van arrives."

"Absolutely! Now please get on board so that they can leave."

Reluctantly, Valeria boarded the ship and sat on the other side of the aisle of the second row so that she could help Don if Julia caused a problem. The door closed and the engine started, startling Diane as Frank held tightly to her hand to reassure her that all was well. Julia, having been sedated hardly reacted to the muffled noise. "We're off," said Jim as he squeezed Henrietta's hand.

Drake turned toward the entrance to the Manor as he kept waiving his left arm in farewell… a final goodbye. Within two hours, the next van would arrive, and he would have to make a decision to go or not to go. After that, the weather was expected to deteriorate, so that no further flights were possible. As he looked at the stuccoed façade of the Manor, he noted the green streaks that had not been cleaned in years, a sign of aging in the increasingly tropical climate. He wondered whether this was another sign that it was his time to leave and start again further north as Alex had suggested. For a long time, he wandered around the now empty hallways and rooms of the Manor and pondered this question.

Once the door to the helivan closed, the engine engaged the rotors that began increasing in speed causing the vehicle to slowly rise above the sodden ground. Inside, the sound was muted but the vibration could be felt by the occupants causing both Henrietta and Diane to reflexively tighten their grip on their seat mate's hands. Julia closed her eyes and hummed quietly, mouthing the words to a spiritual,

When peace like a river, attendeth my way,

When sorrows like sea billows roll
Whatever my lot, Thou hast taught me to know
It is well, it is well, with my soul.[3]

Frank, Don and Jim looked out their respective windows. The flight to Atlanta was to cross over 600 miles. What they were to observe over the next few hours was a bleak landscape damaged over the recent decades by heat and water because of the changing climate.

As they rose higher, they saw Ft Lauderdale and Palm Beach covered with water that they judged to be almost three feet deep. The elegant mansions and boulevards were no longer teeming with people seeking sun and pleasure. On the left, Jim saw Lake Okeechobee whose banks had almost merged with the encroaching ocean. Cape Canaveral on the right where the rockets used to rise majestically to explore the heavens was now covered by the sea as were all the coastal cities and towns. Further on, directly along the path of the helivan was Orlando, safely above sea level, at least for the time being. Crossing into Georgia the land rose ever so gently until reaching the Piedmont Plateau and the city of Atlanta on the Chattahoochee River. Frank was later to jot down his memory of the flight to Atlanta;

Stretched out below us
Was a land transformed.
The fields were bare
No longer green but brown
The farmhouses fallen
Returned to the earth
The forests naked sticks
Like sentinels of doom
Cities on the shore,
Sunken below a rising sea.

As they approached the city, Don and Jim saw outside their windows the many solar farms that had appeared on the landscape in the past decades as the energy needs of the region had increasingly moved away from carbon fuels. Hidden below ground were the battery arrays that stored and metered out the solar energy that had been collect-

---

3 Horacio Spafford, 1873

ed above and dispensed it through the tentacles of wires that spread throughout the region.

"There it is," shouted Don as the many towers of Atlanta came into view. "And there's the stadium. I often used to broadcast from there during major political events."

"I think I'll feel better when we get down on the ground," said Henrietta. "Look at all that traffic. There seem to be planes and copters all over the sky."

"Don't worry, ma'am," interjected the pilot monitor. "It's all under control, I assure you."

"Nothing to worry about. Haven't I heard that phrase before," said Jim under his breath. "That's what they said when the permafrost started to melt."

"Shush," said Henrietta. "I don't want to make the pilot upset."

"This craft is fully automatic. The pilot's got nothing to do but watch a bunch of dials so even if I upset him the craft will simply follow its predetermined path."

"Please," she pleaded," keep still until we land."

Following a tortuous path dictated by the computer to avoid other traffic, the helivan slowly descended and landed without incident adjacent to gate 84. They were met by a travel expediter, a man in a distinctive blue uniform with a military style cap decorated with a single thin red stripe. He had been hired by Drake to expedite the Manor residents to their next flights.

7

THE DIASPORA
Thursday Afternoon

"CALL ME PETER," THE EXPEDITER said. "Please follow me." He escorted the passengers into a private room in the terminal where they were to wait until their continuing connections were ready. As they moved together, they felt the crowds pressing in all directions. People were jostling and pushing each other aside vying for the few available flights, waving their hands in the air and calling out to get the attention from overworked receptionists. There were migrants everywhere, fleeing the southern coastal regions of Mississippi and the Florida panhandle…families with children clinging to their parents and carrying what few belongings they could carry in backpacks and in rolling suitcases rumbling behind them. Throughout the airport there were small groups of young people called the New Greens, dressed in shorts and tee shirts bearing an emblem of the earth with a green band where the arctic circle was. Following Peter, the Manor residents noticed that gates with flights to northern cities were crowded with passengers milling about, frantically eyeing the concession stands that had days earlier run out of food and drinks. Looking toward the runways, they could see flights arriving and leaving every few minutes, most of them autonomous winged vehicles. The electronic control system managing these flights was stretched to the limit and was on the verge of being overwhelmed.

Nervously observing this situation, Val and Don walked on either side of Julia to guide her to a seat in the far corner of the private room that had been reserved for the residents. There, Julia was to wait for Dr Weiner. The Weills sat down at one table near the window over-

86

looking the runways, while Henrietta and Jim sat at another, and all were offered a light snack by a flustered attendant. A half hour later Dr. Weiner arrived saying to Val, "I'm sorry I'm late but this place is like a zoo." He blinked behind horn rimmed glasses and sported a close-cropped beard and pink cheeks that gave him a pixyish appearance. "It's so difficult to get around with so many people waiting for flights."

"That's perfectly all right," said Val. "At least you're here and can take over Miss Smith's care. I gave her a sedative before we left that should be wearing off very soon." Weiner had brought along an orderly to help him with Julia. Val was more than happy to hand over her care to the two of them. Turning to Julia she said, "These good people are going to take care of you to make certain that you get settled. I'm sorry to see you go but I sincerely hope that you will be happy in your new home and I want you to know that it has been a pleasure taking care of you. At this, Julia leapt out of her chair and grasping Val and pulling her close, whispered in her ear, "Are they believers?"

"Yes dear. You can trust them," said Val. Both Dr. Weiner and the orderly held out their hands that Julia slowly grasped saying, "sweet Jesus."

"Well, we're off!" Said Dr. Weiner quietly. Hearing this, Julia's face lit up and she suddenly became animated shouting, "Yes... yes! We're off, we're off to see the Wizard." Becoming more agitated, she began to sing out and locked arms with her two companions and pulled them forward, singing, "We're off... we're off to see the Wizard," causing Dr. Weiner to almost trip as they marched out of the room.

Astonished at this display, everyone was aghast until Don started laughing uncontrollably. This led the others to also laugh...even Diane could not help herself and began to cry with laughter. Val was the only one not amused. She respected Julia's views, however outrageous, even in the way she now thought of God as the Wizard, the man behind the curtain shutting out disbelief.

Peter, who was still in the room, stood with his mouth open and blurted out, "I don't know what just happened, but I have some instructions for the rest of you."

"I'm sorry," interrupted Jim, "but you couldn't possibly know. Anyway, what have you got for us."

Peter then explained that a flight to Nashville for Mrs. Lopez would be leaving in mid-afternoon and that there was a good chance that the flight to Minneapolis for Mr. Garland scheduled for early evening would be canceled. Unfortunately, most flights to the northeast are delayed because of the approaching weather so we have arranged for rooms in the airport hotel for Mr. & Mrs. Weill, Miss Barker, Mr. Robinson and Mr. Garland. Val explained that she would not leave until Drake had safely arrived in Atlanta even if it meant missing her flight. If the weather deteriorated, she was even willing to take a bus. "It's not that far," she said. Prodded by the review of extended bad weather that Jim had forecast, the others decided not to stay at the airport but rather stay in a hotel in town until the projected storm had passed. "Peter, I'm sure you can make those arrangements for us," said Jim. "Whatever the cost, Mr. Drake will pick up the tab. After all, it's part of the cost of getting us to our final destination and, as I understand it, it's part of your job." Peter, although quite flustered, promised to do what he could to satisfy their request.

Within the hour, Peter had arranged for rooms at the Peachtree in Atlanta while Val stayed in the airport to await news of Drake.

"CAN YOU CHECK AGAIN TO see if Mr. Drake has arrived yet," Valeria kept asking of Peter as the hours passed. She had assumed that if he traveled on the helivan that was scheduled to pick him up an hour after the residents had left the Manor, he should have already arrived in Atlanta. Seeing the intensifying grey sky and wind-blown debris flying around outside the lounge window, she became increasingly alarmed and decided to try to call him. "The party you called is not available. Please try your call later," was the reply she received. Meanwhile, Peter returned and told her that landing flights had been temporarily halted because of a malfunction of the control system and some flights had been diverted to other airports. "Can't you get more specific information about Mr. Drake's flight," she asked Peter. "I'll do what I can," he answered. "But you can see that there is a bit of a turmoil here and it's difficult to get timely information."

An hour later, Peter came back with the news that Drake was in Chattanooga, his flight having been unable to land in Atlanta. Hearing this, Val was greatly relieved. *Thank God he didn't decide to stay at the Manor*, and tried to phone him but received no answer. *Maybe the phones aren't working.* She decided to wait and contact him before leaving Atlanta.

After several hours of trying, Drake finally answered the phone. "You gave me quite a scare," said Val. "When you didn't arrive an hour after us, I was worried that you decided to stay."

"I thought about it but in the end, I didn't have the courage to give up. I've still got time and I have people I know who would be happy to have me manage their retirement home or…I could start again on my own. I don't know if I will, but I decided that it's not impossible. So… here I am!"

"Listen," said Val, "you're in Chattanooga and since I can't fly out of here, I was thinking of driving to Nashville. You're on the way and I could pick you up and you could stay with us for a few days while you think about where you want to go."

"I don't know, I don't want to impose."

"Look, the weather's going to be lousy for days and you're not going to get out of Chattanooga anyway so why not let me pick you up. I'm not crazy about driving in this weather so you can help me with the driving."

Val kept arguing until Drake finally agreed and he told her where he would be waiting at Chattanooga airport. Val then made arrangements to rent a car…No easy task because of the confusion in Atlanta but she was persistent until the agent found her a car. To get ahead of the approaching weather, she decided to leave immediately without seeing the residents again. Instead, she composed a letter that was to be delivered after her departure.

> Dear friends,
>
> I wanted you to know that Mr. Drake landed safely, although unfortunately in Chattanooga because of the backup of planes in Atlanta. Since I am on my way to stay with my family in Nashville, I offered to put up Mr. Drake in my home until he can find transportation to his final destination, wherever that may be. He is actually still undecided where that will be, but he is seriously considering following Mr. Simmons' suggestion of managing another home with the same high standards that he followed at the Manor. In any case, I've decided to drive and to pick him up on my way to Nashville.

I am saddened not to be able to see you all again and tell you in person what a privilege it has been to know you all and to provide some comfort for you during your stay at the Manor. I sincerely hope that you all will find a new life away from the encroaching seas that caused us to have to abandon our beautiful Manor. Attached to this note, I have provided my contact information and hope to hear from you when you are settled in your new homes.

One sad note; Mr. Drake told me that the Simmons have not yet been found and that their fate is in doubt. I continue to pray for their safe return.

Your friend,

Valeria Lopez

Meanwhile, Henrietta and the other former residents of the Duck Cove Manor had settled into their hotel rooms in Atlanta. Henrietta's room on the fiftieth floor offered an unobstructed view to the southeast and she could observe the roiling clouds, an early indicator announcing the approach of the storm. This reminded her of the promise she had made to Andy Carlson, so she placed a call to the number he had given her. There was no answer, but she left a message telling him that she was in Atlanta and would be there for some time because of the storm. Just at that moment, Jim knocked on her door and when she opened it, he entered without waiting to be asked. "I'm sorry! I wish we were in adjacent rooms instead of different floors."

"You should consider yourself lucky," said Henrietta, "to have a room considering the turmoil in town."

"I know, I know, but I just didn't want to be away from you."

"Listen, Jim, even though I agreed to sharing an apartment with you when we get to Lehigh, we had agreed to be just friends and nothing more for now. If you hadn't noticed, we're not teenagers, we're adults, actually senior citizens. I like you but please understand that sometimes I need time alone."

Before Jim was able to answer, the phone rang, and Henrietta picked it up and held her free hand out indicating her need for silence.

"It's Andy! I was in a meeting when you called. We were going over some new, disturbing information. I'm afraid you're going to be stuck in Atlanta for a while. There's a second powerful storm that's coming right behind yours."

"That's a fine hello," said Henrietta. "But, it's not the end of the world. At least, not yet! By the way, I had a chance to review my superstorm paper and I believe that it remains a very low probability event."

"I don't know what you'll say about my other good news. There are now two storms in the south Pacific and another one forming off the west coast of Mexico. T'is the season, as they say!"

"That's still a long way from a superstorm scenario. But I assume your folks are keeping tab on this."

"You bet. We're using the Hurricane Center to handle the coordination."

"I have my computer with me so if you could send me the maps, I could stay up to date and let you know if I see a worrisome trend."

"Absolutely! And stay safe," Carlson said before hanging up.

When she was off the phone, Henrietta explained what she had just heard.

"You didn't tell me that we're facing the end of the world," Jim said.

"Now, don't blow it out of proportion. Remember, it's a low probability event."

"Nevertheless…" She is a scientist, thought Jim, and I trust her judgement but what if she's wrong and these storms merge? There was no point in becoming obsessive, so he put such thoughts out of his mind. "Before the phone rang you said you wanted to be alone."

"For heaven's sake, I just meant I need some time alone. Don't take it as a rejection."

"I'm sorry," Jim answered, "I don't mean to seem…I don't know… clinging. These days I just like being with you."

"Fine! Sit down while I unpack."

After some minutes, Jim announced, "This is silly. I'll pick you up for dinner at seven," and left the room.

Later that evening he arrived promptly to find that Henrietta had changed into a stylish blue dress with a white scarf around her neck. "Don't you look lovely tonight," Jim said.

"Thank you, sir," she answered coquettishly as she took his arm to go to the elevator.

They went up to the top of the hotel where the dining room provided a spectacular view of the city and the passing clouds. It had begun to gently rain, causing the view to be distorted by the waves of water flowing down the windows.

"I'm glad we're inside tonight," said Henrietta looking outside. "I keep thinking about the Simmons and wonder if they were ever found?"

"From the letters they left," said Jim, "I don't think they wanted to be found. And, after the kind of storm we expect, I don't think they'll ever be found. But look, this is the first time we've been alone away from the Manor, and I want to just talk about other things...changes, maybe new beginnings."

"First of all, for all the years we were at the Manor, we rarely talked, and you were frankly difficult and not very friendly. Just because you seem to have miraculously become more human in the last few days, I need time to digest it. And then, your reaction to the Simmons situation seems somewhat cold and unfeeling. I can't imagine the heartache that led to their decision. It must have been wrenching. I'm not sure I could ever have made it. I care too much about life no matter how difficult it becomes. On one level, I understand it. They had a fantastic life together and didn't want to live through another displacement. But... Let's order before we continue."

The menu was somewhat limited because the food supply had been interrupted by the approaching storm, but they found a good wine and more than enough food to satisfy them. Henrietta began to relax as Jim sought to talk more sympathetically about what happened the last few days, of course, except anything about their relationship. It was after nine when they left the restaurant and descended to her room. When they arrived in front of the door, Jim kissed her tentatively at first and then more intently. At that point, she pulled away and said, "It's been a lovely evening but we both need our sleep since we don't yet know what tomorrow will bring, so good night." Reluctantly, Jim said, "Good night. I'll see you in the morning."

DON, IN HIS ROOM A dozen floors below Henrietta's let Girl out of the carrier and put water for her in a bowl in the bathroom. "Now you're going to have to be a good girl or they won't let me keep you with me," he said. With the confusion in the lobby, the hotel staff had not noticed that Don had a pet carrier with him. If they had, they would have told him that pets were not permitted in the rooms and that Girl had to stay in a cage in the basement where she could be visited anytime. *That's not good enough for my girl*, thought Don. This brought to mind their uncertain future and caused Don to wonder if any of the old contacts he had in Minneapolis were still around. He dug through his suitcase until he found the memoir he had started when Paolo was still alive. He looked through his description of the early years in Minneapolis to find names of some of the contacts he had there at the time. Most were no longer familiar to him except for two he still recognized. Opening his tablet, he started a search for both and found one in the obituary columns almost five years earlier. *He seemed so young when I knew him. That was only thirty years ago. I wonder what happened?* The other, Wayne Petersen, was a much younger associate at the television station when Don left there. He was still at the station as a senior correspondent. *I'll contact him when we get to Minneapolis. Maybe they could use me to provide the viewpoint of a displaced refugee of the climate crisis. What do you think, Girl?*

DIANE TURNED TO FRANK IN a room on the other side of the same floor, and said, "I'm so tired already, why can't we just continue on to Vermont where I can rest."

"I'm afraid that's not possible. There simply are no flights to take us there for some time. You're just going to have to rest here so you'll be ready to go."

"But..."

"No buts. Please just lie down for a while." After she fell asleep, Frank retrieved the worn leather-bound book from his bag, sat down in the easy chair looking out the window and watched the swirling clouds. He read the prescient words of his great-grandfather.

June 11, 1940

Today, as I feared, I was forced to leave Paris ahead of the advancing German Army. I looked at our house as if for the last time. In the garage, the Peugeot waited for my departure but when I checked the level of petrol, I realized there wasn't enough for the journey, and

I had been told that no more petrol was available. Sadly, I decided there was only one way I could leave; that was to use my bicycle. This limited me since I could only strap one old leather suitcase on the rear rack. I had to leave the trunk that I had previously packed and only repacked in the suitcase what was absolutely necessary for my forced voyage. Among the shirts, trousers, undergarments, and toiletries, I was devasted to only be able to include the music for my last sonata. I had to leave so much behind.

Once on the road, I found it difficult to negotiate my way among other bikers, walkers and the few cars that still had some of the precious petrol. Suddenly, we were attacked from the sky by the Fokkers shooting at us and forcing us off the road to avoid being killed or injured…not once but twice. Why couldn't they have left us in peace. It was bad enough that we had to leave our home… At the end of the day, I was exhausted and fortunately found refuge in an inn outside of Orleans. I was too tired to even eat supper and lay down on the lumpy bed, immediately falling asleep. It was raining when I awoke the next morning and I was happy to find a breakfast of a croissant, boiled egg and coffee. I knew I had to keep moving to stay ahead of the invading forces, so I set out in the rain heading toward Nevers.

I had calculated that it would take me a total of five days to reach Geneva where I hoped to be welcomed as a returning citizen. However, on the second day of my exodus, I was unable to even reach Nevers. Every muscle in my body hurt and I was drenched, so I had to stop early. I realized that I was over fifty years old, no longer young and agile and had not recently ridden a bicycle other than completing leisurely circuits in the park with the family on Sundays. In a small village, a farmer offered to let me stay in his barn where I could spend the night and recharge my aching body. On the third day I regained my momentum but paced myself to continue and stopped only to eat and relieve myself. When I finally arrived at the Swiss border on the sixth day, I felt that my renewed strength could carry me anywhere I wanted to go. But… all I looked forward to, was being reunited with Madeleine and the children in Basle.

"Frank," called Diane, shaking him lightly on the shoulder. "Are you asleep?"

"I was, but not now! Are you all right? Is anything wrong?"

"No! It's nothing. I just thought it was strange to see you slumped over in the chair."

"I was reading Bertrand's diary about his exodus from Paris back in the last century and thinking about how now, here we are, fleeing for our lives from the Manor that was our home for the last ten years," adding after a pause, "but, don't worry! We'll be safe once we reach Vermont just the way Bertrand was safe once he reached Switzerland."

Diane was so anxious to leave, and Frank had to keep reassuring her that it was a few days at most until they could resume their journey.

8
THE STORM STRIKES
Friday

B Y NIGHTFALL THURSDAY, IT BEGAN to rain along the Florida coast, gently at first but it soon developed into a hammering rainfall. Then there was the wind forcing its way inland, blowing from the east, signaling the edge of the cyclonic flow from the offshore hurricane. By Friday morning the force of the wind intensified reaching velocities of 140 mph. Lying on their tarpaulin, the Simmons moved closer together absorbing the punishing power of the combined wind and rain. Alex took the rope he had brought along and wrapped it around his and Dolores' waist so they would not become separated as the storm intensified. "I loved you, always," he whispered in her ear." Dolores replied, "we've had a wonderful life together and I've been so lucky that we ended up together." After a moment, she added, "When we die, do we leave a trace?" "I don't know," he answered.

"Then, let it be quick," she said.

On the open sea, hundred-foot high waves rolled along, sapping some of the power from the high winds while the warmth of the ocean that had been increasing for decades served to increase the force of the wind. These two effects vied for dominance as the hurricane moved slowly closer to shore. With a wind velocity over 180 mph, the forward edge of the storm with waves over thirty feet high smashed onto the Florida shore slightly north of Miami. Powered by the storm surge, the overwhelming force of the wall of water striking the coast caused houses near the shore to be the first to fall. Moving forward at a snail's pace the storm then attacked the Manor whose walls offered little resistance and fell, dragging and toppling the wooden floors along.

Within a matter of minutes all that was left of the Duck Cove Manor was a jumble of wooden sticks, smashed furniture and mashed drywall. The home that the residents had left a day earlier was no more!

When the wave arrived at the site the Simmons chose as their resting place, they were picked up violently and their end came quickly. All that remained was their lifeless bodies tossed about in the roiling waters like two drowned rag dolls. The storm surge carried them almost to the shore of Lake Okeechobee before depositing them in the marshy ground, presented in a perpetual embrace.

The storm crossed Florida in a mere four hours and when it hit the warm waters of the Gulf of Mexico it began to regain strength that it had lost over land. Nourished and renewed the storm turned northward heading for the Mississippi coast. Throughout the day it intensified threatening the very existence of what was left of New Orleans that had by then, already been mostly inundated by the rising seas. While the storm that destroyed their former home raged, the residents of the Manor rested in the comfort of their hotel rooms in Atlanta.

The sound of rain slapping against the hotel windows woke Girl who scratched the bed covers looking for a protective blanket. This caused Don to stir awake. "What is it, Girl? It's not time to get up." The dog jumped on Don's chest and buried herself under the covers. Don was now wide awake and pulled himself out of bed to open the curtain. Although it was past seven, the sky was totally obscured by waves of rain washing down the windows. "I don't think we'll be leaving today, Girl. We'd better settle in for an extended stay." He turned on the telescreen looking for good news but all that was being reported concerned the current state of the weather refugee crisis. Northern cities were being overwhelmed with people seeking a cooler climate. Among them were the New Greens who Don remembered seeing in the airport. They were seeking recruits for their return-to-nature movement reminiscent of the time in the mid twentieth century when the hippie generation sought an alternate lifestyle. They were recruiting candidates for a new life in colonies established in Canada, Alaska, Scandinavia and parts of Siberia meant to restart civilization in the new temperate climate regions of the earth. Some of these were led by cult-like charismatic leaders who closed admittance to their colonies to new recruits not totally committed to the cause of a natural way of life. This week, the government of Canada decided to close the border to the United States as it could no longer deal with these New Green groups as well as other migrants. It was announced that President Davenport was scheduled to meet with the Canadian Prime Minister later in the day to try to develop a compromise position. *There must be some better news somewhere in the world,* thought Don as he flipped through the channels and stopped at the image of a beautiful white polar bear sitting on an ice floe. Instead of good news, the announcer read through a litany of the disappearance of so many species: the polar bears who had long been the image of extinction resulting from climate change, as well as 2/3 of birds, turtles, penguins, koala bears, cod, monarch butterflies, ringed seals…it seemed like a never-ending list that was summarized by the announcer stating that half of all species on earth had either disappeared or become extinct. Disgusted and depressed, Don darkened the telescreen and lay back down in the bed, holding Girl on his chest.

FRANK WOKE UP LATE WHILE Diane still slept. Both suffered from nervous exhaustion from the trip to Atlanta. He opened the curtains a crack to give him enough light to place an order for breakfast before going to the bathroom to get ready for the day. While shaving he suddenly heard a frantic cry, "look, look out there." He rushed out of the bathroom to see Diane, sitting up in bed pointing to the window. He heard what sounded like marbles hitting the window and pulled open the shade to see white pellets of ice, raining down. "It's all right," he said taking Diane's hand in his. "It's just sleet. It doesn't usually last very long. I'm sorry it woke you."

"I thought it was like the war," Diane said, tightly squeezing Frank's hands. "You used to tell me about it." Before becoming editor of a weekly news magazine , Frank had been a foreign correspondent for a news network during the Afghan war. When he returned home, he had lost much of his bravado after seeing too many soldiers with both physical and emotional wounds and innocent civilians injured or killed by a stray bullet. The sound of war is what stayed with him for a long time…deafening explosions, the rat-a-tat of machine guns, the zing of passing bullets, the cries of the injured. Even after he returned, he had recurring nightmares that would not abate and as a consequence, left the news network and never again went into a war zone. Once settled into his new position, he and Diane married.

"There, you see, it's turning into rain just as I said. I've ordered breakfast so why don't you put on your robe and get ready. They should be up shortly."

Sometime later, the Weills sat at a folding table facing the window while eating their breakfast. "It's so grey out there, almost like night-time," said Diane. "I can hardly see any other buildings."

Frank became very concerned that the weather was not improving and that they would not be able to continue their trip to Vermont. He realized that Diane was in a delicate state, and he was not certain how long she would remain calm before again becoming agitated and even possibly aggressive. He needed some assurance that they could contin-ue to their destination so he placed a call to Henrietta whom he was sure would be up to date with the latest forecast.

Jim had called Henrietta in the morning and asked if they could have breakfast together. "I thought we could do it in your room," he said.

"Why don't we meet in the dining room instead," said Henrietta. "I think it would be best because I'm quite disorganized here and I don't have the time to straighten up." She had spent a sleepless night trying to resolve her feelings toward Jim and did not want to be pres-sured by being confined with him in her room. Within a minute after disconnecting the call, she received another call. "Listen Jim," she said immediately. "It will take me twenty min...." The caller interrupted, "Uh!... It's Frank."

"I'm sorry. I thought Jim was calling me back."

"That's all right," said Frank. "And, by the way, I did notice that the two of you were becoming cozier together. If you don't mind my ask-ing, is this the start of a late romance?"

Somewhat flustered, she answered, "Nothing of the sort. We're just friends... So, what can I do for you?"

Sure, thought Frank, *just friends! Even Diane mentioned that she thought something was going on.* "Diane has been pressing me to tell her when we might be able to leave. I need to get her to Vermont as soon as possible so I wonder if you've heard anything new from your sources?"

"I'm sorry, Frank, but I don't really know much more than you must have already seen on the telescreen. I'm afraid it's not clear when this storm will pass and allow flights to resume. Listen, there's nothing we can do today so why don't we meet for breakfast tomorrow morning to work out a plan for the next leg of our trip?"

"That might be nice. We're kind of tired and a day of rest would be good for Diane before we have to start traveling again."

They agreed to let Don and Jim know.

Henrietta took the opportunity to call Carlson and was forced to leave a message as the Science Advisor was occupied. She then took out the maps she had received from Carlson and focused on the two storms in her vicinity, the one that was now headed for New Orleans and the other, still in the Atlantic that seemed unusually close. Since they were both rotating in a counterclockwise direction the region between them would tend to force a separation or cause the following storm to veer north. The second storm, if it continued on its current track, could kiss the first one somewhere over land, like lovers. She had never seen anything quite like it. Was it real or was it an illusion?

Andy Carlson called back an hour later. "I'm sorry," he said. "We were in the midst of an emergency meeting. What's up?"

"That's what I should ask you. The last maps you sent me seemed to indicate a strange phenomenon with two Atlantic hurricanes merging. Can you confirm that?"

"That must be an anomaly. It certainly does not show on this morning's maps. What I do see is your hurricane intensifying as it approaches New Orleans. It should pass west of you and will certainly weaken by the time it reaches your latitude. The second hurricane is still off the coast. But in any case, I imagine you must be experiencing heavy rain and strong winds by now."

"Absolutely! I'm not planning to leave the comfort of this hotel at any time soon. Do you have any idea when all this good weather will pass?"

"I told you, the second hurricane is on your tail so I wouldn't make any plans for a flying departure any time in the next two or three days."

"That's a disappointment, especially for some of the other members of our group. It seems we may have to look into other means of travel." Henrietta wondered how she would break this news to her companions. She was especially concerned about Diane Weill who needs to be settled in her new home as soon as possible, although remembering her sudden lucidity when they were all together for the last supper at the Manor, *maybe the old girl's a bit more adaptable to change*, she thought. But, for the moment there was nothing else she could do.

A half hour later Jim and Henrietta sat facing each other at a small table overlooking the city that was enveloped in grey swirling clouds and a pelting rain. "Here we are again," said Jim. "It's almost as if we never left."

"You're being awfully flip."

"Sorry, I didn't sleep well last night. I was thinking about what you and your friend the president said."

"He's not the president," Henrietta said while smiling. "He's the science advisor to the president."

"OK, OK, but seriously, is the government worried about these storms?"

"It's a combination of the number of storms around the world and their intensity resulting from increased temperatures. That is a concern."

"So, Is this an end of the world scenario?"

"I don't believe it is," said Henrietta clasping her hands together as if in prayer.

"You don't sound very convincing."

"I'm sorry. I have to admit I'm somewhat concerned. I talked to Carlson this morning and studied the storm maps he sent me, and they are a little scary." Taking a deep breath, she continued, "but, being rational, I know there's not enough there to make an intelligent judgment."

Jim looked out the restaurant windows that were still being pelted by rain. "I wonder if we'll ever fly out of here. Perhaps we should think of another way to travel north. There must be trains or busses that go to Pennsylvania. What do you say we look into it?"

"Let's wait and talk to the others. Everyone's a little tired so I've suggested we all rest today and meet tomorrow for lunch," said Henrietta. "There will be five of us and we should be able to come up with some ideas."

When they left the dining room, Jim suggested they spend the day in her room, but Henrietta said she needed the time alone to study the latest maps she had received from Carlson and that she, herself was tired and needed to rest. Jim sensed that there was no point in arguing so he retreated to his own room.

9

VAL & DRAKE
Saturday

Valeria had driven to Chattanooga Friday morning to meet Drake so that they could bring each other up to date. She decided to stay for the night before continuing on and after securing a room had a late supper with Drake. By Saturday morning, the storm had curved northward and was expected to make landfall along the southern Louisiana coast. Inland, the rain had already begun and was projected to intensify during the day. Val was not going to let a little rain stop her and so she woke Drake early to join her for a leisurely breakfast before setting out on the road. Later, when they started out, they discovered that the car's air conditioner was not working. Contacting the rental agency, they were told that no other cars were available and decided to leave anyway. They headed for the interstate, expecting to reach their destination well before lunchtime. For the first hour the traffic was unusually heavy and moved slowly. There were many cars, buses and vans filled mostly with migrants escaping from the heat and the flooding along the southern coasts. Without air conditioning, the windshield kept fogging up and had to be continually wiped clear with a rag. They tried opening the side windows to bring in fresh air to help, but the pelting rain made that impossible and only blew water into the car. Val became tired of fighting the elements and pulled into a rest area to let Drake take over for a while. They quickly changed places but could not avoid getting soaked before setting off again. On the radio, they heard of possible flooding along their route and more significantly, flooding along the Cumberland River. There was also an early warning that parts of Nashville may need to be evacuated. Hearing this, Val called her husband who told her that their part of town near Vanderbilt University was not expected to be flooded. It had happened in the past, but flood control measures had been installed to mitigate against a recurrence of the 2040 flood. "I hope you're right. I just left one flooded house and don't want to have to live in another one."

They had to stop often to wipe away the condensation and be able to see more clearly out of the windshield. Along the road, they passed people walking or camped along the side but did not stop. Suddenly, Drake saw three men in ponchos and floppy hats shielding their faces, illuminated by his headlights blocking the road ahead. As he drove closer, he saw that one of them held a baseball bat. Opening the side window, he yelled out, "Would you mind getting out of the way." The man holding the bat moved closer to the driver's window while the other two stayed in front.

"We just want a ride," the man said.

"I'm sorry, we're not allowed to pick up hitchhikers," said Drake. The man lifted his bat in a threatening manner as Drake pushed open the door causing the man to fall backward onto the pavement. The other two men then ran to either side of the car as Drake stepped on the accelerator causing the car to jump forward and away from the threat.

Val was shaken by this incident. "They only wanted a ride," she said.

"I know those type of people!" said Drake. "If I had stopped, they would have left us bloodied and taken the car. I wasn't about to take a chance on that happening. Make sure your door is locked."

Val was not convinced but stayed quiet for the rest of the ride. Even without any further incidents, it took them almost twice as long as they had expected to travel the 120 odd miles to reach their destination as the rain continued to fall and became ever more intense.

Val had entered the unfamiliar address into the GPS and as they approached Nashville, they followed the voice commands judiciously as she had never before been there. Their destination turned out to be a brick faced apartment building, ten stories high. The Lopez apartment was on the fourth floor facing the tree-lined street. "I don't know what to expect," said Val as they entered the lobby. "All I know is that there are two bedrooms since we wanted a second one for visiting grandchildren."

"At this time, all I care about is that it's indoors! I'll just be glad to get out of this weather and into some dry clothes," said Drake, shaking off water from his jacket.

When Ernesto, Val's husband, opened the door, he wrapped his powerful arms around his wife and kissed her repeatedly on both cheeks before turning toward Drake whose hands he shook effusively. "Thank you for bringing my little Valeria home to me."

As Drake retrieved his hands from Ernest's strong grip he remembered that Val had told him that her husband worked in construction for most of his adult life. As a superintendent leading crews of workers, he learned to maintain his physical strength to underscore his verbal directions. "It's late and I guess you guys had a rough trip with the weather and all. Have a beer and relax," he said as a broad grin spread across his round face. He looked as if he had already long ago started on the beer, based on the color on his shiny bald head that topped a face covered in a three-days growth of beard.

"Ernie baby," Val said, "I guess you didn't wait for us to start on the booze, and you didn't have a chance to shave before we arrived? Listen, we had a tiring trip and perhaps Mr. Drake would prefer to go right to bed."

"Actually," Drake interjected, "a cool cerveza would do me good."

Ernesto happily opened the fridge that seemed to be well stocked with beer but not much else and took one out for Drake and one for himself. Meanwhile Val looked into the cupboards to try to find something to eat. Finding only nuts and some dry crackers, she phoned the local pizzeria and had one delivered. By the time the food arrived, the men were already on their second bottle of beer and devoured the pizza within minutes. Val had by that time excused herself to go to bed. After one more round, it was almost midnight at which time the two men had finished discussing the disasters the world was plunging into and they staggered to bed.

Drake woke late in the morning and slipped into the bathroom to drench his head in cold water to help open his eyes. After a warm then cold shower he dressed and went to the dining room where Val silently poured him a cup of hot coffee. "Thank you! I think I overdid it yesterday," he said.

"I'm afraid that Ernie dragged you along a wicked path."

"No, no! It's just that these past few days were super high stress and I needed to decompress. I'm fine now and I'm going to check out some of my options this morning so I can get out of your hair."

"You're welcome to stay with us as long as you like, Mr. Drake. The weather's still pretty rotten and besides, Ernie likes your company."

"Please Val, after all that's happened, it's Al...no more Mister... And... thank you for the offer. I do have to spend a little time deciding where I'm going to live." He welcomed the chance to rest for a few days and consider options for his future life.

10
A LOST DAY
Saturday

IN ATLANTA, THE WEATHER HAD not improved. At the restaurant where Henrietta had suggested they meet for lunch, the Weills were the first to arrive. Looking around, Diane observed, "there aren't too many people here." Turning to Frank, she added, "Are you sure we should be here? We could eat in our room."

"I'm sure the others will be here in a minute. It will be good to see them again. Why don't we ask the hostess to seat us at a table near the window? It looks as if the weather may improve a bit and we'll finally be able to see the city." He waved to the hostess who led them to a window table.

"I don't want to look out," said Diane. "Can we sit so that I don't have to?"

Before Frank could respond, Don walked in and waved to them. "It's good to see you both. How are you bearing up under this interminable wait for transportation?"

"How's Girl? interrupted Diane.

Looking around, Don said, "shh. They don't know I have her in my room because it's not really allowed."

Putting a finger to her lips, Diane said conspiratorially, "mum's the word."

"What are they going to do if they find out, put you out on the street?" said Frank. "These are not normal times and they have to expect rules to be bent a little."

"I'm not sure the management would see it that way," said Don. "But, more importantly, have you heard any news about our transportation?"

"I called Henrietta this morning, but she had nothing to add to what we heard on the news. By the way, what do you think about she and Jim getting together?" Said Frank.

"I hadn't heard but…there they are, walking in together. Over here," yelled Don waving at the couple.

After they all greeted one another, Diane said, "It's nice to see the two of you getting along together."

Looking embarrassed, Henrietta said, "We just met in the elevator."

'Sure,' whispered Frank under his breath. "Let's eat."

After lunch was served, Jim turned to Henrietta and asked, "Why don't you tell everyone what you heard from the science guy."

Henrietta turned to glare at Jim. "Andy is not just a 'science guy', he's Dr. Andrew Carlson whom I've known for a long time, even before he became the science advisor to the President. I've been in touch with him to check out the latest information about the storm to help us judge when we might be able to continue the journey to our new homes.…Apparently there is another hurricane following on to the one that is set to pass West of us, so he doesn't expect plane travel to be back anytime soon. Looking at the whole country, the northeast is in relatively clear weather but in the southeast, it's going to be rainy and windy for days and there is even the possibility of tornadoes. That's why I suggested we get together and talk about alternatives. Jim, why don't you tell them what you've found out."

"Well, if we can't fly out of here there are a couple of other possibilities. I thought about renting a car and driving to Charlotte, it's less than 200 miles and, even though it's a hub for a couple of airlines, the airport there is less crowded than here in Atlanta."

"I'm sorry to interrupt you," said Henrietta. "But before I left my room, I received a call from Val with some disturbing news."

"Is she all right?" said Diane anxiously. "Has anything happened to her?"

"No, no, she's fine. She and Mr. Drake drove to Nashville where they are safely staying in Val's apartment. Val just told me about what happened to them on the way to Nashville. You know that there are groups of climate migrants moving north… they are along every highway. What is disturbing is that some bad people are mixed in among them. What happened to Val and Drake on the road is that they encountered a group of these thugs who tried to stop them on the road. Well… it seems they clearly wanted to steal the car and Drake, who was driving, just drove them off the road and sped away."

"Good for him," said Don, "it's a crazy world we're living in, where travelers are assaulted by highwaymen. What about a train? There's the ultra-train that was put into service about ten years ago and goes all the way to Philadelphia."

"They move awfully fast, don't they?" said Frank. "Isn't that uncomfortable. I heard they go more than 200 miles an hour. I'm not sure we'd like that."

"You're happy to fly in planes, aren't you, and they go almost three times faster," said Jim. "I can tell you that I've ridden in ultra-trains and the ride is as smooth as glass. The problem is going to be getting a reservation because they're usually booked way in advance."

"There's another problem," said Henrietta. "I've heard that because of the deteriorating weather these past ten years that there have been problems maintaining the roadbed. You certainly can't have any bumps in the road with such a high-speed vehicle, so If there is any softening of the ground, the track is vulnerable, and then, there could be an accident."

"So, where does that leave us?" said Jim, "What about a bus?"

"We might have the same problem," said Frank, "with overcrowding and unavailability of seats."

"It seems to me that a car or van is still our best solution." said Henrietta. "If we're vigilant and careful we should be all right. What do you all say?"

There followed a period of discussion, with Frank questioning if such a trip might not be a good idea for Diane and Don pointing out that he was heading toward Minneapolis which was to the northwest while the group planned to drive to Charlotte which was northeast of Atlanta. Jim pointed out that Charlotte was a great location because flights originated there going in all directions. Finally, everyone agreed to make Jim responsible for trying to rent a van as soon as possible. They also decided to gather again for dinner for an update.

Jim spent the afternoon on the phone checking with every auto rental agency until after almost three hours he found an available vehicle and at once made arrangements to pick it up in the morning. He wanted to immediately tell Henrietta but decided it would be best to wait for the group to gather for dinner. "As I suspected," he said, when they had all been seated, "it was almost impossible to find an available rental. Finally, I found one that I hope you all will find acceptable. It's the only one in town and it's not exactly what we had in mind. It's a limousine, all electric with a 300-mile battery…and kind of snazzy… with a built-in bar and fridge. What do you say?"

They all looked at each other, somewhat flabbergasted. Diane smiled broadly and spoke first. "I love it!" She turned to Frank. "It'll be like graduation. Do you remember?"

"You're kidding," said Henrietta. "You mean that in all of Atlanta, there was nothing else available?"

Jim was clearly annoyed and blurted out, "If you think you can do any better…"

"I'm sorry. I didn't mean to put down your effort, but you must admit that a limo is a bit of an odd choice for us. Of course, if that's all that was offered, I suppose we have no alternative. So, what time shall we leave?"

"I've always wanted to drive a limo," said Don.

"Hey, we'll share the driving," said Jim

"Does that put me in the back with my date," said Frank.

The dinner turned into a celebration with drinking and raucous conversation drowning out the noise caused by the vibration of the windows reacting to the increasing force of the wind outside. When dinner was finished and they began to disperse, Jim whispered in Henrietta's ear, "Can we go to your room for a while?"

She was not at all surprised and nodded, "yes!" They waited until the others had left and then took the elevator and as the doors closed, Jim started to say, "Ever since you talked about my reconnecting with my son, I've thought a great deal about that…"

"Why don't we wait 'till we get to the room before you tell me about it."

"But,…" he started to say, until he realized there was another couple in the elevator. They remained silent until entering her room and before Jim could open his mouth, Henrietta said, "Before you say anything, do we still have an understanding about being friends?"

Somewhat taken aback by this remark, he answered, "I suppose so, but can we not make that a hard and fast rule."

Henrietta smiled and gave his arm a friendly squeeze, saying, "That's fair."

As is typical of hotel rooms there was a bed, a desk with drawers and a single chair. Jim looked around waiting... Seeing him looking puzzled, Henrietta said, "Why don't you sit on the chair, and I'll sit on the edge of the bed."

"I'm glad that's settled," he said. "What I wanted to talk to you about is that since we had the conversation about my son, I've come to a new understanding of that situation. I realized that we're not talking about a child or even a young man. Mike is almost fifty-years old. He's lived practically his whole life without me and the only father he's ever known is his stepfather who raised him and from whom he learned values. He doesn't even carry my name since after my wife and I divorced and she remarried, she insisted that her new husband adopt Mike. All I ever contributed was a seed. That doesn't seem to be enough to impose myself into his life and his family at this late date."

"You talked about grandchildren, and wouldn't they want to know their grandfather."

"Well, they know him and it's Mike's stepfather and not me. It wouldn't be fair to suddenly introduce a stranger in that role. Anyway, I've decided to leave well enough alone and not try to impose myself on them. You know, I've been alone pretty much all my life. It's a choice I made, first because of my profession, being posted all over the world and then, because I became used to it....at least until now." He suddenly felt a pressure in his chest and tears welling up in his eyes. "Now... I don't want to be alone anymore."

Henrietta reached out to him. "Come, sit next to me."

He got up from the chair and moved next to her on the edge of the bed as she put her arm around him and pulled him close. "I'm sorry," he said, as he wiped his eyes with the back of his sleeve. "I didn't mean to burden you with my problem."

"It's all right, I understand. After all I've been very much alone since my husband died, so I know what it's like not to be close to someone."

Falling back on the bed he said, "I'm so tired."

"Why don't you take your shoes off and stretch out," she said.

"You don't mind?"

"No! It's fine."

He lay back on the bed and folded an arm across his eyes while Henrietta went to the bathroom to get ready for bed. By the time she returned dressed in her pajamas, Jim was snoring lightly. She lay down next to him and covered them both with a blanket, snuggling close and was soon asleep herself.

Sometime later, Jim awoke and went to the bathroom. When he came back to bed, he looked down at Henrietta and saw that she was missing the turban that she usually wore. She doesn't need it, he thought. There's nothing wrong with her hair. He stretched out quietly next to her and gently put his arm across her back and soon fell asleep. In the middle of the night, Henrietta woke up and turned to face him and softly kissed his cheek as he stirred awake. He pulled her close and kissed her as they embraced, and soon they no longer heard the rain beating against the windows. Instead, all they heard was the staccato sound of their blended heartbeats....

11
ON TO CHARLOTTE
Sunday

ON SUNDAY MORNING THE INSISTENT buzzing of the alarm woke Henrietta who shook Jim. "Please wake up! We have to get ready to leave and you're going to have to go back to your room and pack."

Jim tried to pull her close to kiss her, but Henrietta pushed him back. "We don't have time for that now," she said.

"Just one kiss? After all, we…"

"Please!" she pleaded. "We have to get ready."

"Oh, all right." He slowly heaved himself off the bed and went to his room as Henrietta went to the bathroom to ready herself for the trip to Charlotte.

The former residents of the Manor slowly gathered in the dining room for breakfast; the Weills were the first and had already ordered when Don and then Henrietta arrived. Jim arrived much later and strode to the table full of energy calling out, "I'm famished, what's there to eat?"

"You'll have to order," said Henrietta, "but in the meantime there are some rolls in the bowl.

"You seem pretty chipper this morning," said Don

"Well, I slept well, I've already picked up the limo and I feel on top of the world this morning."

"I remember what a good sleep will do for you," said Frank with a wink.

Throughout the breakfast, Henrietta was very quiet but stole momentary glances at Jim but otherwise looked out the windows at the city still enveloped in grey. The rain, she noticed, was not as intense as

113

it had been earlier, and she wondered how much time they had before the next storm was to arrive. "I wonder if we shouldn't get going," she said, "while the storm seems to be less severe?"

"Can I have a few minutes to finish my breakfast," said Jim. "I'm trying to get charged up for our little trip. And besides I'm all packed and the limo is downstairs."

"Let the man eat," said Don. "After all we don't know what we'll encounter on the way? I'll get my bags and bring them to the limo."

Don walked to the elevator, followed by the Weills. Once they had left, Henrietta turned to Jim. "I don't know what happened to me last night, but I may have lost my way."

"No, no, you didn't lose your way, but I think maybe we both found something important that was missing in our lives. I don't know what you would call it. It felt like a burst of renewal, a warmth and tenderness that I don't know if I've ever felt in my life. And, I want you to know, I'm not prepared to give it up and I'm willing to fight to keep it. Please tell me you felt it too?"

"I don't know what to say. Last night was such a surprise to me. I felt something that I thought was lost forever but I need time to understand it."

"It's not some intellectual question. Just revel in the feeling, that's all."

Henrietta pushed back her chair. "We'd better go and not keep the others waiting."

As the residents gathered in the hotel lobby awaiting their departure, Henrietta received a text message from Dr. Carlson;

> The second storm is on a path to hit the Georgia coast later today with sustained winds of 130 mph. This is substantially less than the first storm but strong enough to cause severe additional damage when added to the damage caused by coastal flooding that has already been experienced. Remember that the storm surge is expected to be as high as a two-story building. I know you are far from the coast, but you should be aware that from the storm that hit Louisiana, there is now greater danger from tornadoes or even micro-bursts.
>
> I'm concerned for your safety so please call me and let me know

your intentions for leaving Atlanta.

Also, be advised that President Davenport has asked if you would be willing to join a taskforce on adapting to the new environmental norm.

Andy

Henrietta considered immediately calling Carlson back to say how surprised and flattered she was by the President's offer to join an environmental task force. But, on reflection she needed time to consider it. *After all,* she thought, *I've been away from the academic world and the mainstream of thinking on this issue for some time. Is there even a possible solution to the issue? It's a time of revolutionary change. Where can we live, how will we live in our new environment? These are issues that touch on philosophy and politics, not just science. I don't know if I'm qualified to explore this new world. I just don't want to make a fool of myself.* She wished she had time to talk to Jim. He's a rational thinker and together they should be able to decide how to respond …

"Folks, it's time to saddle up," barked Jim. "The weather's not going to get any better and we need all the daylight we can get for this trip."

No time now, thought Henrietta. *When we stop along the way, I'll talk to Jim.*

The Weills captured the settee in the back of the limo while Henrietta took the lounge chair behind the partition separating her from the driver. Jim took his seat as the designated driver with Don next to him. Driving away from the hotel the limo was buffeted by a moderate wind driven rain. Jim drove carefully through the city streets until reaching the interstate in the direction toward Spartanburg. "And, away we go," roared Jim, as he stepped on the pedal to speed up. As they moved away from the environs of the city, Don pointed out a tent city in a clearing on the side of the road. "Must be one of those refugee groups that Drake mentioned they encountered on their way to Nashville."

"I wouldn't worry about it since with the traffic moving so fast no one would be brave enough to walk on the road. Anyway, it's well patrolled and …." Jim suddenly pointed, "See there! There's a National Guard vehicle on the other side of the road. I heard that the governors of many states have called out the Guard to keep order since there are so many refugee groups travelling north." *I'll have to talk to Henrietta about this*, he thought. *Her friend in the President's office should be able to shed some light on the situation. It worries me that this country's turning into an armed camp.*

Don said, "That's not just a vehicle but an armored vehicle the Guard is using. They must be expecting trouble."

"That's funny," said Jim. "I was just thinking that this refugee crisis is subtly moving this country toward a more autocratic state. I wonder how far the administration is prepared to go?"

"Maybe you haven't been watching the news lately, but I've seen recent interviews with the President, and she strikes me as becoming quite imperious. First there was the closure of the border to Mexico and just last week the Canadian PM closed their border with the US to keep out the climate migrants. That means a lot of these migrants are stuck with no place to go and the questions are, what are they going to do and where are they going to end up? Perhaps in one of the border states where we're planning to re-settle? I tell you, Jim. I think there's going to be trouble ahead."

"Maybe you're right. First, we were drowned out of our home at the Manor and now we may end up in a war zone. With all the guns in this country, I can well imagine that many of these refugee groups are well armed."

"Should we share our optimistic outlook with the folks in the back?" asked Don.

"Nah! Let them enjoy the ride."

Frank and Diane were holding hands on the settee in the back of the limousine like two teenagers. "Isn't this romantic?" said Diane. "Do you remember, Frank, when I kept telling you how disappointed I was that I never rode with you in a limo to my senior prom. Well, here we are and only sixty years late."

Frank put his arm around Diane's shoulder and pulled her close. "It's not quite the same. I'm glad you like it, but you know we're not exactly alone here."

"Don't mind me," said Henrietta. "I'll just turn and face the front."

Diane's cheeks burned with embarrassment. "It's not as if we were planning anything… were we, Frank?"

"At our age?"

"Love has no age limit," said Henrietta, smiling!

For the next two hours, they drove without incident, passing several tent cities with climate migrants. The occupants were not visible as the continuing light rain kept them inside. Since it was almost time for lunch, Jim suggested they stop and take a short break. All agreed as the rain had almost ended, and they all welcomed the chance to stretch their legs and take a bathroom break. "Hartwell Lake is just ahead," said Don. "It has a rest area. We can take the sandwiches that the Hotel prepared for us and I'm sure that there are concessions there for us to get drinks and tables where we can sit and enjoy a leisurely lunch.

When they arrived at the rest area, they saw that there were a number of decrepit cars and an old school bus already parked in front. Turning to Frank, Diane said, "I hope they have room for us because I really have to go." When they entered the building, all the tables were occupied, and two dozen pairs of eyes suddenly turned to glare at them. Diane and Henrietta headed for the ladies' room while the men went to the gents. Frank said, "maybe we shouldn't stay. I have a feeling these people don't want us here."

"Nonsense!" said Jim. "We have as much right to be here as they do."

"Yes, but they're not driving around in a limo," said Don.

The men waited around the vending machines for the women to come out of the restrooms and when they did, Don suggested they go back to the car, whispering, "we don't really need to get anything here. Don't forget we have a fully equipped bar in the limo."

"It's creepy here," Diane added as they went outside.

Jim was about to argue when the others blurted out almost in unison, "Let's go somewhere else."

They drove a little further and stopped along the side of the road in a quiet spot overlooking the lake. "This is better," said Diane. "It's stopped raining and we can have a little picnic here. I don't know what was wrong with those people at the rest-stop, but they made me very uncomfortable."

"They looked to me as if they had been traveling for some time," said Don. "The men were unshaven and disheveled, and the women looked bleary-eyed and unkempt. And, did you notice there were no children. I suspect that this group did not consist of families but were simply individuals who were traveling together to get away from un-livable conditions further south…very much like us!"

"It's just as well that we left because they clearly did not want us there," said Frank, "and they looked a bit threatening. Anyway…" He took a throw blanket from the limo and was about to stretch it out on the ground when Jim pointed out that the grass was too wet and why not sit in the back cabin of the limo. There were more than enough seats for all and with the doors open it wouldn't get too hot. Don opened the well -stocked bar and offered the others, hot or cold drinks and even the choice of a chilled bottle of Sauvignon Blanc. "Maybe we should skip the wine until later when we get to Charlotte," said Henri-etta, …"especially for the drivers,".

"Kill joy," said Jim snickering.

After eating and drinking the group relaxed before continuing their journey. Henrietta turned to Jim and asked, "Can we have a few minutes to talk? Something came up this morning that I'd like to dis-cuss with you."

"Sure. What is it?"

"Walk with me!"

They walked away from the group to stand under the shade of an oak tree and Henrietta proceeded to describe the message she had re-ceived from Carlson and her concerns. How was she to respond when she felt so unsure about her ability to fulfill such a position. She was so confused.

"Wait a minute, Henny," interrupted Jim. "You have a doctorate in environmental sciences. You've spent your whole life studying the environment. I don't know anyone who is more qualified than you to serve on such a panel. I have great respect for your knowledge in this field. Hell, I'm even willing to grant that maybe you're right when you talked about the carbon eating, scrubber satellites improving the atmosphere even though it goes against what you wrote in your Ph D thesis."

"You read it? I'm shocked."

"It wasn't difficult to find since it had such a sexy title; *Why the Effort to Reverse Climate Change Must Fail.* Your argument that the problem can only be solved by international action has been proven accurate, and the reality is that it won't work. Year after year, agreements were broken by one country or another for all kinds of reasons; internal politics, cost of the transition to alternative fuels and so on and on and on. Now there are the scrubber satellites funded and operated by only two countries, the US and China. And, the agreement they made was to pressure every other country in the world by excluding them as trading partners unless they commit to a ten-year monitored conversion away from carbon fuels. Look, my base of knowledge is rooted in technology on earth and not in space. I have no idea if the scrubbers will work but I give you credit for supporting it. You *should* be more involved, so please don't turn down the chance to be on this panel. I know you would have much to contribute." Jim took a deep breath before adding, "if you want to worry about something, worry about the increasingly autocratic attitude of the President with troops everywhere controlling the free movement of people."

Dumbfounded, Henrietta stood facing Jim while he presented this rambling argument. She now stepped forward to hug him. "I give up. How can I argue with you when you confront me with such a rational line of reasoning? Thank you." And, she kissed him on the cheek before taking his hand to walk back to the car.

"Is that all the thanks I get," he said, winking.

"All right!" And she kissed him on the other cheek. She then took out her phone and typed in a text message to Carlson. When she finished, she turned the phone so Jim could read it and asked, "Is that to your liking?"

"Perfect," he said as he pushed the send button and then pulled close to kiss her on the lips.

As they walked back to join the others, Henrietta thought to herself, *I think I could learn to love this old guy.*

When they reached the Limo, Don greeted them. "You two have a nice chat together?"

"Actually, Jim was very helpful in solving a problem I was having," said Henrietta.

"You mean, while we were sweating in this heat, you two were discussing technical issues? You could have done that later," said Don as he stepped into the driver's seat.

When the Weills and Henrietta took their seats in the back, Diane took Henrietta's hand and said, "Don't mind him dear, he's just jealous because he has no one to talk to. Frank, why don't you switch seats with Henrietta. That will give the ladies a chance to talk."

As he stared at his wife Frank obeyed, once again surprised at her unpredictability. During the ride to Charlotte, the two ladies engaged in an intimate conversation while Jim and Don, in the front of the Limo stared ahead without communicating with each other.

Watching through the windshield, Jim observed the many camouflages colored military vehicles parked along the side of the road spaced a few miles apart. Guns could be seen sprouting from openings, ready and threatening. As cars, trucks and buses passed these armored vehicles, some were waved down and pulled over by the military and its occupants were asked to show identification and were then interrogated. It made Jim increasingly uncomfortable although he recognized the need for action to control the cascading violence caused by roving bands of climate migrants. *Perhaps*, thought Jim, *I can ask Henny to question Dr. Carlson. After all, he has the ear of the President and could tell us whether this apparent police-state style action is the new normal.* He remembered the note that Henny sent Carlson. It was perfect as it emphasized her independence if she were to be accepted on the President's task force. Once he responded, she would have the perfect opportunity to talk to him about this visible increase in military presence.

In the back of the limo, behind the soundproof separation panel, Frank saw the same sight out of the side window, and he shuddered as it reminded him again of the story of his great grandfather Bertrand's exodus from Paris. He remembered the paragraph he had last read:

> Military troops were everywhere as migrants crowded the roads. People were pulled aside to verify that they had proper credentials and were not enemy infiltrators. It was a dangerous time, and the general population was frightened and had lost confidence in their leaders.

It was clear that democracy was fractured then, as it seemed to be now because of the dislocations caused by the decades long change in the climate. Frank was concerned that this country, his country, was descending into chaos as the population was fracturing into enclaves of frightened entities; some neighborhoods or towns welcoming new settlers while others erecting armed walls to keep them out.

He looked across to Diane, openly talking and responding to Henrietta, seemingly free of any constraints, as if her disease had miraculously withered away. But he knew that if he spoke of the disturbing thoughts that bedeviled his mind, her moment of joy would instantly vanish. He realized that his love for her was too strong to allow that to happen.

It took our voyagers longer than they had anticipated to reach their destination but by late afternoon they arrived at the airport in Charlotte. The terminal was crowded with passengers waiting for flights. People were jostling, pushing each other aside to get attention from the overworked agents. Don elbowed his way through and collared an agent to explain that they had been forced to abandon a retirement community in Miami and had already been traveling for days. Since they were all senior citizens, he hoped that they could be accommodated with flights as soon as possible, explaining the need for three different destinations for the travelers in their group.

The agent, his name tag identified him as Roger Franzen, said, "Listen, mister, everyone here has a story. The best I can do for your group is to take you to the VIP Lounge and let the staff there try to deal with you." Without waiting for a reply, he led them toward the lounge.

The airlines agent took down all the information from our travelers and suggested they take a seat and have an offered refreshment while they waited for her to see what arrangements she could make. A half hour later she called them to her counter and explained, "I've done my best and here is what I can offer you." She proceeded again to explain the reasons for the restricted number of flights both because of the weather and the crush of migrants. "Mr. Garland, I've been able to book you on a flight to Minneapolis early tomorrow morning. Mr. and Mrs. Weill, I've booked you on a flight to Burlington tomorrow midday. Ms. Barker and Mr. Robinson, Allentown is the closest airport to your destination and I'm afraid, we have no seats available for those flights for the next three days."

"I assume you've checked alternatives," said Henrietta.

"Of course! I might be able to get you to Philadelphia earlier, but you would have to find other transportation from there to Bethlehem."

"Give us a minute to discuss this," said Jim and taking Henrietta aside, he suggested they have another option which was to continue to drive. It's about 500 miles and he felt that they could easily make it in two days.

"I'm not comfortable with that," said Henrietta. "It would mean finding a motel on the way and with all those migrants on the road that might prove to be impossible."

"Remember, we have a limo and we could sleep in the back, you on the banquette and me on the floor. How about it?"

"I don't know?"

"Would you rather wait here for who knows how long? There's no guarantee we can ever get out of here."

Taking a deep breath, Henrietta said, "I suppose you're right. But let's see about accommodations for tonight so we can at least have a leisurely farewell dinner with Don and the Weills." The agent, after a quick search offered the group either a roadside motel or a deluxe hotel in town. Without waiting for a response from the others, Don said, "We'll take the downtown hotel."

Jim drove the group to the hotel and after checking in, they agreed to meet for dinner in the rooftop restaurant. Once settled in her room, Henrietta checked her messages and found one from Carlson in which he congratulated her for accepting to serve on the President's task force and asking her to call to arrange a meeting in Washington. Before placing that call, she contacted Jim who reminded her of his concerns about the increasing military presence they had experienced during their drive to Charlotte and the signs of an increasingly autocratic administration. He asked her to bring this up in her conversation with Carlson.

Henrietta was able to reach Carlson after a half hour arguing with layers of secretaries.

"Where are you now?" he said, when she was finally able to speak to him. "The last time I heard from you, you were still in Atlanta."

"We're in Charlotte now, and it looks as if a friend and I will be driving to Bethlehem because flights are limited. Judging from the weather here, I gather that the second storm is dissipating over land at this time. "

"That's right. And, you might as well know that the Pacific storms have not developed as we expected so the possibility of a superstorm has declined to almost zero. It seems that the current conditions have changed drastically."

"Since you mentioned the current condition, that's one thing I wanted to talk to you about. On our drive from Atlanta, we encountered another kind of storm that was quite disturbing. Among the climate migrants we saw, we were confronted by a somewhat threatening rogue group. And also, we noticed military vehicles all along the route that were stopping and interrogating travelers. Is this a direction that is coming from the administration?"

"You have to understand, Henrietta, that these are dangerous times. Not only have we had to deal with this crazy weather but the movement of masses of people northward is unprecedented. The states are usually responsible for maintaining order but since this is a national problem, the President has directed the national guard to take over. I know it must seem somewhat draconian but believe me, there have already been too many incidents of violence coming from groups such as the one you encountered. President Davenport is well aware of the dangers of an increasingly repressive government clampdown, but this situation requires decisive action to prevent a total breakdown of civilized behavior." Henrietta pulled the phone from her ear and held it in her lap while she tried to think how to answer. "Hello, hello. Are you still there," called out Carlson!

"Yes, I'm here....I was mulling over what you said. Frankly, in view of this situation, I'd like a little more time to reconsider whether I should join the task force. Let me first get settled in Bethlehem. I assume there's no great urgency and I really need to decide if it's something I should undertake."

"I don't mind waiting a few days but hope I didn't discourage you," said Carlson.

"No, no! There are so many changes taking place in my life right now and I just need time."

Carlson did not argue and agreed to wait for her decision.

12
THE INTREPID FIVE

Aᴼᴼᴼᴼ HANGING UP FROM HIS quick call from Henrietta, Jim lay down on his bed for a brief nap. He realized that the drive from Atlanta had tired him out even though he had shared it with Don. In his travels around the world carrying out engineering projects he was often called upon to drive long distances to remote sites on less than favorable roads. He considered these trips to be adventures that made him feel energized and excited. Of course, that was many years ago, and now he realized.... *I guess I'm not as young as I used to be,* As he closed his eyes, he tried to suppress the aches in his back and very slowly descended into a deep, dark and ever darker tunnel.

The rhythmic buzzing of his cell phone rudely woke him, and he mumbled loudly, "yes!" even before picking it up to answer.

"You haven't forgotten we were to meet for supper?" asked Henrietta. "We're all here waiting for you."

"Sorry, I must have fallen asleep. I'll be right up."

The rooftop dining room faced the city enveloped in a light drizzle. While waiting for Jim to arrive Don said, "It's too bad we're not higher up. Also, if it were clearer, and of course, in daylight, you could just about be able to see the tops of the Blueridge mountains. Incidentally, do you know how they got their name? It's something I once had to describe in a news program. It seems that the spruce-fir forests exude a hydrocarbon gas that gives off a blueish tinge when seen from a distance."

"Well, that's very interesting but, of course, it's so dark outside that all I can see are the lights from all the buildings in town," said Frank and looking at the door, added, "Anyway, I see Jim has decided to join us."

Jim took a seat next to Henrietta. "Sorry folks. I'm afraid I fell asleep. But I'm glad to see all of you… perhaps for the last time."

"Well, as you know, nothing is forever," interjected Diane, turning to face her husband. "…As Frank keeps reminding me!"

"It's wonderful we're all here and I must admit I'll miss you when we all leave for different destinations tomorrow," said Jim.

The five of them, or as Frank came to call them, the INTREPID FIVE, started talking almost simultaneously. Henrietta first asked if the Weills and Don had received confirmation of their flights and asked how they planned to spend the time until their planned flights. Then, Frank and Don turned to Jim, and quietly asked about the development of his relationship with Henrietta. Jim made it clear that it was none of their business, but they were insistent and pressed him to be more open about what happened! "If you asked me a month ago that the two of you would get together," said Don. "I would have told you, that you were crazy. But I have to tell you, Jim, that it seems to have made you a better man."

"I still don't want to talk about it, but…..thanks."

Diane spoke to Henrietta, saying that she was so happy to see that Jim and she were getting along so well. "It's important to have someone with whom to share your life, especially at your age, dear. I know that I would be lost without Frank, more than ever since I developed this problem."

"I understand," Henrietta answered. "But it happened so quickly and I'm not sure it's real."

"Trust your heart dear, trust your heart. The two of you are lucky. Look at poor Don who has no one."

As the evening was winding down, the conversations drifted toward a passionate discussion of the future. Both Frank and Diane, practically stepping over each other's words, said how much they were looking forward to seeing their sons again. "And don't forget about the little ones," said Diane. "It's been so long since we've seen them. I hope they're not too old to let me hug and kiss them."

Henrietta stated that she hoped that she and Jim would benefit from being closer to a university environment; that it would do them good to collaborate on a professional level… and in the process bring them closer together. Jim seemed somewhat embarrassed by her statement but smiled and squeezed her shoulder with his left hand.

Don listened nervously and suddenly slapped the table causing coffee cups to rattle and Diane to whimper and grab Frank's arm. "Look out there," he practically screamed. "Don't you see what's happening? All those years at the Manor I feel we were in a cocoon. Sure, I used to watch the news on the telescreen but to be in the middle of what's happening all around us now is a totally different story. I've become desperately worried after these few short days we've been traveling since having been forced to abandon our home in Miami. Actually, seeing what's been happening to the people and to the environment has been a shock, a real eye opener. I spent so many years reporting the news; at first it was about runaway population growth that went from eight billion and zoomed up to ten billion within forty years and then as the climate disaster became apparent, reporting on its impact in Southeast Asia with inundating seas and in Africa with rising temperatures causing so many deaths as a result of a new virus strain. My God! Think about it, not far from here, in the breadbasket of the country was a drought a few years back that caused the failure of grain, wheat and corn crops causing dire food shortages. I reported on all that and also about those scientists," he lingered on the word with reverence, "who since the last century warned us about rising seas and rising temperatures. I wasn't just reporting the news, I lived through it. And the shame of it is, that I was just as naïve as all of you about the consequences, thinking that our leaders would not let such things happen to our planet…that they would trust in the science…. And, on top of all that, today we see those migrants. Hell! We're the lucky ones. We're migrants as well but we have safe havens to go to, but the ones we saw on the road, where are they going to end up. These people and others like them all over the world are fighting to settle in the few remaining habitable places on earth. But, no one wants them. Canada's closed her borders, and the northern states have soldiers trying to keep people out and herding those who won't go back into camps to starve and die from diseases. I've come to realize now that we're on a runaway train and it's too late for us, for civilization. I see instead that those who survive are going to have to adapt and plan for a different future, different from anything we've known. That means us, folks! We've finally been forced to see it in these past few days and it's not pretty…"

"Stop it," Diane cried out. I don't want to hear any more. My boys, they still have a future and I don't want to hear otherwise."

Frank pushed back his chair and gently pulled Diane out of hers. "Can't you see you're upsetting Diane. There's no need to continue like that. I'm sorry but we're leaving!"

"Can't you accept the truth," shouted Don as Frank escorted a crying Diane out of the room. "It's your future as well that I'm talking about."

"That was very cruel," said Henrietta. "There was no need to paint such a negative picture…and in front of the Weills, especially Diane. You're entitled to your opinion, but that's all it is. There's no need to destroy their hope for whatever time they have left."

"Of all people, you know that I'm right. There is no hope!"

Jim jumped in, "You don't know that! Christ, even I'm not willing to grant you that. First of all, much of what you described has become a political issue and is no longer just about climate change. If you're worried about the government becoming too autocratic, we still have representatives in Washington to whom we can express our concerns. We're certainly not helpless! And as far as the science, Henny, here, knows a hell of a lot more than you about that and I'm sure she doesn't go along with your bleak picture."

"Thank you, Jim. I can speak for myself," interrupted Henrietta. "Don, first of all, you're lecturing us the way Drake did on our last night at the Manor. That's not necessary because we're all adults and know what's been happening in the world. Furthermore, you have to understand that there are efforts being made not just by our own government but others around the world to take actions that will hopefully alleviate some of the climate problems we're living through and in time, lead us toward cooler temperatures and falling sea levels. I mentioned the scrubber satellites in the past and there is another proposal being developed to increase the formation of clouds that have the effect of reflecting sunlight resulting in a cooling of the earth. With all this heat, there have already been more cloud formations and some cooling but a scientist in England believes we can multiply what nature already provides. Of course, these proposals take time and in the interim, our government couldn't allow our world to descend into anarchy. Believe me, I've been concerned myself about the role of the army that we saw, and I expressed those concerns to the President's science advisor. I challenged him, saying that we seemed to be moving away from democratic principles. I've been assured that the military that we saw along the highways while driving here, were needed only temporarily to control the migrants."

"I'm sorry, Henrietta, but I just don't buy it. Of course, everything you're talking about takes time. After all, it took almost two centuries to arrive at the catastrophic situation we're in now. Even if your miracle proposals are fully implemented, by the time the environment will return to that existing in the nineteenth century, we'll all be long gone."

"That's rather narrow minded of you. Don't you think future generations deserve better prospects?"

"It's not that I don't think about that. I may not have children of my own, but I have nieces and nephews who deserve a good life. It's just that I have no faith that science can repair what science, in effect, caused. Scientific progress in the 19th century led to the industrial revolution which then led to rampant use of fossil fuels which led to the release of carbon dioxide into the atmosphere which put us in the pickle we're now in!"

"Just a minute," Jim interrupted. "That's a pretty simplistic analysis of a very complex situation. Science, invention, engineering, whatever you want to call it created the means for industry to flourish. People were perfectly happy to enjoy the benefits of all the new mechanical innovations but when scientist began to warn about the consequences of all that carbon trapped in the upper atmosphere and the greenhouse effect, those same people were not willing to modify their newfound lifestyles."

"And…" Henrietta added, "the politicians were complicit in being seduced by money they accepted from fossil fuel industries. Aren't you willing to give science a chance, Don, even if as you say it will take time? I've been asked by the President to serve on a task force to propose solutions and I didn't think that I could contribute anything worthwhile. But… this discussion we've had convinces me that I have a duty to try. I don't deny your pessimistic outlook, but I don't accept it either. I believe we owe it to the survival of future generations to make an effort."

"That's very noble of you and maybe when I settle in Minneapolis,

I'll find a reason to change my pessimistic outlook but in the meantime all I can say is, I'm not sure."

"I'll drink to that," said Jim. "In fact, let's all have one last drink together to celebrate the possibility of civilization's future."

The three of them raised their glasses as Don toasted, "To the time when the sun has lost its vigor and the seas have found their level."

After a few more toasts, Don thanked Jim and Henrietta for the open discussion and said that he would not forget them and try to be a little more optimistic about the future. He jotted down his contact information and hoped they could stay in touch. He promised to let them know his address, once he was settled. Since he had to leave early in the morning for the airport he said, "So, this is goodbye. I've enjoyed knowing you both and wish you a safe trip to wherever you're going tomorrow and," he added with a smile, "of course, good luck on saving the planet!"

After Don left, Jim turned to Henrietta and said, "You know that Don is right when he said that time is not on our side."

13
A NEW DIRECTION

*W*HERE DO *I START,* THOUGHT Drake? *When the Manor drowned, I lost everything that my parents had spent their whole lives building up. They left it to me, and I failed to act in time to move…No! What could I have done? Close the home years ago and at least walk away with something? You're kidding yourself. What kind of money could I have gotten when everyone knew the seas would eventually overwhelm the place? And… flood insurance along the coast had over a decade earlier been no longer available. No! it was a total loss and I'm lucky that I still had some savings so I'm not out on the street. I still have friends!*

Drake opened his address book and started to contact friends and colleagues he had met over the years while managing the Manor. He hoped they might provide him with leads…perhaps even an opportunity to manage a community like the Manor. On the third day, he reached a contact who told him about an opportunity to manage a facility on the shore of Lake Ontario that was popular with retired faculty from Syracuse University. It was similar to the Manor as it was owned by an individual, William O'Donnell, and not a corporation. Mr. O'Donnell had expressed an interest in retiring and turning over day to day management of the facility to someone sympathetic to the needs of active retired people such as he had been all his life. Drake was immediately attracted to this possibility and contacted O'Donnell. There followed an exchange of information over the next few days, culminating in an invitation to visit the facility, called Maple View. As the weather was still unsettled, Drake was not able to arrange transportation until the following Monday. He rushed out of his bedroom and confronted Val and Ernie. "Friends, I think I've found a home to manage. It is very similar to the Manor and the owner has invited me to visit and to see if we can come to an understanding. It's on Lake Ontario which means that it's not going to be drowned out. In fact, I understand that over time, the level of the lake is actually receding and not climbing even though it seesaws up and down depending on the season." He enthusiastically went on to describe what he saw online about the Maple View Home, as well as the results of his discussion with O'Donnell. "Doesn't that seem wonderful? I was thinking that perhaps you guys could even move up there with me, and Val can pick up where she left off at the Manor…and Ernie, you could handle construction and maintenance. What do you say?"

"What I hear from Val," said Ernie with a quizzical look on his face, "You're a good guy and terrific manager so I'm sure you'll do great. But as far as our moving up there, we've got our kids here."

Val added, "If it's as perfect as you describe it I know you'll make a go of it. Of course, you haven't seen it yet and don't know what they need so let's not rush into talk of moving up there. I haven't even had a chance to settle in here and as Ernie said, we have to think about our new grandson that I'd like to know better."

"Well, never mind that for now! Maybe I'm getting ahead of myself. But, there is still cause for celebration. So, what do you say we go out for dinner tonight?"

"Why not! There's a great, tapas place I know that I'm sure you'd enjoy," said Ernesto. "Good food and a quiet atmosphere for talking."

When they arrived at El Mercado, the owner greeted Ernesto like an old friend causing Val to ask, "I guess you've been having a good time while I was fleeing the rising ocean."

"No, no, I've only been here once or twice with little Freddie." Federico was taller than both his parents and was now the father of a three-year old son of his own.

"So!" asked Drake, "What do you recommend?"

They shared a large number of small plates while Drake kept gushing over his good fortune and kept coming back to the possibility of a place for the Lopez's in his new community. Val reminded him that he had never even seen Maple View and had no signed deal. Before planning to ask them to join him, perhaps he should wait until he had met the owner/manager, seen the facility and concluded an arrangement.

Toward the end of the evening and after a few beers, Drake confessed that he would miss having Val around as she had become his family and that in the short time that he had been in Nashville, he learned to love Ernie like a brother. The Lopez's were evasive but said that they too enjoyed his company.

On Monday morning, Ernie drove Drake to the airport and wished him success in his negotiations while Val had stayed behind to get together with her grandson.

When the plane took off, Drake looked out the window at the shrinking view of Nashville and felt sad once more to be alone. The flight went directly to Syracuse where Drake took a helicab for the trip to Maple View, just east of Oswego. Looking at the lake, he noticed the exposed shoreline as the lake level was unexpectedly low, quite a contrast to the last view he had of the Manor where the sea was licking at its foundation. A great lawn separated the Maple View facility from the water's edge. He noticed a group of residents playing croquet. It reminded him of images he had seen of early twentieth century resort hotels. Upon landing near the entrance to the facility, he was met by Bill O'Donnell, a man with a big smile and a crown of wavy white hair. After the customary introductions, the two men went to the manager's office where O'Donnell offered Drake a cup of coffee before beginning their discussion. "Welcome," he said. "I understand you had a pretty rough time of it toward the end in Miami."

"It started over a year ago when it became clear that we couldn't stay there. Of course, I lost pretty much everything in having to abandon the Manor. It was the saddest day of my life. You know that my parents opened the place and…well, it's too late to do anything about that. I just decided that I'm not giving up so easily and when I heard about your situation, I thought this would give me the opportunity to put my life back together."

"Well, young man, it's not so perfect here either. You know about the migrants. We've got groups of them trying to go across the lake to Canada. Of course, that lake can be pretty treacherous when the weather turns and lately the weather's been unpredictable with sudden storms cropping up. It's sad but we've had quite a few drownings when these people in their skimpy boats were not prepared…this isn't just a little lake. It can be as mean and rough as the ocean sometimes."

"'Can't be worse than what I've seen these last few years along the coast."

"You'd be surprised. But let's talk about how you could fit in here."

O'Connell proceeded to explain how Maple View was managed. He also explained that he was prepared to give Drake an interest in the facility after the first year if everything worked out to their mutual satisfaction.

"That's very generous of you," Drake said.

"To be perfectly honest, I had you checked out pretty thoroughly and I think you're the right man for the job. So, let me show you around and have you meet some of the staff and residents." As they walked around, Drake admired the relaxed atmosphere and asked about staff turnover. "Most of our staff has been with us for over ten years and we have a few who spent the major part of their working life with us."

"That's a wonderful recommendation of their loyalty to you. I imagine you've been an ideal boss."

"We've been very fortunate in having such a loyal staff. We've had very few changes because both the staff and the residents feel very safe here. You may have noticed the safety precautions we've had to take lately because of the migrants. The compound has had to be fenced in and we've had to hire guards at the entrance gate. I don't like it, but it's proven to be necessary."

Drake spent the next few days becoming familiar with the facility and meeting many of the residents and staff members. He also learned more about O'Donnell, whose wife had died a year earlier, an event that precipitated his desire to retire. Also, there was a daughter about whom he had little to say other than she and a partner had settled into a commune in Canada and had foresworn bringing children into this chaotic world. As he revealed this, O'Donnell lowered his eyes and remained silent for a long period. Perking up, he asked, "So, when can you move in."

"There's nothing holding me back. How about right now!"

Once he had been offered the position of manager of the Maple View facility, Drake placed a call to Valeria Lopez describing the beauty of the place on the lake and the friendliness shown him by the residents of the home as well as Mr. O'Donnell, the original owner. He urged her to consider moving her family north, also pointing out that they would be further from the seemingly unstoppable northward march of the stifling heat and humidity. Val reminded him that she wanted to be close to her only grandson. "Get them to come north as well. Wouldn't you like to have your grandson see snow in the winter? And, as far as Federico is concerned, I'm sure he can get a job around here. By the way, what does he do?"

"He's a bookkeeper…"

"That's great. Maybe Maple View needs a new financial person. If not, there's a university in Oswego and many firms around here that use bookkeepers. Think about it…..please," he pleaded. "Remember, I've been given free rein to fill out the staff and you and Ernie can certainly work here."

Val agreed to let him know in a week if moving with her family is even possible.

At the end of the week, Drake received a message from Val saying that the family had decided to stay in Nashville for the time being. They had made friends in the area and Federico had a good job that he was not ready to abandon. They appreciated the offer, but the time was not right. As he read the message, Drake was visibly disappointed but answered that he hoped they might change their minds in the near future.

14
HENRIETTA & JIM
Monday

JIM WOKE EARLY IN THE morning, packed his bag and went to the garage to load the Limo and make certain that the battery had been fully charged. He planned the trip with stops along the way to recharge the electric car's battery and provide options for an overnight stay. Before going to Henrietta's room, he stopped at the reception desk to confirm that Don had left on time. It was still raining in Charlotte, a leftover from the dissipating second storm but the winds had died down, so he assumed that Don was now on his way to Minneapolis. He also left a message for the Weills suggesting they meet for a quick breakfast before heading out to the airport.

In her room, Henrietta was finishing dressing when the phone rang. "Good morning. This is Frank. I just saw a note from Jim suggesting we meet for a bite. I'm afraid we don't have time for that because we have to leave in half an hour."

"That's a shame. Why don't we get together in the lobby before you leave? We can be down there as soon as I reach Jim." As she hung up, Jim arrived. and she quickly explained the need to go down to the lobby to see the Weills before they had to board their airport shuttle.

"I'm sorry that we had to make this parting so short," said Frank when he walked up to Henrietta and Jim as they exited the elevator, "but the airline wanted us to be at the airport early because of the controls they instituted to prevent problems. It's such a crazy time with so many migrants around."

Henrietta embraced Diane, saying, "I'm saddened that we couldn't have more time to say goodbye."

135

Diane tearfully explained that she was sorry about last night and the confrontation with Don. There was really nothing to say that had not already been said before, so the four of them said their goodbyes with embraces and handshakes and an exchange of contact information ending with waves from Jim and Henrietta as the Weills boarded their airport shuttle.

"Well, that's that," said Jim. "I guess we'd better get going ourselves. I've already put my bags in the limo."

Henrietta suggested that they have breakfast first, after which they went back to her room to fetch her suitcase and bring it to the limo. As they drove away from their hotel, Jim explained his planned route of travel. They would drive north, hugging the eastern edge of the Appalachian Mountains until they reached Hagerstown, Virginia. Then they would continue toward Harrisburg, Pennsylvania and finally to Allentown adjacent to their final destination. He suggested they stop for the night roughly half way along the route at a charming old town in the Shenandoah Valley, Staunton, Virginia.

Henrietta was still not very enthusiastic about the prospect of this two-day trip with Jim as she was still working her way through her feelings for him. But, as she leaned back in her seat and tried to close her eyes, she said, "I'm sure you've worked this out well and I appreciate it." The streets leading out of town were crowded with pedestrians and vehicles carrying people to their workplaces. Around the entrance to the malls located between the city and the suburbs, shoppers were pushing each other seeking to be the first to buy some of the food that had just been delivered on this Monday morning. Because of the heat as well as the shortages of water, food had become a precious commodity. This was exacerbated by the large number of migrants moving through the area who, like locusts, quickly grabbed and exhausted the available food supply. Even with her eyes, half closed, Henrietta still saw enough to make her wonder what's happened to this country? People are acting like feral animals. No wonder the government is using the military to try to control the situation. Yet, she still hoped to exert her influence toward a gentler future. "Jim," she said. "Does it bother you as much as it does me to see this country falling into a militaristic trap?"

"Of course, it bothers me. I remember the last viral pandemic when

I was just out of college; the lockdowns, the rules established by the government to limit the spread of the virus and then using government agents to control violators. I was in my early twenties then, and I remember that it felt like being in jail. It's one reason I took a job overseas, building a dam in an area of the world with few people and fewer rules. By the time I returned home almost three years later, millions around the world had died from the virus. But what really bothered me then, was the realization that many innocents here at home had died when government agents fired into crowds of peaceful but unruly protesters in the streets. It made me understand that using the military to control civilians at home is dangerous. What we're seeing now is also a pandemic but instead of a virus it's a migration pandemic. You've got a third of the world's population displaced and moving out of the equatorial latitudes. How can you possibly control that?"

"Well, you can see what the President has done. The National Guard is everywhere. We saw them last Sunday driving from Atlanta and now we see them again as we're driving north. Carlson told me it's only temporary but....I don't know?

"I'd rather think about something else," said Jim. As they drove onto the interstate that would carry them all the way to Allentown, he tried to put aside thoughts of the current state of the world and concentrated on driving. But it was no use because within minutes, they were stopped at a checkpoint and after waiting in line, were interrogated by a guard who entered their information onto a tablet. When Henrietta mentioned that she was going to meet the President's science advisor, they were asked to wait while that information was verified. After an interminable time, the guard came back and said, "sorry, ma'am, I apologize for the delay, but people try to pass through here with all kinds of wild stories. Here," he added, "Put this blue card inside your windshield and you will be able to bypass other checkpoints along your route."

As they drove away, Jim said, "Well, I'm glad to be traveling with a big shot. If we had a siren, we could really zip along."

"Stop making fun of this. You should feel lucky that I have a friend in high places. Did you see that car in front of us with a family with two small children forced to sit on the ground with armed soldiers guarding them! It's so sad to have to see that happening in our country. I'm sure all they were trying to do was to go where they could bring up their children in safety, away from the oppressive heat or encroaching ocean."

"I guess you're right. I know it's shitty what's happening, but I feel kind of helpless, so I try to make light of it."

"Don't take this the wrong way but you often do that."

Smiling, Jim answered, "with a teacher like you, I feel that I'm not too old to change bad habits and learn to do better."

"I hope so because I'm not sure that otherwise we have much of a future."

For the next ninety minutes, they drove in silence as they approached the Blue Ridge in the foothills of the Appalachian Mountains. A blue-green vapor emanated from the dense forests in the west, just as Don had described. It imparted to the landscape a mystical air from which ghosts could be imagined appearing, lit by the orange sun in the southern sky. There was something warm and magical about this image that became more intense as they burrowed deeper into the mountains. All along the sides of the road were stands of oak trees with blackened scars from bears who long ago scratched them in passing. Near them at ground level were the stumps of chestnuts that had been attacked by blight in the past.

They drove on through the verdant hills with its stands of majestic oak and hickory trees that were occasionally interrupted by grassy meadows where the forest had been cleared. Henrietta closed her eyes and was transported back over forty years to the time when she and Crandall spent their honeymoon. They had driven along the Blue Ridge Parkway all the way down to Asheville where they stayed and spent one afternoon visiting the sprawling and opulent Biltmore mansion that they both agreed was a shameful example of nineteenth century greed. The highlight of their trip, however, was the subsequent drive through the Great Smoky Mountains, encountering bears along the road who would come right up to the cars begging for a sweet treat. The forest ranger had warned them not to open car windows as the bears who seemed so docile were actually wild animals that with one swipe of their paws could wound them severely. Being young and reckless they considered petting a bear who approached their car but at the last minute quickly closed the car windows. It was such a heavenly time as she and Crandall were so much in love, spending their nights in each other's arms making love in shabby roadside motels. Less than six years later he was gone, and the honeymoon was over. The memory of that time brought tears to her eyes that she wiped away with the back of her hand.

As he turned to look at her, Jim asked, "Are you crying?"

"I'm sorry, something must have flown into my eye," she said wanting to keep her memory safe. It was different with Jim. Her feelings for him were strong but the ardor of her youth had waned. Yet she cared for this man in a way she had not cared for another since Crandall Barker died.

As they drove on, they encountered few other vehicles until they came upon another checkpoint. The guard, seeing the blue card with the eagle insignia in the windshield, waved them on. Looking west, Henrietta exclaimed, "Jim, look over there on the meadow adjacent to the woods. It looks like a tent colony but enclosed with a fence with guard towers?"

"I think it's a detention center for migrant," said Jim. "I'm afraid we're going to see a lot of those because the government doesn't know what to do with all those people moving north." Seeing Henny staring at the scene, her brow furrowed in pain, he added, "I'm sorry that we have to see scenes such as this but for now, we're helpless to do anything about it. But listen, I'm getting a little hungry so why don't we stop for lunch next to that lake just ahead.?"

"Good idea. And, you're right. We can't change what's happening, but it certainly gives me a lot of ammunition for the next time I talk to Carlson. When you stop, I'll get everything setup in the back with the sandwiches I brought along from the hotel," said Henrietta.

As they approached the lake, they saw many groups of people scattered along the shore. Some seemed to be families with children, resting before continuing their journey north. One group of men lying on the grass, stood up when they saw the vehicle approaching. At first, they stared and then began moving toward the limousine in what Henrietta interpreted as a threatening manner.

"Jim, I don't think we're welcome here," said Henrietta.

Jim answered, "I think you're right. Let's get back to the interstate and we'll find a spot along the side of the road to eat in peace. As he turned the car around, one of the men separated from the rest and approached the limo on the driver's side. "You people going north?" he asked through the half open window.

"We're on government business to survey the movement of migrants," said Jim. "See that blue card in the windshield. Please step away from the car."

"Hey, I just asked," the man said as he stepped back to let the limo leave.

Once back on the interstate, Jim parked along the side of the road and he and Henny went into the main cabin to have their lunch. They kept the door open to take advantage of the view of the hills. "It's a hell of a way to have a picnic," said Jim, "locked in a limo instead of stretched out on the grass but I just don't know who else is going to come along asking for a ride."

"I think we've both become a little paranoid. The man by the lake only asked a question that we didn't even answer. Maybe he was just curious? After all we're two old folks driving in a limousine. That must have struck him as quite peculiar."

"I don't know! I didn't see a car, so I assumed he was looking for a ride...and his buddies didn't look any too wholesome," said Jim.

"Let's just enjoy the view," said Henny. "I've always loved these hills. Driving through them is so peaceful and full of memories."

Oh, God! she thought, *I keep remembering Crandall, but I'm having trouble seeing his image. He was so different from Jim. Even at our age, Jim is so much more athletic looking. I can imagine what he looked like in his twenties. No, no, it's Crandall I'm trying to bring to mind, not Jim. It's so confusing. On that last night in Atlanta, when we made love, he was so tender, yet strong and insistent. So different from Crandall who was always gentle and responsive but seemed somehow distant, but I know he loved me. And now, I believe Jim really cares for me as well. It's so jumbled up.*

"Are you OK," asked Jim. "You seem, I don't know, somehow confused."

"It's all right. Let's just clean up and get moving again. I'm just a bit anxious to get settled in our new home."

Jim was momentarily puzzled. *Did she mean our, that is, the two of us or was it simply a figure of speech.* But... he was not about to question her about it. He preferred to think that maybe they had a future together as more than just friends. "Let me help you put everything away," he said as he took the plates that she had just rinsed and folded them into a towel that he held in his hands.

"That's sweet of you," she said. "But you have to drive, so let me finish up." He does have such a nice smile, she thought.

As she was putting away the dishes, she glanced back and saw a woman walking along the road holding the hand of a small child. As they neared the limo they quickened their steps and the woman held up her free hand and screamed, "Help me, please help me."

Jim saw this and said, "Let's go," to which Henrietta said, "Wait! She looks as if she really needs help."

"We don't know who else is lurking in the woods on the side of the road. Come on! We can't take a chance."

"No!" replied Henrietta, "the child can hardly walk. Let's at least talk to them. Have a little compassion."

As the mother approached, she kept repeating, "We can't walk any more. Please help us." In the distance the wail of a siren could be heard.

Henrietta opened the back door of the limo and said, "Sit down while I get you some water. You look parched." They sat on the edge of the floorboard with the child's feet dangling free while Henrietta brought them water and crackers. The wail of the siren increased. An olive drab painted military vehicle pulled up behind the parked limo. Two soldiers stepped out and walked toward the limo, one with his hand pressed against the holster of his pistol. The shorter of the two asked to see identification as Jim said, "What's the problem?" while pointing to the blue card with the gold eagle in the windshield.

"Sorry, sir, we've been asked to find wanderers."

"As you can see, we're on official business," said Henrietta confidently.

"And what about you two?" said the soldier pointing to the woman who pulled the child close.

The woman explained that she was going home, and this nice couple offered them some water. The soldier asked her for identification that she could not produce. The taller soldier then asked the woman and child to step into their vehicle while Henrietta said that she could take them where they wanted to go. "Do you know them?" the soldier asked. When Jim said, "No," the soldier reached for the woman's arm. "Hey, you don't have to be so rough," said Jim as the child began to cry. "We're only doing our job," said the soldier. "We don't allow hitchhikers," said the soldier as the brusquely led the woman and child into his vehicle and quickly drove away. Henrietta and Jim were both shaken by what they had just witnessed and were unable to move for the longest time. "How could they be so heartless," Henrietta finally said as Jim put his arm around her shoulder to comfort her. Then, Jim turned and leaning down wiped the crumbs from the half-eaten crackers on the stoop of the back door of the limo. Without another word, the two of them stepped back into the limo and drove away.

They were on the road again heading for Staunton where they were to spend the night. "There's a beautiful nineteenth century hotel in town," he said. "Would you mind calling them to see if we can get rooms."

"I thought we were going to try to stay in the limo for the night?"

"That was before this last encounter along the road. I don't know any more whether we should be afraid of the migrants or the soldiers? I really think it would be safer in town or even in a motel."

"Maybe you're right. I'll try to call." Henny tried the historic hotel but found they were totally booked. They recommended another hotel that, when she called, told her that they only had one room left. She thought about that for a moment and without consulting Jim, booked the room. *I really need him to hold me tonight after what we've just experienced. We're not strangers,* she thought, *after all we had even been lovers although for only one night.* She told Jim who simply nodded in response as he was still upset and deep in thought from their encounter on the road. Her feelings for him were becoming difficult to deal with. *Wait,* she thought. *Wait until we've had time to settle in Pennsylvania. Then, I'll be able to resolve my feelings for Jim and decide if we can have a life together. Right now, we're both still dealing with a disturbing present.*

As they drove through the gentle hills of the Shenandoah Valley, the sky overhead was streaked with a wash of lavender illuminating the brilliant foliage on the mountaintops. Those same hills appeared to lovingly embrace the town of Staunton with its three- and four- story Victorian buildings at its historic center. They found their hotel on the outskirts of the center, adjacent to a lovely small park. After a quiet but pleasant dinner, they settled into their room. Quickly changing into pajamas, Jim said a cursory goodnight and practically fell into bed and under the covers and was soon asleep. Henny thought he must be tired because of all the driving and the emotional reaction to the afternoon's conflict, but nevertheless she was disappointed that their evening ended so abruptly.

The next morning, Jim awoke refreshed and ready for the last leg of their trip. After dressing, he shook Henny who was still sleeping and said, "Look outside! It's a beautiful day with the sun out and no more rain after the remains of the storms moved north."

Henny, who had read for a long time before falling asleep, covered her eyes with her hands and said, "For heaven's sake. Can't you let me sleep a little longer. We're not on a deadline."

He leaned over and kissed the hands covering her eyes. "You told me you were anxious to get to our new home," emphasizing the word, 'our'. "Let's have breakfast and get going."

Sometime later they were on their way into Pennsylvania. As they left the pastoral landscape of the highlands, the road ahead became hypnotically duller and they stopped numerous times to stretch and relieve aching muscles. Two hours into their trip they stopped to get a quick bite of lunch. They had noticed that the further north they drove there were fewer checkpoints, except when they crossed into Pennsylvania. There, a major border-like control point reminded Jim of his days crossing from one country to the next in Middle East... document check, face scan, search of the vehicle...even the pass they had in the windshield was examined for authenticity, making them both nervous. After what seemed like an interminable delay, they were finally allowed to proceed.

Throughout the next part of their ride they were both quiet, as each was absorbed in thought. For her part, Henny wondered what she would encounter when and if she were to participate in the President's task force. She also began to question whether she could commit her-self to Jim. The thought of then losing him...after all, he was older... she was not certain that she could live through such a loss a second time in her life.

Jim kept imagining whether he could sustain being in a close relationship. He had failed once. But he tried to convince himself that Henny was different. Although she could be brusque in her judgements sometime, these last days being alone together has brought her closer. He wasn't young anymore and he wanted to spend the rest of his life with someone he loved, and he was certain that it should be Henny…there was no one else.

They drove in silence until reaching the Lehigh Valley. Jim opened his side window and exclaimed, "It's not that much cooler here than it was down south."

"You're exaggerating," said Henny. "It's a good ten degrees cooler. Remember that we went from stifling hot to what I would consider pleasant summer weather."

"Yes, but we're now in the fall!"

"You know perfectly well that this is the new normal. Temperatures have been moving north for the last fifty years. Wishing it were otherwise is not going to change it. It's too late. But look around; trees are brilliantly green; flowers are blooming in all colors. That's not so terrible."

"Yes, but I remember the colors in the fall. The reds and yellows. You now have to go into Canada to still see such colors. I miss them."

"If I were you, I would be a little more concerned about all those pioneers going into northern Canada seeking a new life. They are bound to be disappointed if they expected to find the same rich topsoil that they left down south. Instead, they will find that the soil there is not fertile enough to grow the food they will need to survive."

"Who's being negative now," said Jim.

As she recognized the neighborhood where she used to live while teaching at Lehigh, Henny suddenly said, "I remember some of these houses, It's just outside the university area. We should soon be coming to Hillcrest. It's supposed to be close to the University."

"According to the red dot on the moving map display, I would say it's about another mile. I don't know about you, but I'll be very happy to finally get there." As they drove closer, Jim added, "That must be it, our final destination, those buildings at the base of the hill, set back from the road." Turning a corner, he was suddenly faced with a gate that barred the entrance to Hillcrest. On either side of the gate, a high fence in front of a heavily wooded area appeared to wrap around the property. "It's a gated community. Not at all what I expected," he said.

"I wonder if Drake was aware of this when he made the arrangements for us. It's a little bizarre…hopefully, they can explain it when we go in?"

Jim spoke into a box on the side of the road and after identifying himself, asked to be let in. The gate opened and they drove a short distance to a parking area in front of three chalet-style buildings. A middle-aged man with a slight stoop guided the limousine into a parking spot in front the center building. At four stories, it was higher than the buildings on either side and was clearly the administrative and community center of the complex.

"I didn't know what to expect when I signed on to come here," Henny said, "but, it looks rather charming, almost like a Swiss village, with carved wooden balconies and an overhanging roof. From the outside, it certainly looks better than I expected…except for that fence."

When he stepped out of the vehicle, Jim said, "I'll be so glad to get rid of this limo," he said. "It's just not me! As soon as we get settled, I'm calling the rental people to pick it up."

After introducing themselves to the receptionist, they were met by the manager of the facility and Jim immediately asked him about the gate and fence. The manager dressed in a dark blue suit and tie, sported a thin mustache and wire-rimmed glasses and was clearly the opposite of Drake, who usually walked around in a colorful sport shirt and slacks. He explained that the fencing and gate had been added about five years ago when climate migrants began to show up and tried to camp on the property. "We couldn't let that happen as it would upset our residents," he said. "But let me tell you about Hillcrest. This building is the center for all activities including dining, exercise, a meeting room and a medical suite." He then led them to their apartment on the second floor of the east building. Henny admired the view from the living room window looking north across the valley. As she walked into the first bedroom and saw the double bed, she hesitated as she was suddenly reminded of the fact that she had consented to live with this man in such an intimate setting. *Just friends, that's what he agreed.* Even though there was a second bedroom, the physical reality of the situation made her question her decision.

"This looks cozy," said Jim.

"Remember our agreement."

"Of course." *Perhaps, in time she'll relent,* he thought. But in the meantime, he did not want to do anything to upset her and what he believed was their improving relationship.

After settling into their new apartment, each in a separate bedroom, Henny suggested they contact their old friends from the Manor to see if they are all safe.

15
DON
Monday

Early on Monday morning, while his companions from the Manor were still asleep, Don left for the Charlotte airport just as the sun was peeking out behind the few lingering clouds left behind from the passage of the weakened hurricane. He hoped the dying winds would clear the sky before his flight was scheduled to depart. Arriving at the airport, the bus he was on was scrutinized by guards who checked the flight document of all departing passengers before they were allowed into the waiting area. Once inside, Don looked at the electronic flight display and saw that the departure time for his flight was indicated as INDETERMINATE. Upset by this news, he walked directly to the ticket counter and confronted the agent saying, "What the hell is going on here. I was told last night that there was no problem with my flight."

After requesting Don's flight number, the agent said, "I'm sorry sir but we're awaiting the arrival of the incoming flight that will have to be cleared and refueled before we can establish a new departure time."

"Look Miss whatever your name is, I've been held up by a storm and now this!!! Can't you give me your best estimate?"

"It's Mrs. McDonald, and all I can tell you is that it will be at least two hours. In the meanwhile, I can offer you a stay in the executive lounge to make you more comfortable while you wait."

Don grudgingly accepted the flight agent's offer and after checking in his bag and taking his dog for a walk in a special area reserved for dog walking, went up to the lounge located on the mezzanine with Girl comfortably settled in the dog carrier. He then requested a cup of coffee and a croissant and decided to call Frank Weill who was preparing to leave for the airport. "Frank! I'm glad I caught you. Listen, my flight has been delayed and I'm sitting here in the executive lounge. I thought when you and Diane arrive here, you might have time to join me while we all wait for our flights."

An hour later, Frank and Diane presented themselves to the receptionist in the executive lounge and asked for Donald Garland who, ran up and put his arms out to embrace Diane, saying. "I was so hoping to see you both before you left. Diane, I'm afraid I upset you last night. Believe me it was unintentional."

Diane, with a frown on her face, turned away to face Frank who answered, "It was quite thoughtless in view of the circumstances, but I convinced Diane that you did not mean that our sons wouldn't have a good life. So, why don't we drop it."

Don explained why he was still at the airport instead of being on the way to Minneapolis and hoped that their plane was not similarly delayed. "We've got twenty minutes before we have to be at the gate," said Frank. "Just enough time to join you for a coffee and one of those delicious looking croissants that I see you've already bitten into." Don quickly placed an order from the passing waiter, and they spent their remaining waiting time drinking, eating, exchanging in a pleasant conversation, and avoiding any mention of an uncertain future that would have upset Diane. Finally, the Weills left for the departure gate after a final round of hugs and a tap on the top of the dog carrier that woke Girl out of a sound sleep. After quieting her down, Don was now left alone, to wonder if he can yet find a partner with whom to share the rest of his life. The Weills, for all their difficulties seemed so genuinely warm and close to each other. It made him miss Paolo but... it's time to let go. Once he was settled in Minneapolis, he felt certain that he would find the path to a personal renewal even as the world remained in turmoil.

As he waited impatiently for his flight, Don retrieved a tablet from his shoulder bag and first checked the news headlines. He focused on an item discussing an announcement from President Davenport that warned of increasing travel restrictions to prevent northern communities from being overwhelmed by the movement of climate migrants. The National Guard had been instructed to turn back migrants along an east-west line (just above the 30th parallel) roughly defined by the southern border of Virginia. All northbound flights from locations to the south of that line are being scrutinized to prevent passengers without proper travel documentation and Northern addresses, from boarding. *No wonder this airport is jammed with people*, he thought. *I'd better check again on my flight.* The good news, he was told, was that his flight had arrived and was being readied for departure but that was an hour from now. *Thank God, I can get out of here. This place is like a zoo.* He then searched through his contacts in Minneapolis and placed a call to Wayne Petersen, the old colleague from his broadcasting days,. After the third ring, a hoarse voice coughed and answered, "Hello!"

"This is Don, Don Garland. I don't know if you remember me, but I certainly remember that cough of yours."

"Don! For Christ' sake, how are you...and where are you?"

"Actually, I'm flying up to Minneapolis in half an hour and wondered if I could come and see you after I'm settled in."

They agreed to meet at four the following afternoon in a downtown bar favored by the TV news team, just as Don's flight was announced as being ready for departure. Once in the air, the flight proceeded smoothly and a little over two hours later landed in Minneapolis. The passengers were allowed to disembark and proceeded to the arrivals area where they were asked to pass through a checkpoint monitored by armed National Guard personnel. Each passenger was asked for identification and a local address. As Don passed through, he asked the guard, "Why all this security?"

"We're looking for non-residents to make certain that they have a legitimate reason to be here."

With a smile and a chuckle, Don answered, "Well, I'm glad I've got all my documents with me."

The guard was annoyed and said, "This is serious business and nothing to laugh about, sir."

It's incredible, thought Don. *This is not the same country I remember from the time before I went to the Manor. There were changes taking place even then because of the climate problem but this, what's happening now is looking more like the creation of a police state. When I first started working at the station, we would interview scientists who warned that it was almost too late to do anything about the causes of climate change. Hell, that was almost fifty years ago. They talked about fractions of a degree change in temperature that we thought gave us time to press for a reduction in fossil fuel use. Those little fractions began to add up and within twenty years temperatures began a precipitous climb until today, even with the almost total elimination in the use of fossil fuels those same scientists don't know how to stop it. Maybe Henrietta was right when she said that we need to take extreme measures such as the ones she's promoting. I don't know why I'm getting all worked up about this. I'm here, back in Minneapolis and looking forward to meeting old friends and seeing if I can find someone with whom to share this rotten life.*

Leaving the airport, he took a cab to go directly to Longview House, his new home. As the cab left the airport, Don was further shocked by what he saw. The city seemed like a medieval town surrounded by a wall with a limited number of controlled access points. But perhaps he was letting his mind imagine it as there was no real wall but rather a new circumferential highway that seemed like a wall since it prevented the free flow from the surrounding countryside into the city. It reminded him of Paris, that had built a similar highway around the city well over a century ago with access points defined by the gates of the ancient city.

As the cab stopped in front of Longview House, Don looked up at a twelve-story stone and glass, modern building peppered with small windows shaded by concrete eyebrows to control the sun. *Well,* he thought, *this is certainly not the Mediterranean style he was accustomed to at the Manor.* It looked more like a luxury hotel. *I hope I'll learn to like it.* As he entered the outer lobby a disemboweled voice asked, "Please state your name." Once he did, the inner door opened and the voice said, "Welcome. Please proceed to the registration counter on your left." Where, he wondered were the grassy lawns that he promised Girl?

Completing the registration process, he was given an electronic key that he could use to access both the front door of the building and his suite located on the eighth floor. He was pleasantly surprised to find that his suite consisted of three rooms, a sitting room with kitchenette, a bedroom and a study. "What do you think of our new home, Girl?"

150

he said as the dog was sniffing every corner of the suite. Looking out from the sitting room window toward the west he saw a city transformed from the one he had last seen decades ago. Gone were the sheer glass skyscrapers whose facades were now adorned with smaller windows of various shape, square, round, triangular, in response to the increasing local temperatures. Skywalks that had been built in response to the city's cold winters were now expanded and air-conditioned to deal with the almost constant heat.

On Tuesday morning he awoke late after having enjoyed a delicious dinner in the elegant dining room of Longview House and spent most of the day walking around, exploring his new surroundings, and finding a small park where Girl delighted by rolling in the grass.

At four that afternoon he pushed open the swinging door of the bar where he had agreed to meet his old colleague. As he looked around the less than crowded room, he pictured Wayne Petersen and his wild bushy light brown hair, a round face with protruding large ears and eyes shaded by heavy eyebrows. At the time, of course, Wayne was a dozen years younger than Don who now tried to imagine what he must look like today. Suddenly, a man jumped up from a booth in a far corner and waved wildly as he approached Don saying, "I would have recognized that handsome face of yours anywhere. You haven't changed a bit except for the grey hair. Come on, I have a table and I want you to meet my wife."

"I didn't know you were married?"

"Well, you know we didn't exactly move in the same circles outside of work. Anyway, it's great to see you. What are you doing back here after all these years?"

"It's a long story. I'll give you the gory details after I've met your wife."

Wayne introduced his wife, Francine, an attractive woman in her early fifties with coiffed blond hair and full painted lips that looked artificially enhanced. The two men ordered scotch while Francine said she would prefer a gimlet and a bowl of those nice peanuts for the table. While waiting for their drinks, Don asked the Petersens about their family as Wayne explained that they've been married over thirty years and had a daughter and two beautiful grandkids. "But, how about you," asked Wayne. "Where have you been these past years?"

Don explained that when he left the station, he first took a cruise around the world to unwind before moving to Florida. From his reporting about rising oceans for over forty years he should have known that a home near the ocean was not a good destination, but he had naively thought that it would not flood in his lifetime. "I wasn't the only one to make that mistake," he added. "But I had my four-legged friend with me, and I enjoyed the location and the many wonderful fellow residents. It was a good time and I wish it would have lasted. However, I now realize I was in a cocoon. What I've seen in the last week since I left Miami frightens me for the future of this country and actually, the world. I wonder if you feel the same way about the current situation?"

"I worry about my grandchildren," Francine said. What kind of future will they have?"

"Honey, it's not just about the kids," said Wayne. "But where are we going to be in five or ten years? We've been talking among the guys at the station about how the government is handling this situation. It's all been done so quietly without pronouncements from the administration. I'd like to hear from the President what led her to decide that it was necessary to mobilize the National Guard and deploy them all over this country?

"I may be able to find out," said Don. "One of my fellow former residents at the Manor has been offered a position on a Presidential Task Force. I'm sure she'll be anxious to find that out for herself. But listen, you've been very kind to meet me so we can catch up a bit. There's something else. I wonder if you can help me with local contacts so I can find people with whom I can socialize."

"What? We're not enough for you?"

"You know what I mean."

"Well, there is one guy I met recently that I think you might enjoy. He helped us decorate the apartment. His name is Richard Deighton, and he knows all the hoy-ploy in this town."

"The name doesn't sound familiar. No, I don't think I ever met him."

"He's really nice and I think you guys would get along. Don't you agree, Francine?"

"Absolutely! He's such a sweet man. I'll arrange a small dinner party and invite him."

"That's very kind of you. Now I hope you'll allow me to pick up the check here."

"You don't see me reaching for it," said Wayne with a broad smile on his face.

Don spent the next few days discovering the city. Wayne had arranged to have him come to the TV station to see his old haunt. Walking around and seeing the people who worked at the station, Don realized that most of his old colleagues were either gone or dead. This realization suddenly made him feel old. During his short stay in Longview House he had yet to meet people with whom he could develop a close relationship. It was so unlike the Manor where there was an intimacy and a warmth that was lacking at Longview. Most of the residents here had existing relationships as most had lived in the area for most of their lives and for Don as an outsider, it was clearly difficult for him to insert himself. He began to look forward to the dinner party that Francine had arranged on Saturday night and the chance to meet new people.

When he arrived at the Petersen's apartment and rang the bell, Wayne came to the door. "Welcome," he said. "Don't just stand there, come in, come in. Francine's in the kitchen but the others are on the terrace having drinks." The Petersen's apartment was on a high floor of a new high-rise condominium in which the top floors stepped inward giving the tenants on those floors, terraces along the whole length of their apartments.

"This is pretty snazzy for a retired newsman," observed Don. "Who did you have to kill to get it?"

"Actually, I did quite well in the market but," he added quietly, " to be honest, this place came out of Francine's inheritance. Come on, let me introduce you to the other guests. But, let me get you a drink first."

A scotch and soda in hand, Don was first introduced to a couple in their early sixties, Sam & Betty Lockhart. Sam, a real estate broker, dressed in a plaid sweater vest and sporting a broad smile, greeted Don effusively, shaking his hand up and down, hard. "Sam," cautioned Betty, "careful now, you've almost caused the poor man's drink to spill." Turning to look directly at Don, she added, "I'm sorry for my clumsy husband. He's sometimes too enthusiastic when meeting new people. We've been friends of the Petersens since Sam found this beautiful apartment for them. I hear you used to work with Wayne." Betty's wide-open green eyes looked as if they had been pulled up with a crane and her red cheeks blazed with a little too much rouge, but her smile was genuinely warm as she held Don's free hand between hers.

"That was a long time ago. I don't know too many people in town so it's a pleasure meeting the two of you."

"Then I don't suppose you've met Rick yet," said Betty as she gestured to the man who was leaning forward from a chair to stand with the aid of a cane. "Rick is connected to our firm as an independent interior designer. I had brought him in to help the Petersens with the design of their apartment interiors. They just didn't have anything that was right for this spectacular place."

Richard Deighton looked like an aging preppie, dressed as he was, in tan slacks and a yellow short-sleeved sweater over a light blue button-down shirt. His lightly wrinkled, pale face was partly covered in a neatly trimmed white beard. With his light blue eyes, he looked directly at Don. "Sorry about the cane," he said in a clear baritone voice. "It's a leftover from last winter's ski accident."

"Where did you find snow in this heat and what happened?"

"A group of us went to Montana where the snow was great but, unfortunately, I took one run too many at the end of the day. I fractured a tibia and at my age it takes a devil of a time to heal but I've been told I should be good as new in another month."

"You don't seem otherwise the worst for wear," said Don. "Tell me, are you from around here?"

"Actually, I'm one of the few genuine natives as my parents settled here when they arrived from England."

"I'd love to hear more about that."

Just then, Francine came out to the terrace. "I hate to interrupt the conversation, but you must be quite hot out here and I've fixed a lovely dinner in our air-conditioned dining room that I hope you will appreciate. Bring your drinks if you don't mind."

Holding his drink in one hand, Don followed the Lockharts into the dining room while placing his free hand on Richard's shoulder to guide him. Rick turned his head and smiled.

At the end of the evening, Rick asked Don if they could get together another time so that he could learn more about life in the news business. Don agreed to call him once he was fully settled into his new residence.

Rick was still working part time and had several important commissions. Many involved modifying upper-class residences in response to the increasing atmospheric temperatures. He tried a number of approaches including reducing window sizes, providing shading devices over windows, adding insulation to walls and ceilings. Most were needed because added air conditioning was not available as power was limited and unable to respond to the explosive increase in demand. This work kept him very busy. Nevertheless, within a week, he and Don found time to get together. Rick was interested to learn about Don's world-wide experiences as a newscaster and Don wanted to hear about Rick's involvement in the local arts scene. At their meeting the following week, Rick asked, "I hear you came from Miami just before that big storm hit?"

"I had planned to spend the rest of my life there but unfortunately nature conspired against me."

"Really? I thought everyone knew that the coast was going to be flooded one day. It's happened in the distant past and it was bound to happen again."

"What do you mean? This change in climate that's been going on for over a century is not just some cyclical event but is tied directly to what man, you and I and billions of others have done to create this blanket of carbon dust that's insulating the earth, causing all this heating."

"I'm not sure I can accept that," said Rick. "We're just pin pricks on the face of the planet. How can we be responsible for covering the seemingly infinite sky with enough material to create such an insulating blanket?"

"I can point you to the scientific literature, but I have a feeling that your mind is made up."

"I don't think we're getting anywhere with this. Why don't we switch subjects?"

"It's late," said Don, "and I have to get up early tomorrow so why don't we call it a night. I'll get back to you to see when we can next meet."

Don had no intention of contacting Richard Deighton again. It was clear to him that they were not compatible, at least in the area of understanding scientific facts. It was inconceivable to Don that anyone living in the world today could not be aware of the cause of the current climate crisis. Suddenly, he missed his friends from the Manor. At least they understood the reality of what was happening in the world, so he made a mental note to call Jim and Henrietta in the morning. They were certain to be settled in their new home by now. When he returned to Longview House that evening, he also decided that he must make more of an effort to meet some of his fellow residents, convinced that some of them must be more open minded than Deighton.

16
THE WEILLS
Monday

A FTER THE WEILLS LEFT DON in the executive lounge, they went directly to their gate. "I'm glad we had a chance to get together with Don one last time," said Diane. "I hated to leave while there were still bad feelings between us. I rather like him, even though he seems like such a lost soul."

"The problem is that he's too attached to that dog of his. He needs to find some human attachment."

"What do you have against that sweet dog?"

Frank felt it was a yappy dog but was relieved not to have to answer, as their flight was called, and they had to begin boarding. "Here we go," he said as he led Diane through the crowd pushing to get aboard.

"Ladies and gentlemen, please stay in line," the gate agent said. "There are seats for everyone, but I need to check your boarding passes before you can cross the boarding bridge."

Diane nervously held on tightly to Frank's arm. "I don't like this."

"They are just being careful and once we're on the plane, it will be fine," he said. Once cleared, he guided her to the window seat in the second row. When all the passengers were seated, Frank saw that every seat was taken. There were a large number of older passengers and several families with children and babies. He guessed that most going home or were escaping the excessive heat and had relatives up North with whom they can stay. He had observed that the gate agent carefully examined the boarding documents as passengers filed past, undoubtedly making certain that the information matched the individual's general description. Since everyone carried an electronic instrument, a phone or E-Tag, on which the flight information and the passenger's description was stored, it was easy to verify both. Frank saw that one passenger ahead of him had been pulled aside by an armed guard and taken to a nearby room. A standby passenger was then called to take that seat. Diane missed that event as she was enthralled by a baby sleeping in her mother's arms and thought, *a few hours and I'll see my babies.*

The flight to Burlington proceeded without incident and landed two hours later. When the cabin door opened, a gust of fresh air filled the cabin. 'Still warm,' thought Frank. 'But nowhere as oppressive as the heat we left behind.' Diane, her eyes wide open in anticipation, pushed Frank out of his seat. "Hurry! let's get off this plane. The children must be waiting." As the line of exiting passengers moved slowly, Diane became increasingly anxious. She clutched Frank's arm causing him to wince in pain. "Easy," he said, "you're hurting me. We'll be out in a minute." In the waiting area, Diane looked around nervously trying to find a familiar face. "Where are they?"

"There," Frank pointed, to not one or two, but a group of seven people, four adults and three youngsters waving wildly. This caused Diane to tense up and cling desperately to Frank, who said, "Isn't that wonderful. The boys brought their whole families." As they walked toward the family, Diane buried her face in Frank's chest while breathing fitfully saying, "I can't."

Frank called over his oldest son. Frank Jr. and told him how happy he was to see them all, but that mother was not feeling well and needed to rest before getting together with them. "I hope you understand!"

"Of course, Dad, you'd better get her settled at Lakeshore and we'll be in touch. Anyway, it's good to see you both." After a moment, he added, "Look, let me explain it to the family and I'll drive you there."

In the car, Frank and Diane sat in the back while their bags were in the front seat next to Junior. The drive to the shore of Lake Champlain took only a little over thirty minutes and as they arrived at the gatehouse of Lakeshore Residence, Diane suddenly looked up. "Frankie, Is that you?"

"Yes, Mom," he said stopping in front of a three-story white-clad building. "We're just arriving at your new home."

After getting out of the car, Diane embraced her son fiercely, refusing to release him until Frank gently pulled her away saying, "We'd better check in and get settled. We'll see Frankie again soon."

It took a while to say goodbye and to go through the check-in process. The Weills apartment was on the second floor and consisted of a bedroom, a living room, and a dining alcove with kitchenette. However, what delighted Diane was the terrace overlooking the lake. She immediately stepped out there and looking pensively, she sat watching a sailboat moving gently, pushed by a light wind while loons glided silently overhead.

With Diane settled comfortably on the terrace, Frank called his two sons and made arrangements to meet each separately, with their wives but without the grandchildren. He explained that Diane is more comfortable with small gatherings. Over the next ten days the Weills met with various combinations of their children and grandchildren, always on the terrace where Diane proudly showed each the view she now so admired. To his sons Frank expressed his joy at how easily Diane had adapted to her new home. "You don't know what a relief it is for me that your mother is now with the family that she loves. She seems so much more open and relaxed than I've seen her in a long time." Both Frank Jr. and Arthur, each in his own way, reproached their father, "Dad, you should have come here a year ago when you knew that the rising sea would eventually make it impossible to live in Miami." Frank tried to explain that they had not been free to leave the Manor until arrangements could be made so that the Lakeside Residence would accept them. When they arrived at the Manor, it seemed that the changes that were taking place causing increased temperatures and rising ocean levels moved so slowly that they could have spent their remaining years there. He did not realize that although change was slow, it was accelerating, finally putting them in the position of precipitously having to leave. But here they were close to their families, settled in a comfortable environment, hopefully for the rest of their lives. He could not imagine having to move once more. He thought again of the Simmons, who after a life well lived, decided to let nature govern their end by staying in the face of the inevitable storm surge. When he was first made aware of this, he condemned them as cowards but now, he was no longer so certain. But that was not a decision he even had to contemplate. Of course, he and Diane were safe now except…. No! push away negative thoughts. After all Henrietta was optimistic about a future in which the earth would again begin to cool. That's good enough for me he thought, at least for the remaining years of our live

17
THE EXILES
Wednesday

IN HIS OFFICE IN THE west wing of the White House, Andrew Carlson was leaning back in his chair mulling over in his mind the last conversation he had with Henrietta Barker. He had offered her the position on the task force that he thought she would immediately accept. He looked forward to her participation as he respected her opinions in matters of climate change. Instead, she seemed reluctant to get involved because of the military presence that the president had engaged to control the northward movement of migrants. It seemed to him that as a scientist, she should be able to separate herself from political issues. Of course, he remembered that when he was her teaching assistant while in graduate school, she had supported student protests against US government involvement limiting migration of Central Africans into South Africa. That was over twenty years ago and the beginning of a major increase in worldwide migration of populations away from tropical heat. It had started as a trickle and has now become a tidal wave. Henrietta was outspoken then, warning that taking draconian steps to control migration could lead to the rise of autocratic regimes around the world. Yet, he should be able to convince her that uncontrolled migration could lead to armed resistance among established populations. That's exactly what was happening in many areas of the country. Although he sympathized with the migrants, he recognized President Davenport's need to maintain order in the country. Yet…!

He left his office in the warren of rooms in the lowest level of the West Wing and went directly up to the entrance to the oval office where he asked the appointment secretary, "Is the President free by any chance?" and was told, "I'm sorry, Dr. Carlson, she's tied up for another hour, but you're welcome to wait. She has open time after the current visitor leaves."

It was closer to ninety minutes before the door to the oval office opened and the Homeland Secretary walked out and greeted Carlson. "How're you doing, Andy." And added in a whisper, "she's spitting fire today, so you better be careful."

Carlson was escorted into the office and greeted Margaret Davenport. "Good morning, Madame President."

Without looking up and while sorting through some papers on her desk, she said, "Sit down Andy, while I finish going through this mess that Homeland brought me." After five minutes, she added, exasperated, "I didn't expect to see you today, Andy. I hope it's not another problem. I think I've had more than enough of those for one day." Pushing away from her desk, she walked around to sit in an easy chair opposite Andy. "Well, what is it?"

"It's got nothing to do with the storms we talked about ten days ago. In fact, those storms have dissipated and maybe I was a bit premature in raising an alarm about their multiplying."

"Well, that's good news."

"I hate to bring up another subject of concern. I've been trying to recruit Dr. Barker to join your environmental task force and she's expressed unease about the extent of military presence she encountered since leaving Miami... Perhaps, I'd better explain. She left Miami when her residence there was wiped out because of the recent storm, and she has been traveling to her new home near Lehigh University. All along the way she and a partner encountered National Guard units controlling the movement of people along every highway. She wonders if this is the beginning of a major shift toward a more intrusive government."

"Let me stop you there. This is exactly what I've been worried about and actually discussed with Homeland just before you arrived. I sympathize with poor people who have been flooded out by the encroaching ocean or can no longer live in excessively hot areas of the country. But maybe I haven't made it clear to our citizens that we cannot allow this country to descend into anarchy."

"Couldn't you let the local police handle this situation?"

"They tried at first, but they were overwhelmed by the sheer mass of people trying to move North."

"I'm your science advisor and can tell you that from the viewpoint of the environment, it can only get worse. But as a citizen, I don't want this country turned into a police state."

"Speaking as your friend, Andy, neither do I. But as President, I have a duty to take whatever actions are necessary to keep this country safe, even from the disruptiveness of a group of its own citizens." Just then, the phone rang, and the President went to her desk to answer it. "I'm sorry, Andy but you'll have to excuse me. I have an emergency. Perhaps we can pick this up later."

As he left, Andy noticed a flurry of activity near the Oval office with cabinet members and their aides talking excitedly among themselves, many with worried expressions on their faces. "What's going on?" he asked one of the aides he knew.

"There's been a shooting incident in Northern Virginia," the aide whispered as he rushed off.

Over the next hour, Andy learned that there was a confrontation between an armed group of migrants and a Guard unit near the border between Virginia and West Virginia. As the Guard tried to direct the migrants to turn back south, shots rang out. There were a number of deaths and injuries on both sides. The Guard called in reinforcements and surrounded the migrants, who in the face of overwhelming odds, eventually raised their hands as ordered and surrendered. Andy was concerned because he remembered that Henrietta was on that same route on her way to Pennsylvania. Back in his office, he placed a call. "Where are you," he asked anxiously when she answered."

Surprised to hear from him, she said, "Andy? We're just outside Lehigh. Why do you ask?"

"I'm so glad you're all right. There's been a shooting along the road that I believe you traveled on and I was worried about you."

"We're fine. Of course, we did encounter some migrants along the way who seemed somewhat scary, but Jim handled it. I can easily imagine that some of those migrants were armed and that could have led to shots being fired by one side or the other. Frankly, such a possibility did concern us as we traveled north. It's the heavy presence of the military and the almost police state atmosphere that exists now that is deeply disturbing."

"I was just about to discuss this very same issue with the President when we were interrupted with the news of the shooting."

"To be perfectly frank, Andy, I'm not sure that I'm comfortable serving on your task force for an administration that is leading this country toward autocracy. I've been discussing this with Jim and…"

"Who's Jim?

"He's a friend from my years at the Manor. His name is Jim Robinson, and he's an engineer with extensive international experience. He feels as I do that there must be a more humane way to deal with the climate migrants than to simply push back. We both agree that this is a long-term issue that's not going to be resolved with guns."

"Let me talk to him," interrupted Jim as he reached for the phone.

Surprised by his sudden outburst, Henrietta was at first reluctant to give up the phone but seeing how insistent Jim was, she put it on speaker mode so they could both talk!

"Guns will only lead to further conflict," Jim said. "What will happen next is that more groups of the migrants will arm themselves for protection and suddenly you've got a minor war starting. I've seen this happen time again in my years working in the Middle East. It escalates more quickly than anyone can act to change course."

"I agree with you, so why don't both of you join me in developing an alternate policy and presenting it to the administration."

"That's up to Henrietta," he said.

Henrietta looked at Jim and when he shook his head up and down, she said, "Very well, if you can assure us that our voices will not be drowned out."

"That's up to the both of you but I have a feeling that Jim would not let that happen. And Jim, let me add that I look forward to meeting you… in person, that is!"

After disconnecting, Henrietta now realized that she had made the right decision to invite Jim into her life. He was not only a loving person, but his voice will clearly add to her efforts in finding a way out of the current direction that the administration has taken in connection with the climate migrants. In the past he seemed so dismissive when she talked about finding ways to deal with the insulating layer of carbon in the upper atmosphere that is now causing the planet to wilt. Perhaps she can even engage Jim in rationally evaluating technologies to remove this offending carbon. She recognized that it was important for her to have him at her side, no longer as an observer but a participant in her work and life. "I hope you're serious about engaging with the task force."

"When I make a promise, I stick to it. You got me involved, and now I'm out to win. I thought you understood that. After all, that's how I managed to get you to care for me and maybe even love me."

"You certainly have a huge ego, Mr. Robinson, to think that you can manipulate me so that I would fall for you. For your information, I felt sorry for you at first. You were such a needy puppy. Then I found you weren't all bad and rather kind of sweet. That's the reason that I care for you now. And, for your information, it's too early to call it love," said Henrietta walking to her room and adding as she closed the door, "Let's see what time brings...."

18

THE CALLS

Henrietta sent a message to Don, the Weills and Drake offering to arrange a video call once they had all settled into their new homes. The call was arranged for the following weekend as Henrietta looked forward to seeing her old friends, even virtually. On the appointed hour, one by one, the images appeared on the screen; Don looking somewhat downcast against a view of a grey city; Frank and Diane sitting side by side on a couch with a Grandma Moses print on the wall behind them; the back of Albert Drake's head looking out at a lake on which three sailboats could be seen reaching across the wind; finally, there were Jim and Henrietta sitting on the small terrace outside their living room with a view of the verdant hills behind them. Diane could hardly contain herself and blurted out, "It's so wonderful to see you all. I wish we were all in the same room so I could hug you all."

"It seems we've all safely settled into our new homes," said Henrietta. "Mr. Drake, I'm not exactly sure where you are?"

Drake told them about his time with Val and how he stumbled onto a new position managing a home not too dissimilar from the Manor. He also explained that he very much enjoyed meeting Val's family and that he was trying to get Val and her family to move up to Oswego where the climate was an improvement over that in the south. He also described what he experienced since leaving the Manor and how it reinforced the negative feelings he had about the future and the increasingly autocratic way in which the government is dealing with the migrants.

"I'm also afraid for the future," Frank added. We just didn't know any of this was happening. How come we didn't see it when we were at the Manor. It's as if we were isolated from the world while we were there."

Jim jumped in saying, "I know how you feel. Henrietta and I saw many of the same angry people along the road as we drove north and then there was the military, and you all must have heard about the shooting! Actually, we're meeting with the President's science advisor in a few days as part of a task force to look at possible alternatives to the way the government is currently dealing with the climate migrants." "That's not soon enough," said Don. I'm looking out my window right now at a heavy rainstorm that's heading your way. And that's happening after a dry summer that killed lawns and a lot of greenery around here. Now, of course we'll get washouts and floods. Believe me, this disastrous climate is becoming more and more unpredictable." 'Why do I have to face this alone, he thought to himself. Why can't I find a soulmate to share these days with me?', He promised himself to make more of an effort to meet his new neighbors once he was off this call.

"Diane, you seemed to be so happy to see us," said Henrietta. "I hope we haven't upset you with all this talk of migrants and soldiers. It's just that it's on our minds and we wish it were different."

"It's all right. I understand. Even though it's so beautiful here, we're always reminded that the border with Canada is near and bad people are trying to go there."

"They're not really bad people. They're just trying to restart their lives in a better environment than the one they left. Remember, they're not as lucky as we were in having Mr. Drake arrange to settle us in new homes after the Manor drowned."

Diane looked at Frank and took his hands in hers. "I guess, I am lucky. I do have my boys and my grandchildren near, so I can see them anytime I want. But...please don't let the future hurt my family." Before the call ended, Drake, the Weills, Don, Henrietta and Jim promised not lose touch with each other.

Once she had hung up from the call, Henrietta confronted Jim saying, "I can't get that woman and child we met along the way out of my mind. They were lost souls looking for some help and the response from the government was to put them in a detention camp. I just don't think that's the way to deal with this situation."

"What would you do instead?"

"I have to believe that there are areas of this country, perhaps in the upper Midwest, that can still accept such migrants. I would create resettlement areas there: new towns and cities that can absorb the people who were forced to leave their old homes. Just like the westward expansion in the nineteenth century, these people would bring their skills and professions to provide work. It would be a whole new world."

"I'm afraid that the few people who currently live in those parts of the country would resent the newcomers just as the residents of the more densely crowded areas of the country are pushing back against the migrants. Even though there's more open space where you could house these migrants, the current population like their open spaces and don't want it to change. Quite honestly, I don't know what the answer is. Tens of millions of people have been displaced by the heat and advancing waters. If the government doesn't do anything to house them, they'll become an army of resistance and could overwhelm all our democratic institutions. I've been thinking about this since we talked to Carlson and it seems we've got to meet with the task force to understand what is being planned."

Henrietta was equally distressed by what she had seen in these past weeks and agreed that now that they were settled in their new home, a meeting needed to be arranged in Washington with Carlson's group. They called Carlson, who welcomed the idea. It took a few days to establish a location and contact the other members of the task force. The capitol was no longer a suitable location since the Potomac had for years been licking at the land, threatening to drown it. Even though dykes had been built to protect the city, there remained the constant threat of inundation. Therefore, the President had offered Camp David as the appropriate venue for the meeting. Located in the Catoctin Mountains about 60 miles NNW of Washington, it was away from the pressure of the Capital and would provide a degree of privacy and an unhurried atmosphere for the development of a plan for the future. Once all was set, Carlson offered to have Henrietta and Jim picked up by a government helivan on the first day of the meeting.

On a grey, overcast day in late fall, Henrietta and Jim landed at Camp David and were led to the main building by a Marine Guard. They were then shown the quarters they were to occupy during the duration of the meeting, a two-room suite. Jim noticed the sleeping arrangement with double beds and smiled to himself while Henrietta seemed nonchalant. Once settled in, they were escorted to a conference room in Laurel Lodge where they were to meet the other participants. Jim was somewhat uncomfortable with the formality of the process until the moment he was greeted by Andy Carlson, a man in his early fifties, somewhat stout but with an energetic handshake and a winning smile. Jim relaxed as Henrietta said, "Andy, It's been a long time since graduate school. I see you've rounded out a bit since then."

"Good to see you again after so many years." Carlson replied, and added sarcastically, "Unfortunately, in this job there are too many pizzas and not enough salads… So, Jim it's good to meet you in person, but first, let me introduce you both to the other members of the team." He went around the room and stopped in front of a man wearing thick black rimmed glasses topped with a bald head except for a thin fringe toward the back. "Herman, I'd like to introduce you to Henrietta Barker and Jim Robinson. Henrietta is an environmental scientist and Jim is an engineer." Turning to face Henrietta, he added, "Herman is a professor of political science and was the consultant to Maine's senator." Herman Mickleworth extended a limp hand toward Jim and Henrietta. "I'm sorry," he said. "I've been suffering from a muscle weakness otherwise I would gladly shake your hand."

One after another, Carlson introduced the other members of the team. Gabriella Rivera, a former assistant secretary of state; Benjamin Dapore, the current advisor to Homeland Security, Morio Sasaki, a climatologist and Wanda Zingoni, a social scientist. For the next hour the task force members circulated around the room, becoming acquainted and chatting, feeling each other out to understand where each fit into the mix of expertise and personalities. Henrietta and Morio quickly realized that they had met, or at least corresponded over two decades ago when he commented on a paper she had written. Jim and Ben Dapore spent time to discuss the changes that had taken place to the cities along coast of Africa since the times each had worked there. "I hear," said Ben, "that Mogadishu has become a city on stilts with waterways instead of roads and boats instead of cars."

"I guess that's one way to adapt to the rising sea level," said Jim.

Andy circulated around the room and the adjacent porch and encouraged the participants to begin to think about concrete proposals to deal with the northward climate migrants and the need to establish new centers of habitation, commerce and manufacturing.

Wanda shook her head waving away the black bob above her eyes to clear her brain as she pulled Henrietta close to say in a confidential tone, "I don't think these people know how serious the problem is! In this country alone, we're talking about the migration of tens of millions of people and in the world as a whole..." pausing to take a deep breath, "there are close to a billion. My God, these are numbers no one has ever seen before. It's a societal calamity!"

"You must remember the 1918 and 2020 Pandemics," Henrietta answered. "In their day they were equally frightening."

"Except that those were caused by a bug over which we had no control. This new climate has resulted from what we did and what we failed to correct."

"I thought we're here to come up with an approach that the government can take to avoid further militarization and find a humane alternative in resettling all these people?"

"But the size of the problem.....'said Wanda as she moved away, looking around for another ear to capture.

Just then, Jim came over with Ben who said, "I guess you've just gotten an earful from miss gloom and doom. You'll find she's OK once we start looking at solutions."

Jim added, "It turns out that Ben and I were in East Africa at about the same time when he was on a military mission and I was relocating a railroad inland."

"It's nice you boys have something in common. It also turns out that Morio and I had corresponded in the past."

"Well, I guess we're just one happy family," said Jim. "Why don't we see if we can get Andy to start the festivities."

At Carlson's urging, the task force members slowly took their seats as he addressed them. "I've been asked by the President to bring you all together and see if we can come up with the pressing issue of developing a strategy for dealing with the climate migrants. I know that some of you have experienced the problem first hand and can help us understand the human side of the issue. On the part of the government we have to insure that we don't allow this to descend into chaos and anarchy. At the same time, we're getting a lot of pushbacks from the governors of the northern states who have urged a more aggressive role from the National Guard to stop the movement of the migrants into their states. Then, of course there remains the overriding issue of where we stand in the science arena in trying to reverse this warming trend. You represent all aspects of the problem and I'm hoping that you can come up with strategies to deal with all of them. I realize that it's a herculean task, but you represent some of the brightest minds in the country, and I put the future of our country and even the world, in your hands."

Over the next week there were meetings between individual participants and group discussions as the outline of a series of recommendations began to take shape. On some evenings the group met for a dinner in the common dining room while on others, individual members preferred to dine alone while considering their work. Jim and Henrietta often dined together in their suite. Discussion over dinners were usually followed by a shared bed as their feelings for each other were intensified to counter the grim tone of the discussions by the group. They realized that the future was too uncertain, and that they may only have an indeterminate time together and needed to accept their feelings for each other rather than waste time by questioning them.

On the fifth morning, Gabriella Rivera addressed the group and said, "I've been taking some notes and believe we have a problem. It seems we have been thinking too much about the actions that this administration should take, forgetting that we are not isolated but have neighbors, even across the oceans; all are facing the same effects of climate change. After all, climate does not recognize borders. It would be great if we could simply transfer our climate migrants across into Canada just as Russia can ease part of their population into Siberia."

"So, what are you suggesting?" said Ben Dapore

"Unless we find ways to restrict ourselves to solutions that are limited to those that we can implement within our borders, we need to bring our neighboring countries into this discussion."

Carlson reminded everyone that the President had closed the Mexican border some time ago and the Canadians had closed their border to the US although there are ongoing discussions about that issue between their Prime Minister and the President. "But, I think Gabriella is right," he added, "Let's concentrate on recommending action within our borders and pass the bigger issue of climate migration to the UN where it belongs."

There was some grumbling among some of the participants who felt that this group should not have been called together in the first place, wasting their time.

"I'd be happy if we could just clarify the role of the National Guard," said Henrietta, "and come up with recommendations to avoid having them behave as an arm of a police state."

"Now, wait a minute," interrupted Ben Dapore. "If the Guard hadn't been deployed, we'd have riots in the streets with migrants running amuck."

"I'm not saying they shouldn't be there, but Jim and I saw cases where they were treating some of these poor people like criminals."

"I assume those were isolated cases with overzealous guardsmen."

"Maybe! But, that's why I'm saying, let's define their role."

Ben shook his head up and down in ascent as some of the participants sat down around the large conference table, prepared to start work in this new direction.

Morio Sasaki turned to Carlson and said, "I'm afraid you won't need my expertise if you go in this direction. It seems more in the national political/security arena." Then both Gabriela Rivera and Wanda Zingoni said that they felt their contribution would be more appreciated in the UN where the multi-national issues could be debated and resolved and therefore they decided to leave. Henrietta and Jim expressed the view that although they could not contribute directly to any proposals dealing with management of the Guard, they could help steer any actions toward a more compassionate direction. Carlson agreed as did Mickleworth and Dapore who were the only two original participants left. On hearing this, Rivera said, "maybe I could stay and listen and, of course, interject my opinions."

"Absolutely! With your extensive background in negotiations, we would welcome your participation," said Carlson.

There followed discussions over the next two days among the five remaining members of the task force with Carlson acting as monitor. This led to the drafting of a four-page document defining the precise objectives of the Guard's deployment, the actions they are authorized to take and the limitations of their powers. Concurrently, the Interior

Department was to be tasked to arrange for the study and evaluation of resettlement issues.

That evening, Henrietta thanked Carlson for the invitation and added, "I'm glad that we were able to help draft a document that should hopefully lead to a more equitable way of dealing with those poor migrants. After all, they really weren't to blame for having to leave their homes. Both Jim and I were also forced to leave our home because of the combination of heat and rising seas so I have some empathy for those migrants. We were fortunate to have a new home to go to, they are not."

"I'm also happy," said Carlson, "that you found someone in your life. I like Jim. He seems to be a good person and I can see that he is devoted to you. He's a keeper!"

Somewhat embarrassed, Henrietta responded, "We'll see what the future brings."

"Take it from a lifelong bachelor, don't be afraid to take a chance and express your feelings and don't pass up the chance for happiness. It doesn't come often."

"When did you become so wise?"

"By not following my own advice! I've let chances pass me by."

Henrietta hugged Carlson before leaving to join Jim in their suite. The next morning, they left to return to Hillcrest, their new home.

As the helivan lifted off from Camp David, Jim noted, "I like the service these people offer. I think I could learn to live like this. It's my kind of style."

"Don't get used to it because I don't think we'll be back. Remember, all we accomplished was to deal with only one aspect of the problem, and I'm not sure that it will be resolved so easily. Look out the window. What do you see?"

Jim looked down and observed a line of military vehicles heading North on the interstate. "Maybe they haven't had time to institute our recommendations yet."

"Or maybe the President is not certain whether she should. I can imagine that she's under a great deal of pressure from some of her cabinet members to maintain order as a first priority. And, don't forget the other part of our discussions; involving the UN. That will take time.... I think we'll just have to be patient and see what develops in the next few weeks or even months."

As the helivan gently settled down onto the lawn in front of Hillcrest, Henrietta glanced at Jim and thought, *We're home. It feels somehow so right. I never thought that at my age, I'd find someone with whom to share my life. But I think I need more time to get used to it,* as she absentmindedly raked her hand through Jim's hair.

"What's that for?"

"I don't know. I suppose I'm just glad to be home."

19
RENEWAL

DRAKE CHECKED HIS MAIL AFTER the call between the friends from the Manor. He saw that there was a message from Val.

> Mr. Drake,
> Ernesto and I were wondering if your offer was still open? We had thought that with the changing season, there would be some relief from the hot and humid weather. As we get closer to winter, we expected that conditions would improve. It's not happening. So, we've been talking to Federico, and he agrees that he may prefer raising his family further north. He has also explored the market and finds that there are real opportunities for him. So, if it's not too late…
> With anticipation,
> Val

Drake felt his pulse quicken as he read this note. He had not realized how disappointed he had been in possibly losing his newfound family and immediately sent an answer urging the Lopez's to set a date. Val's response dampened his expectations since she explained that it would take some time for her family to make all the necessary arrangements. In response he enthusiastically offered to help Federico in finding a position in the area and set about contacting local firms. Contrary to Val's note, most firms told him that the market was bursting with people looking for work since the migration north included many professionals. It took several weeks of discouraging responses until Mr. O'Donnell offered to contact a friend at the University in Oswego. The relations between the University and Maple View were close, as many of their retired professors were residents. It appeared that an opening existed for an experienced bookkeeper and Drake urged Federico to apply, mentioning the Maple View connection. A video interview resulted and after some back-and-forth exchange of information, Federico was offered a job at his current salary, which of course he accepted.

Drake immediately called O'Donnell. "Bill, I'm eternally grateful to you for your help in getting my friend this job."

"You're very welcome. I did it for you since we'll be working together for a while and as you're settling in, I want you to be happy at Maple View."

"I think I had mentioned that Val worked for me for many years, and I had a great deal of respect for her ability to bond with the residents at the Manor. I only met her family recently but really enjoyed them…I know this may sound strange but in this short time I've begun to feel they're the family I never had."

"This is a strange time, and we can all use friends and family to help us get through it. So, by all means, bring these people closer to you."

Once Valeria received word that her son was offered a job at Oswego and that she and Ernesto could work at Maple View, she began to anticipate moving north to escape the heat that was becoming more oppressive the longer they stayed in the South. She remembered her youth when she had looked forward to the arrival of summers in northern Florida enjoying the warmth of the sun while walking on a forsaken beach after the tourists had left. Of course, the winters were not cold, but she preferred the broiling sun. These days she would have been happy to return to those hot summer days rather than to the scorching temperatures that now even oppressed her in Nashville. So, she urged Ernesto and Federico to hurry and prepare to leave for their new homes up north. Three weeks later, the two men loaded Ernesto's van and Federico's car for the two-day trip. Their route would take them through Kentucky, Ohio, and along the west side of Pennsylvania and New York State before finally arriving at their destination near Oswego. It would be a long drive that they hoped would not be interrupted by the type of event with migrants that Valeria experienced on the way to Nashville.

As they left the city, they were immediately stopped at a checkpoint. "Where are you headed," the officer asked, looking at them suspiciously. "You from south of the border?"

Ernesto explained that they, "that is, my wife and I and our son and his family in the car behind us." were going to Oswego for new jobs. Fortunately, Val had copies of the messages from Drake setting out the offers of jobs, that she passed to the officer. After a delay during which the officer walked over to the other car where he peered through the window and then went into the guard vehicle parked on the side of the road to consult his superior. Minutes later, he returned, gave Val back her papers and placed a green sticker with the image of the flag and one word, *PASS,* on the windshield of both cars. He did all this without a smile or a word.

As they drove away, Val breathed a sigh of relief. "I don't know what's happening to this country, but I don't like it."

"I'm sure it's just because of the migrants," said Ernie. "Look at it this way; At least we have someplace to go. Any remnants of our family south of the border are stuck between a rising ocean and a closed border."

"What are you talking about? We're second generation... as American as that guard who looked down on us... And, as you know, we don't happen to have any family left in Mexico. Anyway, I resent the way he treated us with suspicion."

"Can't we just relax. We've got our green stickers now, so it should be smooth sailing all the way."

Val kept muttering to herself for a while before descending into a pattern of rhythmic breathing and slowly dozed off as Ernie, when looking down at her, smiled.

As the hours passed, Ernie became aware of an eerie emptiness on the roads that had very few vehicles on them, as if they had been magically swept clean. And, as for the legendary migrant groups, they had vanished, having retreated to the shadows within the occasional forests away from the roads. Of course, Ernie passed periodic checkpoints manned by armed soldiers who, when they saw the green stickers, waved the two Lopez vehicles through. *No problems*, thought Ernie before nudging Val awake.

"Is there something wrong," she said as she wiped the fog from her eyes.

"No, no! I just wanted you to know that we're getting close to the lunch place you had called." Valeria, always the planner, had researched their route and identified restaurants and motels where she wanted to stop along the way. She had also made a reservation at a midway motel although she had been assured that it was not necessary, since as a result of travel restrictions there were few casual voyagers on the roads. When they stopped at the restaurant, there were few cars in the parking area and when they entered, the few patrons and the one waitress looked at them suspiciously. However, they enjoyed the lunch and the chance to stretch and use the facilities. After an hour, the waitress seemed sorry to have them leave and said, "Thank you so much for stopping by and have a safe rest of your trip." Once back on the road, the trip continued without incident passing through one characterless interstate after another until they reached Lake Ontario at Rochester. They then drove on a local road along the lake for the few miles to their destination. In a cove partially hidden from the road, Ernie spotted a group of people pushing a boat into the water and setting out for what seemed like an evening cruise on the lake. The group included men, women and a few children. "Look at that," said Ernie to Val. "It seems to be a little late in the fall for a moonlight cruise, especially with the wind and threatening sky." The boat soon disappeared in the darkness and Ernie thought no more about it as they approached the Maple View facility where they were to meet Drake. At the gate they were stopped by a guard and were allowed to proceed only after acknowledgement was received from Drake who met them at the front entrance to the main building. "Damn! It's so good to see all of you here," he said. "I've been so looking forward to having you arrive."

Val went up to Drake and hugged him tightly. "Thank you, thank you for inviting us. I was so glad to get away from the insufferable heat down south. This place looks as beautiful as you described it. I know we'll be happy here. But, look, you've met everyone, except my beautiful, almost three-year old grandson. He's a little sleepy now, after the long ride but you'll see what a little devil he can be in the morning."

"What's his name?"

"Albert! I had suggested the name to the children, and they liked it. Of course, everyone calls him Al."

Drake looked down at the sleeping child and gently stroked his little hand. "I'm flattered," he whispered.

"Hey! you're not the only Albert in the world you know," said Val brusquely, but quietly added, "Although I admit I thought of you when I suggested the name. My years at the Manor had been happy and I thought it's a good name for the little fellow to grow into."

"I don't know what to say but....come on, let's go inside. Once in the lobby, Drake explained that he had rooms for them for the night and that tomorrow, he would take them to a house nearby that he was certain would please them as their permanent home. Turning to Ernesto, he said, "I'm sure you can do with a cool beer after such a long drive. And for the rest of you a bit of supper!"

"That would hit the spot!" said Ernie

"Let's sit out on the porch while the others start eating."

"Great!" Once settled in two rocking chairs overlooking the lake, Ernie added, "Let me ask you a question. Not long before we arrived here I saw a group of people going out on a boat. It didn't seem like such a good idea with the wind picking up the way it was."

"Sounds as if some migrants," said Drake, "were trying to make it to Canada in the dark, attempting to evade the patrol boats from both sides of the border. I'm afraid that they're not the first and frankly they don't stand much of a chance. Apart from the fact that the lake can get pretty rough, the patrols have advanced radar covering most of the lake and can spot boats easily."

"What's going to happen to them?"

"Well, if they don't drown, they'll be captured and interned on one side of the border or the other. But, listen, gulp down what's left of your beer and let's join the others…I'm getting kind of hungry."

After supper the Lopez family retired to the two visitors rooms that Drake had reserved for them and were all soon sound asleep. In the middle of the night none of them heard the wail of a patrol boat's siren announcing an incident on the lake.

The morning light falling on the west side of Maple View was diffused by a light but steady rain. In the rooms where the Lopez's slept, the reduced light easily pierced the sheer curtains, waking little Albert. When he opened his eyes, he started whimpering as he looked around at the unfamiliar surroundings. This woke his mother, Isabel, who in turn woke Federico, who was told to find out where the kitchen was located and to get a glass of milk for Little Albert.

Meanwhile, in his suite on the top floor of the building, Drake who had been restless, happily dreaming about his new family, finally turned over in his bed and fell into a restful sleep. A warm rain fell all morning driven against the windows by a wind strong enough to cause a rattling sound that later woke Drake out of his reverie. Looking at his watch, he bellowed out, "Oh my God, it's ten o'clock." He quickly dressed and went down to the dining room where he saw Val and a group of residents chatting with Little Albert. "I see that you've already met Valeria and her grandson," he said. "Val will be my assistant, helping with any problems you may have."

"I hope she'll bring over that sweet little boy as often as possible," said one of the residents. "We love to interact with a little child once in a while…just to keep us on our toes."

"We'll see," said Drake impatiently as he pulled Val and Little Albert away from the residents, saying, "We'd better get you and the family settled in your new house this morning."

The house that Drake had found for the Lopez's was about thirty minutes south of Maple View. It continued to rain as they left with Val riding in Drake's car while the other two cars driven by Ernesto and Federico followed. "Is this rain normal around here so close to Thanksgiving?" asked Val.

"You know I've only lived here for less than a month, but I've been told that this is the new normal."

"I also thought it would be a lot cooler."

"Remember what Henrietta told us before we left the Manor; That we won't find what we still think of as *normal* fall weather until we look further north into Canada."

"Well, at least it's not as bad as the heat we suffered through down South," said Val.

"We all have to get used to the fact that the climate is still changing!"

Drake turned off the country road toward a two-story clapboard faced house with a separate barn/garage. In the back of the house was a row of trees that separated the property from a wheat field owned by a neighboring farmer. Val, Isabel and Little Albert excitedly explored the house itself, which with four bedrooms was clearly sufficient for the needs of the Lopez family. Ernie and Drake checked out the barn that Ernie declared had sufficient room for his workshop. "This place is perfect," declared Val as she ran up to Drake in the barn shaking out her umbrella. "Thank you. So, if you don't mind going home alone, I think we should meet with the real estate agent this afternoon and take it from here."

A week later, Federico was officially hired as a bookkeeper by the University and both Val and Ernie had their positions at Maple View verified by the bank. Then, the Lopez's proudly completed a purchase agreement for the house.

Drake couldn't be happier and had much to be thankful for on this day, a day of thanksgiving! After the terrible loss of Duck Cove Manor to the Hurricane's storm surge, he now had begun managing another retirement home that one day might be his, and best of all he had this new family around him including Little Albert. The appearance of that little boy had vanquished all the pessimistic projections that he had espoused and over which he had agonized over for so long. Now, he even imagined that one day in the future, Little Albert would follow him as the manager of Maple View. Considering all that's happened, maybe there is a future! Soon it will be Christmas followed by the start of a New Year.

In Minneapolis, don, far from Drake and his new family, contemplated his future while alone in his sitting room with Girl sleeping at his feet. Since his conversation with his friends from the Manor, he pursued every opportunity to meet some of his neighbors. He started taking his meals in the dining room of Longview House and introduced himself to a number of the other residents. Many, he discovered were set in their ways as some older people tend to be. But there were a number of others, especially some older widows, who welcomed the approach of a handsome, well-spoken and elegantly groomed, grey haired gentleman. One, Ms. Susan Chalmers as she called herself, had lost her husband a decade ago and looked forward to Don's attention. "There are so few single gentlemen here," she said. "I do tire of gossiping with the ladies all the time and anticipate some intelligent conversation." In need of a confidant, Don found Susan a good listener and really intelligent, quite the opposite of Richard Deighton, who was so closed minded... certainly about the consequences of climate change. When Don broached the subject to Susan, she spent a moment in thought and then said, "My late husband, in his last days apologized to me saying, *I'm sorry I'm leaving you with a planet on its last legs.* In his declining years, he understood what was happening but felt powerless to do anything about it. Can you imagine that! Actually, we had often talked about the changes that had occurred in our lifetime and worried for our grandchildren by leaving them with a damaged world." Susan had a beguiling smile and the deepest blue eyes that Don had ever seen. He guessed that she was about his age, not particularly thin but with a straight back that seemed held up by a rope from the heavens. In a way, she reminded him of Henrietta, confident yet somewhat vulnerable.

Don decided to introduce Susan to the Petersens. Francine immediately responded by suggesting he bring her along to a dinner the following weekend. "Don't worry, I won't ask Rick as I gather you two didn't quite hit it off. I know he can be a bit stuffy!" On the appointed date in early December, a light drizzle was falling as Don and Susan were picked up by a taxi in front of Longview House. "I remember the old days when we would have had snow by this time in the fall," said Susan as she was folding her umbrella to get in the car.

"It's all part of the new normal," said Don. "I don't think I'll ever get used to it. I miss the clear delineations of the seasons when you could guess what month it is by just looking at the thermometer."

"By the way, how do you know these people we are to see?"

"Wayne had just started at the station when I was a newsman there and Francine, I just met recently. They're really nice people and I thought you would enjoy a younger crowd from the ones we usually see at Longview."

When they arrived at the Petersen's condo, Francine welcomed them gushingly. "Don, it's so nice to see you again and Susan, welcome to our humble home."

"I certainly wouldn't call it humble," said Susan. "It looks magnificent. And the view out your windows is spectacular. I imagine that on a clear day you can see St. Paul."

Wayne introduced himself and pulled Don aside. "I hope you ladies will excuse us for a minute, but I have something to talk to Don about."

Left alone, Francine took Susan to the living room and offered her a drink and some crudités with a lightly spicy dip that she had prepared. "I understand, that the two of you live together." She stopped herself. "Well, I don't mean 'together' but in the same, what do you call it?" She thought, *old people's home*, but said, "residence."

"You might as well call it what it is; a retirement community with people living out the rest of their days in relative comfort."

"Neither of you seem what I think of as, old."

"Frankly, after my husband died I began to feel old but now, finding a friend like Don has been blessing for me. Someone with whom I can have an intelligent conversation and who is concerned for this crazy world we're now living in."

"But you know he is.."

"I think I know what you mean," Susan said curtly, clearly disturbed by the intimation. "He's a lovely man and I'm glad he reached out to me."

"I'm sorry if I upset you. But tell me, have you lived here long?"

"I feel I have lived here all my life…" Susan went on to describe when she and her late husband first moved to Minneapolis over forty years ago, settled and raised their family with two wonderful children. This led to Francine presenting her life story…in abbreviated form. In the meantime, Wayne spoke to Don in the study. "I'm sorry old buddy, but when I introduced you to Rick, I thought you two might have something in common."

"I don't understand how anyone today could not accept the fact that we bear responsibility for climate change? In any case, I'm not planning to see him again. I assume you don't mind?"

"Of course not. Anyway, I'm glad you found someone with whom you feel comfortable."

"I had decided to try to meet some of the folks at Longview and when I met Susan, I found her to be intelligent and delightful. But listen, there's something else I've been thinking about that I wanted to discuss with you. You know about the great migration that's going on with people moving north to get away from the unhealthy heat.

Since I feel fully settled here, I now feel it is important for me to try to help some of these migrants. I've encountered them ever since I left the Manor and I've been particularly upset about the way the government is treating them. It seems so heavy handed. All these poor people are trying to do is to move their families to more habitable regions of the planet. They're not the bad guys. After all they didn't create this problem. It's as I've said before, climate change is something for which we're all somewhat responsible. In any case, I'd like to help some of these migrants, perhaps finding a way for them to get to Canada?"

"Are you suggesting subverting the government?"

"No! Well, perhaps just bending the rules a bit."

"I didn't hear that! So… how do you plan to help them?"

"I just started exploring ways and I thought you could help me coming up with ideas."

Wayne started walking around the room and stopped directly in front of Don and in a low voice, practically whispering said, "Listen, old buddy, I've got a good position here at the station and have a bunch of conservative friends in important positions through Francine's family. I'm not really able to upset her or any of her friends. So, you understand that in this situation, I really can't help you. In fact, the less I know about it, the less guilty I'll feel. Sorry, buddy !"

"I understand. You have your obligations, but I have to be honest with you, it is disappointing." They rejoined the ladies for dinner. Francine had prepared a delicious dish with broiled salmon with a peppered-lime sauce, tart and delicately spicy, but Don only nibbled at the edges prompting Francine to ask, "Is there a problem with the food?"

"No! I think my stomach is a little upset." Susan looked toward him and saw that he was uncomfortable. She asked, "Do we need to go home?"

"No, no! I'll be fine. Let's finish this delicious dinner and then, perhaps we can leave a little early."

Wayne and Don hardly spoke through the rest of the dinner leaving it to the ladies to carry on the conversation. After desert Susan suggested they leave after thanking Francine profusely and apologizing for their early departure. On the cab ride home, Susan asked Don if there was something wrong at which point he told her about his idea concerning the migrants and the negative reaction he had received from Wayne.

"Can we talk about this another time," she said. "I'm feeling a little tired tonight. Call me in the late morning and we can have a brunch together and discuss your ideas."

Don was disappointed for a second time that evening but promised to call in the morning. When they met the next morning for Sunday brunch, Susan was anxious to hear about Don's idea. "I thought about it before going to sleep last night and couldn't wait to hear more about it."

Feeling newly motivated Don proceeded to explain why he thought that the migrants were being treated badly by the administration. "They're being hounded instead of being helped. I know that I can't change that, but I have friends who are close to the President and are sympathetic to the issue. They're involved on a task force to come up with suggestions to change the military's attitude. But I feel that I should do something as well... even in a small way. "

"What do you have in mind?"

He had been thinking about it for some time and explained that he had studied the areas of the state near the border to Canada and noticed that the wooded wetlands near the Rainy river seemed ideal as crossing point into Canada since it is thinly settled. With the approach of winter, he thought he could lead a small group of migrants and provide them with a rubber raft allowing them to cross over.

Susan took a bite of the omelet on her plate and chewed thoroughly washing it down with a long swallow of coffee before she felt she could answer, while Don looked at her apprehensively seeking a sign of approval. "Don," she said looking at him directly. "Don't you think you're a little old to play the adventurer, running around in the north woods with a group of people you're trying to save?"

"But...?"

"I know you must be frustrated by what you've seen these past months but...wouldn't it be more appropriate for you to perhaps work with the local government, trying to convince them to set up temporary shelters until a more permanent solution to the refugee's plight can be worked out?"

"You must think I'm an old fool,"

"Not at all. It's just that a man with your experience as a reporter and commentator must have many friends in government whom you might contact to start something like a shelter program. I'm not suggesting that it's the only path but perhaps you can think of another that will not having you trek through wetlands and possibly catching pneumonia."

Don looked down at his plate and began breaking up the bacon with his fork. It was crisp, on the verge of being burnt, just the way he liked it. He answered sheepishly, "I didn't think of that. It's just that I remembered the time when I was a correspondent in the Middle East helping to save migrants from one of their many wars."

"And how long ago was that?"

He picked up a broken piece of bacon and put it in his mouth. "A long, long time ago….Maybe you're right. I'm not …But I do still have good contacts and especially with the coming winter, the migrants will need shelter. It may not be as cold as it used to be in the past but hell! It's still damn cold if you have to live outside." His face brightened and he suddenly felt energized. "Say, we could organize a group right here at Longview. I bet there are people who would help, and some might even have good contacts to advance the idea." He suddenly realized that he felt comfortable sharing ideas with Susan just the way he used to do with Paolo. In all this time he had been looking for a clone of Paolo but that was silly. What he needed was not necessarily a lover but a friend with whom he could relate and interact just the way he is now doing with Susan. In all the years at the Manor he could have been more open but instead held on to Girl as his confidant while keeping people at bay; Henrietta, Jim, the Weills; they could all have been his friends. Now, here at Longview there must be more people like Susan. He suddenly pushed his chair back and stood addressing the few other diners. "Folks, my name is Don Garland. I used to be a correspondent on your local TV station until I retired. Actually, the manager of the station fired me because they thought I was too old. Anyway, you're all aware of what's happening as a result of climate change. There are masses of people leaving areas of the country that are no longer livable. They are migrating north, and I've personally seen how the administration is dealing with them. These people who are only looking for a place where they can settle and restart their lives, these mostly good people are being treated like criminals, detained and hounded by the law. I've decided to do something about it by contacting folks in authority that I have known over the years and asking them to help treat these migrants more humanely. It occurred to me that many of you also have important contacts in city, state or the federal government and if you feel as I do that these migrants deserve a break, then you could activate your contacts to do something to correct this outrage."

A man with a trimmed grey goatee spoke up, "I remember you Don. You were a terrific newsman. Wasn't there a time that you were broadcasting from the Middle East about some migrants from that war?"

"'That was a good three decades ago but you're right, that was a situation not unlike this one where migrants were herded into camps instead of being helped to resettle."

"Yes," said an elderly woman at another table. "I remember that, and If I remember correctly, as a result of your reports, the government built a new town to accommodate the migrants."

A number of the diners stood and walked over to Don and extending their hands said they were glad to meet him. Some offered to help with the refugee situation as Susan watched, satisfied that she was able to redirect Don's enthusiasm in a more appropriate direction.

That evening, Don called Wayne to ask if he would be willing under the new plan to use his influence with staff at the station to have them report on what is taking place with migrants. He pointed out that this is a reportage issue and has nothing to do with the 'extra-legal' approach he had discussed at their dinner and added, "Susan convinced me that what I was suggesting made no sense and since then I've received offers of support from some of the folks here at Longview." Wayne promised to take it up with the station manager and agreed that it is a legitimate news issue that should be reported on. Don then called Henrietta and Jim to bring them up to date with his newfound direction, hoping also to hear what they learned from their meetings with the science task force.

JIM AND HENRIETTA, SINCE THEIR return from Camp David, received weekly updates of the progress in establishing a new policy to handle the problem of the treatment of the migrants. It turned out to be more complicated than anyone had anticipated but as Christmas approached, the flow of migrants had slowed as the weather in the south had somewhat cooled. At the same time, the northern states had been hammered with heavy rains causing flooding along major roads, an event that also contributed to holding down the movement of migrant groups. Carlson shared some of the difficulties he had encountered to get President Davenport to restrain the Guard. It seems that the Homeland secretary expressed the view that a firm approach was important, and that any relaxation of the Guards' decisiveness could lead to insurrections. Although the President was sympathetic to the conclusions that the committee had reached she expressed the view that a more balanced approach including firm control of the migrants' movements may be preferred.

Jim was incensed when he heard about Washington's response to their efforts of the previous weeks and wanted to immediately call Carlson. "They ask for advice and then choose to ignore it," he said as he paced around their living room sloshing coffee from the cup in his hand.

"Please put that cup down. You're spilling coffee on the rug, "said Henrietta. "I'm as upset as you are but there's no need to destroy our new apartment while you rant and rave. And get a sponge to wipe up that spill!"

"I'm sorry, but I'm not used to having my advice ignored."

"That's obvious. Haven't you learned the art of negotiation and compromise in your dealings with governments on some of your projects in the Middle East?"

"That was different. I was hired to do a job because of my expertise and the client listened to me. And besides, most of those governments were led by autocrats so my word became an extension of their authority."

"Welcome to democracy! Somehow your powers of persuasion don't carry the same weight here. You need to be more patient and learn the art of negotiation and compromise. Maybe that might have helped you earlier in your life in dealing with your son."

"That reminds me, he said. "There's something else,"

A few days after returning to Hillcrest, Jim had been surprised to receive a message from Mike's wife.

My name is Olga Murray. I'm Mike's wife and because the two

of you have been estranged for most of his life, we have never met. But now, something has come up that has led me to contact you. We have a daughter, Katherine, who just turned 20 and is in college. I don't know what triggered this, but she suddenly announced that she wanted to know something about her biological grandfather. It may have been in response to one of her courses. Naturally Mike was angry and refused to tell her anything about you and said that she already had a grandfather and didn't need a second one. Katherine can be very persistent and asked me to find your address which I finally obtained from Mike's mother. I have always supported Mike's wishes concerning keeping you out of his life but for the sake of my daughter I'm asking you to please contact her.

Olga

After he showed her the message, Henrietta, encouraged him to follow through. "Why didn't you tell me about this before? This is your chance to connect with Mike and his family."

"Maybe I was afraid that she'll reject me the way her father did."

Henrietta put her arms around Jim, pulling him close and kissed him on his cheek. "You owe it to this child to try," she whispered. "Please contact her!"

Pouring himself a fresh cup of coffee, Jim spoke into his electronic pad and watched the words being displayed. It took him a long time to dictate his message, after which he showed it to Henrietta who made a few suggestions for changes. Finally, when both were satisfied, he sent it, breathing a sigh of relief.

The next day, a reply arrived on his electronic pad including an image of a young lady with short cut brown hair and a broad smile.

I'm not sure what to call you but I understand you are my grandfather, and I would like to know more about you. I'm in my first year in college and I took a course in sociology that had a section on extended families. That's when I decided to get in touch with you because I don't know what happened that caused you to break off your relationship with my father. I'm trying not to be angry with you, but I need help with that. Please, can we arrange a time for a long talk.

Katherine

As he read the note, Jim felt tears blinding his eyes as the words began to leak down the page. Henrietta, when she saw his pain, enveloped him in her arms saying, "It's all right to care so much. You've held in your pain much too long. Maybe now you can reclaim your family. It's not too late."

With her help, Jim composed an answer…maybe more of an apology for not being more insistent in finding a way to maintain his relationship with Mike. Yet, at the same time he tried to convey to her the fact that he did make an effort in keeping open the conversation until Mike no longer responded. He also expressed the desire to talk to her; there was so much he wanted to know about her family and so much he would like to share about his life. Finally, he wanted to add that she had opened an emotional door that he thought had been locked forever…but Henrietta advised that this was not something he should say now, so he relented.

For the next two days Jim waited anxiously for a response from Katherine until one morning, a curt statement appeared on his electronic inbox saying, 'call me' and giving a number and suggested time that afternoon. "What should I say to her?" he asked Henrietta nervously.

"Don't overthink," she answered. "Just tell her what's in your heart. She's your granddaughter and remember that you're trying to get to know her and have her get to know you. It's going to be a little awkward at first but I'm sure you'll get into the rhythm of the conversation."

He placed the call and when Katherine answered, he saw a young lady who reminded him of his former wife. Her light brown hair was cut just above the shoulder and framed a long oval face punctuated with striking wide-open blue-grey eyes that stared directly at him on the screen. After the customary hellos, he told her how much she resembled her grandmother. "Thank you," she said in a warm alto voice. "She is beautiful, isn't she? Why didn't you stay with her?"

Taken aback by her directness Jim was stymied for a moment but then began to explain that engineering assignments in the country were not easy to get at that time. So, work took him overseas to areas that he felt were not safe for a woman with a new baby. Over time, he received offers for more and more responsible positions for work that he enjoyed and brought him satisfaction. As conditions changed in the countries where he worked, he tried to get Mike's mother to join him, but she felt that Mike was then in school and had local friends and so on....Also, she just didn't like the idea of moving overseas. Finally, she asked for a divorce as she had met someone. "After that time, I tried to stay in contact with your father and to visit him when I was in the States but when he became a teenager, he cut me off."

"You were the adult," she said. "It was up to you to keep trying."

"Maybe when you're older, you'll realize that sometimes some things just can't be fixed. Even at your age, you must have had relationships that didn't work out."

"Sure, but I wasn't married with a child."

Jim was quiet for a long moment because he did not know what to say that could excuse the past. Finally, he asked, "Why don't you tell me a little about yourself ...what do they call you at home?...what you're studying and where you are in college? I assume that you grew up in Cleveland."

"Well, they call me Kate, and we live in Shaker Heights in a lovely mid-twentieth century house. My dad, as you know is a doctor, actually a surgeon. I went to public school there and ended up going to Villanova because I might go into nursing and they have a good nursing school. Dad is trying to get me to move into medicine but I'm not sure yet that it's right for me...perhaps I'll change my mind before I graduate."

Jim suddenly spoke up as he realized, "Isn't Villanova near Philly? You know that we're less than an hour north of you. That's amazing. We would love to come and visit you so that we can get to know each other better."

"Who's *we*? she asked.

"Henrietta and I have an apartment in a retirement community near Lehigh. She's an environmental scientist and we met in Miami before the ocean wiped out the place a few months ago."

"Weren't you frightened when that happened?"

"We left a few days before it actually happened, but listen, why don't we arrange for you to come up to see us perhaps for a weekend before Christmas. I assume you'll be with your family at Christmas."

"Honestly, this is not a good time for me to get away because there are exams and papers due."

"Well, we could come down to see you for lunch one day. That won't take away from your schoolwork too much."

There was a note of hesitancy in her voice, but Kate finally agreed on a date.

As Jim had no other living relatives, other than Mike, he was anxiously looking forward to bonding with his only granddaughter and spent the days before their meeting aimlessly puttering around the apartment. "For God's sake," Henrietta exclaimed one afternoon, "Can't you just sit down and read a book or something. Your aimless wandering around the apartment is making me nervous." Of course, she was at the same time trying to hide her own concerns about this meeting. Overhearing the phone conversation between Jim and Kate, she detected a note of disapproval or blame in Kate's response to Jim's explanation of his separation from Mike. She felt protective toward Jim and worried that he would be heartbroken if the luncheon with Kate were to turn out badly.

There was a light chill in the air on this December morning. Looking at the rain falling on the wooded hills facing Hillcrest, Jim was apprehensive about the coming luncheon. Perhaps, he thought, that the depressing weather caused him to view the future negatively. After all, it was close to Christmas and there had not been even a hint of snow. Nothing but lukewarm rain even on this cool day. He thought back to the graph he had drawn on the wall of his room in the Manor showing an accelerating rise in the sea level. But that was behind him and he was away from the shore and on dry land. "It's funny that it can be called *dry land* when I can clearly see that it's wet and getting wetter." Before they had left their friends in Charlotte, Henrietta reminded him that in the northeast where they would settle, they should expect warm but wetter weather and likely no White Christmas. Yet, he remembered his youth, growing up in Ohio and seeing snow in early December. He was so excited that he would go down to the yard and immediately push what snow there was into a mound, the first step in building a snowman… two sticks for eyes, a carrot for a nose, a short stick for a mouth and a log for a rimless top hat. *This damn weather*, he thought. In his memory of his youth there was also smoke coming out of the chimney and a gas-guzzling truck parked in the driveway. *My family was just as responsible as everyone else in causing this change in the climate. Now there's Mike's family and Kate whom I've barely come to know. What kind of future is there for them?*

"Jim, I think we had better get ready to leave," said Henrietta when she saw him looking out the window with his hands flat against the glass. Jim was suddenly pulled out of his reverie and left to pick up the car he had rented for the drive down to Villanova. Later, when they were on the road, Henrietta asked him, "You seemed distracted earlier this morning. Is anything wrong? I hope you're not nervous about meeting Kate?"

"No, it's not that exactly. I suddenly wondered about her future with what's happening with climate and even with the migrations.?"

"I hope you'll be a little more optimistic when we meet her. After all, even though the present may look dire, there is still the hope that some of the positive steps we discussed in Washington will lead to a better future."

"I guess I'm not as optimistic as you are but....OK, I'll put on a happy face and be more positive. To be honest, I'm a little scared to meet her for the first time. You heard her the other day. I think she is critical of me, thinking that I abandoned her father."

"I'm not sure I would put it quite that strongly." But Henrietta was not really convinced of that and hoped that Kate understood Jim's explanation.

When they arrived in front of the main entrance to the campus they saw Kate waiting under an umbrella. Jim waved to her to get into the back seat of the car. Once safely seated, Kate turned to Henrietta and asked, "So, are the two of you married?"

Surprised by the directness of the question, Henrietta said confidently, "We're good friends who happen to live in the same apartment."

Jim jumped in quickly before Kate had a chance to comment saying, "Let's get to the Inn and we can talk at lunch."

There was a total silence during the short ride to the Inn until they were seated at a table in the dining room when Henrietta asked, "Kate, what made you suddenly want to contact your grandfather? I gather that your father certainly tried to discourage you from doing so."

Kate was clearly not comfortable being interrogated by this woman, her grandfather's 'girl friend?' and turned to face Jim before answering. "I had never even heard about you until I was about twelve years old and didn't understand at first how I could have two grandfathers. And of course, the family was very secretive and didn't really explain the situation. Finally, when I got to college, I asked my mother that I wanted to talk to you so that I could try to understand…"

"I can see that it would have been confusing, but I tried to tell you the other day that I did make an effort to stay close to your father, but it just didn't work out."

"Maybe you should have tried harder."

Henrietta interrupted, "Don't be so quick to judge Jim. In the time I've known him, one thing you can say is that he does put much effort into a relationship."

"That's different, you're his girlfriend and you're both old."

"Now wait a minute," said Jim in anger. "Yes! I'm older than you and that means that in my *long life*, I've learned much more than you have. It also means that I know more about life and about relationships and…"

"Jim! Please don't get upset," said Henrietta. "Why don't you excuse yourself and let the ladies talk together for a while."

"But…"

"Please…"

Once Jim had left the table, Henrietta started to explain, "You must understand that Jim was very nervous about meeting you because he never really dealt with young people especially one quite so forthright as you. When you get to know him, you'll find that he is really very sweet and warm hearted. And….when he heard from you he was so excited to meet you and get to know you. You're someone who was missing in his life"

"Maybe I expected something different. I thought he would be… I don't know,…apologetic for leaving my father. I know he says he tried hard, but I still wonder why he gave up."

"Perhaps you've never had the experience of being totally rejected, otherwise you might better understand how he felt when your father cut him out of his life."

"I don't know…"

"That's right, you don't. So, why don't you consider giving him a little leeway."

"Maybe you're right. He can't be too bad when I see that you two seem to get along so well."

"We found each other, which at our age is a blessing. Listen, why don't you go out and ask Jim to come back in?"

Kate left the restaurant and found Jim in the lobby, sitting with his head in his hands. Somewhat hesitantly, she lightly placed her hand on his shoulder. He looked up, rose from his chair and gently took her in his arms. Together they returned to the restaurant and spent the next few hours talking and slowly getting to know each other...under Henrietta's watchful guidance.

On the drive back to Hillcrest, Jim told Henrietta what a lovely and bright young woman, Kate was and how he felt so lucky that fate had brought them together. But on a darker note, it made him realize that he would not want any harm to befall her, This brought him back to the reality of the destructive effects projected by the future climate. He was no longer a passive observer and told Henrietta that they must become more active in participating in Carlson's group not just in connection with the security issues posed by the presence of the Guard but in the mitigating proposals to reverse the adverse effects of a warming planet. "It's personal," he said.

"Jim, I'm glad that you found Kate in your life, but don't forget that my whole career has been involved in dealing with this climate issue and it's not that simple."

"Henny, I truly respect you and I know that among the concepts for moving back from the current disaster, many of which you've talked about, there must be some that will avoid what I see as a possible end of our civilization."

"Remember your wall graph. The line that you drew on the wall that showed the rise in the ocean level...it was a shallow slope which meant that change occurred very slowly. The same is true for the general climate. Temperatures have been moving up, again slowly. The problem has been that we keep feeding the climate change monster by pumping more gases into the atmosphere, first carbon and now, methane. Why don't you get in touch with Dr. Sasaki whom we met at Camp David? He's the one who can tell you about the current projections and what is being done to reverse the temperature increase."

Once back at Hillcrest, Jim contacted Sasaki who told him of the efforts that had been made to try to either begin to remove some of the accumulated carbon in the atmosphere using some of the techniques that Henrietta had previously discussed. He then hesitated a moment and asked to speak to Henrietta. "I think I can speak to you in confidence," he told her. "There is a new concept that has been proposed by a group of Chinese climatologists which is yet unproven but could be important."

"Can you tell me about it, in confidence, of course?"

"This must not be revealed yet but since you are in the same field. These scientists propose to release reflective clouds over the Arctic and Antarctic regions which would have the effect of supercooling those regions. Natural circulation patterns would move cool air near the surface toward the equator. It is hoped that this will result in a long-term cooling of the earth…yet…it will be years before this will be known for certain."

Henrietta was conflicted because she saw this as a real possibility but had promised not to discuss it outside of her professional colleagues. She wanted to tell Jim but thought that he would either put it down or blow it out of proportion and want to tell all their friends. She realized that they all wanted hope but as a scientist she knew that the chance of success was slim until actual testing was completed. But hope was needed!

ON THIS EARLY DECEMBER MORNING the air was warmed by a blazing sun allowing Frank to sit in a rocking chair looking out at the lake. He felt at peace in his new home and opened the last pages of his great-grandfather's diary.

> As I write this, I feel relaxed for the first time since leaving Paris. At last, the nervous energy that held me together has finally slipped away. At long last, I was in a protected environment and together with Madeleine and the children again. I had left the war on the other side of the Swiss border and fleetingly wondered about those other migrants, the ones who had no secure destination but were doomed to keep wandering, seeking a safe harbor. I worry that the safety I feel, being inside this fortress was an illusion since the Axis

forces on all sides could easily breach it and overwhelm this sheltered island. The war was never far away. Some days I could hear the sounds of war, the big boom of a bomb dropped from an allied bomber only miles away or the rat-a-tat of a machine gun aimed at a refugee trying to outrun a deadly bullet before crawling under the razor wire at the border. Madeleine urged me to find a way to help one of these lost souls who were desperately seeking the freedom we had gained. But… what could we do?

"Do you hear them?" said Diane as she joined him on the porch. "It's the wail of the children out there, on the other side of the fence. Those poor children. I hear them every night. Frank, you have to do something for them…Please!"

"All right," he said. But he had heard nothing! Diane had become obsessed with the plight of the migrant children. Although there were none near her new home, she insisted that they were just outside the gates. She wanted to see them, talk to them, feed them and hug them to give them comfort in the realization that someone cared. Frank tried to reason with her and offered to walk down to the gate to show her that there was no one there, but she kept telling him, "Please, you go. Tell them that I care." It was enough for her to believe that she heard them, and it was not necessary to see them. Once, when a grandson visited she would hold him tightly and whisper, "It's all right. I'll keep you safe. You don't have to walk any further." The child didn't know how to respond as Frank patted Diane on the shoulder and said, "It's all right dear, he knows you love him, and he doesn't have to leave." These were awkward moments for one or another of the grandchildren who no longer felt comfortable visiting grandma. Frank tried to explain to them that their grandmother was a little confused by all that had changed in her life in the past few months but that she was so happy to see them.

"Do you know what day this is?" Asked Frank. "It's St. Nicholas day, December 6th. Remember when the boys were young, you would put treats in their shoes outside the door to their room. They would discover them in the morning with screams of joy. God, there was so much joy in the house then…"

"I remember! Frank Jr was always the first to open the door and tear into his shoes to find his favorite chocolates. I wonder if he does that with his children?"

"We'll call them, and you can wish them a happy St. Nicholas day."

Frank placed the call, but no one was home and within a short time, Diane no longer remembered what she was waiting for and lay down in her room for a rest.

It's three weeks to Christmas, thought Frank, *and I hope that Diane will be able to enjoy her first Christmas in years in which she would be surrounded by her sons and grandchildren.* It had saddened him to watch her continuing decline. It's been only months since they had been forced to leave the Manor and in that time he had noticed that she had fewer periods when she seemed untroubled and more of fear. At the Manor, he had sensed that she was more responsive to their friends. Now, even her children caused her to be afraid. He decided to arrange a virtual get together with their friends from the Manor. *Yes*, he thought. *Maybe that will cheer her up. I wonder how they're doing and what their plans are in view of the changing weather.* When Diane awoke from her nap, he told her about his plan, and she seemed happy at the thought of seeing her friends.

The next morning one by one, the friends from the Manor appeared on the screen. First to arrive were Val and Drake followed almost instantly by Don. They waved as Diane threw them kisses with both her hands flying out toward the screen. When Jim and Henrietta appeared, there were tears in Diane's eyes as she said, "It's so wonderful to see you all. I can't tell you how much I missed you these past months. Don, you're so far away. Did you find what you were looking for?" Don recounted how he had made new friends in Longview House although he did not reveal that he had found a special friend with whom he felt comfortable and was able to communicate openly, something he had never felt at the Manor.

Diane was so happy when Drake proudly described how Val's grandson was named Albert and called him, uncle Al. "That's so sweet," she said.

"That little fellow is special," Drake answered. "I'm thinking he could take over my job when he grows up."

"So," asked Frank addressing Jim , "What have you and Henrietta been up to?" He was about to add… *in your little love nest* but thought better of it.

"Did I hear a hint of reproach in your voice?" said Jim.

Diane punched Frank on his side saying, "We're so glad you two are together. Perhaps Frank is jealous?" adding, "We'd love to know what is happening with your man in the White House?"

Henrietta answered, "I'm afraid that meeting we attended had mostly to do with the administration's handling of the migrant situation. The long-term issue of how to reverse the warming climate has been passed into the hands of the UN since it is global in nature. We've all encountered migrants moving north and seen how they're treated. Both of us saw shameful situations where some of these people were treated like criminals and placed in detention camps. The administration is now looking for more humane ways of handling this."

"They asked for our advice and now they're ignoring it," interjected Jim. "I must say that I expected a better response."

"I'm afraid Jim expected a miracle. I explained that this takes time and if know Carlson, he'll keep pressing until things change in the treatment of the migrants."

Don jumped in, "I still have friends in the media, and I've recently convinced a former colleague right here in Minneapolis to start a campaign to influence the White House to modify their migrant policy relying less on the military."

"I didn't think of it," said Henrietta, "but I have a friend at Lehigh with whom I collaborated on a blog called 'The Climate Timeline' and we could update it with current notes publicizing the urgency of the situation."

Frank added, "I'm not sure what we can contribute to this, but I'll talk to the boys and see if they have any ideas. After all they must have local connections that could be tapped."

Drake was silent. Since Little Al was in his life he felt a sense of responsibility for the future. Yet, his innate pessimism still plagued him causing him to retain a measure of futility. Was it within the realm of possibility for ten billion people on earth to do the right thing? And as to the science proposed to reverse global warming, it seemed too far-fetched. "I'm afraid there's nothing I can do to help," he said. "I don't have your folks contacts." Diane held Frank's hands during this discussion and as Drake talked, she squeezed hard causing Frank to wince. He said, "I'm afraid we have to leave now but I will definitely be in touch once I find out what my boys can do to help." He did not feel it necessary to explain his departure.

As in seeking a vaccine in the period of a pandemic, the effort to reverse climate change takes time. In the interim, the problem worsens, more people die, the arable land needed for the sustenance life turns to dust, water descends from melting glaciers and the seas rise. But man holds on to hope while some act. At the moment this virtual meeting was taking place, a satellite passed overhead sweeping the atmosphere of the carbon detritus that had accumulated since the start of the industrial revolution. It was only one of hundreds more that had been sent to accomplish the task. Ever so slowly, bit by bit this waste was gathered and shot into space making it some other celestial body's problem. The atmospheric balance that had existed in pre-industrial times was expected to return in decades, how many was not yet known.

ELEGY

For Julia Smith it's the end of time
For the Simmons, the end of the line
For Garland there is renewal
But what of the rest of us?
Ever so slowly, the climate will change
While the icebergs continue to melt
And the oceans continue to rise
The atmosphere will warm.
Disrupting the patterns of weather.
The air will heat up
Life will go on
But it's the children who will suffer
The Weill's children and grandchildren
Jim's newfound granddaughter Kate,
Shared with Henrietta.
Valeria's children and grandchildren
Shared with Drake…
What will the future look like ..
What will change to provide hope…
Is there time to save the earth
For these children and grandchildren…
These questions remain unanswered.

ABOUT THE AUTHOR

Matthys P. Levy is a founding principal and chairman emeritus of Weidlinger Associates. His credits as principal structural designer include the Rose Center for Earth and Space at the American Museum of Natural History, the Javits Convention Center, and the Marriott Marquis Hotel, all in New York City; the Georgia Dome in Atlanta, and the La Plata Stadium in Argentina, which features his patented Tenstar Dome.

Levy is co-author of *Why Buildings Fall Down; Structural Design in Architecture; Why the Earth Quakes, Earthquakes, Volcanoes & Tsunamis;* and *Engineering the City.* He is also the author of *Why the Wind Blows: a History of Weather and Global Warming,* published in 2007. He published his first novel, *Building Eden* in 2018.

He is a founding director of the Salvadori Center, which teaches New York City youngsters mathematics and science through hands-on learning about the built environment. He was born in Switzerland and holds a BSCE degree from City College of New York and Master's and CE degrees from Columbia University.

CPSIA information can be obtained
at www.ICGtesting.com
Printed in the USA
BVHW041121100522
636459BV00005B/144